WHEN THE SKY FALLS

BOOKS BY B.R. SPANGLER

DARK SKIES APOCALYPSE

When the Sky Falls

When the Dawn Breaks

DETECTIVE CASEY WHITE SERIES

Where Lost Girls Go

The Innocent Girls

Saltwater Graves

The Crying House

The Memory Bones

The Lighthouse Girls

Taken Before Dawn

Their Resting Place

Two Little Souls

Our Sister's Grave

Her Last Hour

WHEN THE SKY FALLS

B.R. SPANGLER

SECOND SKY

Published by Second Sky in 2024

An imprint of Storyfire Ltd.
Carmelite House
50 Victoria Embankment
London EC4Y 0DZ

www.secondskybooks.com

ISBN: 978-1-83525-852-1
eBook ISBN: 978-1-83525-851-4

PART ONE

ONE

"Emily... I need you to wake up!"

The warm touch of someone's hand.

"Huh?"

"Come on now!" a voice cracked.

"Wha—" Groggy and disoriented.

"Emily! Girl, it's an emergency!"

In a sliver of fuzzy dim light, Emily found the outline of a familiar figure.

"Mom?"

"Come on now!" her mom said, standing over her. "We have to go, now!"

"Huh?" Her throat was scratchy and dry. Emily peered out the bedroom window and tried to focus, the sight of a hazy streetlight urging her back to sleep. "It's early."

"Emily!" A shake jolted her. "Now, girl!"

"Why!?" Emily's eyelids sprang open. More alert. "What is it?"

"Emily, there's no time," her mom cried. "Something's wrong... terribly wrong!"

"Mom—" Distant rustling came from beyond the room, a frantic stirring. Emily's eyes cleared enough to get a good look, her mom's face stricken with fright. She searched the gray light for her father, panic seizing her. *What's happened to him?* Before she could ask, her mom yanked the blanket, cold air rushing over her bare legs. "Mom, you're scaring me."

"Good! You need to get moving!"

"Is it Dad?" she asked. She was awake now, worry shaking her voice. Her mom stopped and let the blanket fall to the floor. "Is he okay?"

"I'm fine, but we have to go!" her father answered. His tall silhouette appeared in the doorframe, the hallway light splintering. "We need to get to the car; the house isn't going to last much longer!"

"I'm moving." Emily swung her feet over the edge of the bed and stood up. She gripped the carpet, squeezing her toes. The lure of sleep loosened its hold as she shook off the early chill and felt the need to pee. Whatever the emergency, it'd have to wait until she was done. Emily glanced at her window again and touched the glass. The streetlight growing dim, its color off.

"Don't!" her mom snapped, clutching Emily's hand as though she were a child daring to touch a flame. "Emily, let's get moving."

"How early is it?"

"Almost morning," her mom answered, throwing loose clothing onto the bed. "I'll pack you a few things."

Must be another storm, Emily thought and rubbed the slumber from her eyes. That would explain everything. *An evacuation,* she concluded dismissively, recalling times before when they'd packed to stay at the shopping mall for safety. Her breath seized when the house shook, a crack peeling open across the ceiling. She raised her arms instinctively, guarding against falling clumps of plaster. Dust shimmered in the broken light, and she opened her mouth to scream, a second crash stealing the words as it rumbled onto her feet.

"What was that?" she asked, a distant cry wailing from her little sister.

"It's the house!" her father answered sharply, staring upward. He shuffled what was in his hands, stopping a moment to look at her with firm eyes. "Listen to us and get moving!"

"Okay," she said, breathing shakily. She turned an ear toward the window. *No wind.* There was no wind, not even a breeze. Living near the ocean meant there was the breaking surf to listen for, especially when the seasonal storms blew through. But now, there was nothing, the outside eerily silent. There should have been *something*.

Two more thumps. But these came from below the window, outside from the street. A neighbor? A car door creaked open. It was followed by the slamming of a trunk lid and a holler that escalated to a yell, telling someone that they needed to hurry. A second car door opened and then closed with a thump, metal on metal clanking. Whatever was happening, it was happening to everyone; their neighbors were awake and in motion.

A scream. It came as a shriek first, a shrill rising into her bedroom. It cut through her brain with a chill racing up her spine. Emily jumped and searched her parents' faces, her mom cupping a hand over her trembling lips while her father's jaw fell wide open. The screams had a throaty and raw sound, tortured in a way she didn't understand. It was blood-curdling.

"Dad! What was that?" Tears pricked her eyes, the fright too much. "Mom! Why did it sound like—"

"Wait." Her father raised his hand, shushing her. For a moment, they just stood in her room, motionless and listening. The screams turned wretched, throaty and wet and drowning. Worse yet, it became marred and deformed and made Emily cover her ears. Muffled, there were a few words that stood out.

They said, "*Stay inside!*" The cries ended abruptly, punctuated by the crumpling sound of someone falling. Silence followed. Her father's hand stayed in the air.

"Their car never started," he whispered, talking to himself more than to her or her mom. "It's so strong and fast. Very fast."

"What do you mean? *Fast?* What's fast?" Emily asked. "They might still be alive. We have to help them!" But she knew what she'd heard. There was no mistaking that it was a body collapsing onto the pavement.

"No. We can't," he answered hoarsely. He lowered his hand and leveled his eyes. "We can't help anyone but ourselves now."

"But they're right outside!"

"Emily!" he scolded. She flinched, hurt by the tone. He dipped his face and spoke in a soft voice. "Please, Emily, can you hurry and get your things?"

Emily bit down on her lower lip and rushed past her parents. She said nothing, keeping her focus on the floor as she crossed the hall. Another scream came from outside, slowing her steps, questions and confusion circling. She picked up her feet as if she could run from the screaming and slammed the bathroom door behind her. The door was thin, though, and only muffled the horror. What nightmare was this? What did she wake up to?

Alone and hidden from the world, the tears wet her face, dropping onto the tiled floor. The toilet seat was cold, but she hardly noticed it. From the bedroom, there was a volley of sharp words as another set of screams crept beneath the door. When it turned quiet again, her mom started to yell.

"Did you do this?" Her voice was loud and shaking. "Tell me you didn't do this, please, Phil! Tell me!"

"Barb, I don't know what happened," he replied coldly. "None of our models ever showed a reaction like this. The conditions are incorrect... it's got to be wrong!"

"*Incorrect? Wrong?*" Emily's mom cried sarcastically.

"People are dying, Phil! Don't you hear them? Did one of your *precious* machines do this?"

"I'll fix it," he answered flatly, resigned even. "I can fix this."

Her mom's crying slowed to hushed sobs. Footsteps moved outside the bathroom, shadows appearing on the floor. Quick knocks rapped against the door. "Hurry it up, Emily," she demanded. "I need help with Sammi."

"In a minute!"

The lights flickered, the electricity bouncing. A second later, it was gone. Blackness swallowed the room in a blink, and she gulped dryly. She told herself that the power did that sometimes. But she sensed this was very different. Much worse. Emily took a breath and caught the bitter taste of salt. The muscles in her neck suddenly strained with a tart bite filling her mouth. It wasn't like the ocean breeze she knew. This was strong and chemical.

"Dad, the lights!" she yelled when they flicked on again.

"The power is going to go out for good soon. It's the substation... we're losing it."

"What do you mean? Losing it?" No answer. "I'm scared."

"I know, honey. We all are... Hurry it up now," he answered. The electricity popped, sounding a crisp break this time, shutting off all the lights. It forced Emily's eyes wide, a thin rail of light stretching beneath the bathroom door where shadow feet were passing again. The quick pace and the short steps told her it was her mom. Her father followed behind, continuing the argument from earlier. They were on the stairs and moving down to the foyer.

Her world became silent. The outside. Her parents. She welcomed the quiet but thought of the dead body. Or was it *bodies?* The dead make no sounds. Her stomach tightened, a sudden urge to heave bending her over. She coughed out the burn until starry tails zipped across the bathroom floor. The swirly dance ended with a new distraction, an itch burrowing across every inch of exposed skin. Whatever it was outside was beginning to seep into the house and walls and find her. *Dad's right, the house isn't going to last.* Emily wiped herself, dropped the tissue, and pulled up her underwear. Her nightie fell over her itching legs as she rushed out of the bathroom.

Clutching some pants, she shoved her feet into them, pivoting onto her bed while jerking them over her bottom. She did the same with a shirt while watching the sun begin to rise. Only, it was different—off. The colors were washed out, a gray world arriving through the bedroom window. There were no buildings or cars. No birds or trees. The streetlight she'd focused on earlier had disappeared entirely. In their places was a heavy fog, the outside reduced to a gray square of roiling mist.

"Oh my God!" she cried with a jump as car horns blared and doors opened and slammed shut. There were more people venturing outside. They were rushing into a toxic soup that was threatening to melt her home. She drove fingernails into her skin, the itch burning. It was nearly bone-deep, and a nightmarish thought of melting had her tearing up again. She swiped errantly at her eyes, the burn in them too painful to cry. A scream broke her attention, the voice failing with what sounded like a heavy sack flung to the ground. She pinched her eyelids shut when the terse yells of a woman pleaded for help, the tortured words screaming about being boiled alive.

Run, she thought, gripping the stairwell railing for the last time in her life. When she neared the bottom steps, a notion to say goodbye to her room stopped her. It was silly. Maybe stupidly sentimental too. But to her, sentimental was sometimes everything. A wave of new screams got her feet moving again, the last steps skipped with a jump. She landed hard onto the foyer's wood floors, a sharp twinge in her ankle, rocking her sideways.

"Mom!" she yelled, her heart leaping into her throat. In the middle of the floor was her mother's body. She limped over, begging in her mind, *Did the poison get to her? Please God no!* Her mom's face was hidden beneath fingers, her shoulders shaking with braying sobs. Emily knelt and braced an arm, concern replaced with sympathy. "Oh Mom, please don't cry."

Her father entered the foyer, air rushing over her when he came to their side. The sour smell of sweat followed; his face tight with composure. "Barbara, I'm going to fix this," he insisted, wiping spittle from his chin. "I promise you, guys!"

More tortured screams, the sounds haunting and louder this time. A commotion joined the screams. Shoes on the patio, a body leaning into their front door. Her mother's crying stopped, and they stood when a woman's voice called out. Heartbeat thudding, Emily's heart raced, and she dared to lean in closer.

"I'm dying. Please help me," the woman begged, voice raspy like the others. It was Ms. Quigly, the neighbor from across the street. The old woman had probably gone outside for her cat and gotten caught in the fog. Emily cupped the doorknob, thinking to turn it, her father rushing over with a harsh shove.

"Don't you open that door!" he screamed. "It isn't safe!"

"We have to help," her mom pleaded. Emily took hold of the cold handle again. She'd open the door. Just enough. Just long enough for Ms. Quigly to get inside.

"You can't!" he shouted, fear and alarm mixing in his expression. He had a crazed look which darted from her to her mom. "Ms. Quigly was doomed to die the moment she left her home. She just didn't know it."

"Barbara? Phil?" the old woman called, fingers drumming. They said nothing but clung to one another, waiting. "Barbara, please."

"I can't take it," her mom whispered with a soft cry. She reached for Emily, pulling her close, the space filling with warm breath. "We have to stay together."

"Why is this happening?" Emily asked. Her father only stared at the door, lips moving without words.

"Plea—" the old woman's voice turning wet. Blood perhaps. Fingernails clawed the length of the door. Fear and shame crushed Emily's chest, making it hard to breathe. When the woman's body thumped against the patio, their neighbor was dead.

"I hate you for this," Emily's mom told her father. Leaving for the kitchen, she squeezed Emily's fingers. Emily followed but glanced over her shoulder; her father's head slumped as he brushed his hand across his face. The sight of him frightened her more than the nightmare outside.

"Dad!" Emily shouted, begging him to follow. Arm stretched, he took hold of her hand, their eyes locking on the first visible signs of what the poison was doing. Blotchy red patches had formed on her skin, some of them raised to watery blisters.

"Emily, girl, let me see," he said, lifting her hand. "You're so much fairer than me. Sammi too. You guys have to cover up a lot, understand? Long sleeves! You need to cover everything." He showed her his arms, which were clear of any welts. He ran his hand along the side of her long red hair, then leaned in, kissing her cheek. "You and your sister have got your mom's hair and complexion."

"Dad?" He lifted his head, eyes filled with a look she didn't know. "Can you taste it too?" Emily asked. He nodded with a raspy cough.

"It's the salt." His tone was settled while he glanced into their kitchen.

"Salt?"

He started to speak, but then stopped. She sensed his uncertainty while he rummaged through a kitchen drawer. "From the ocean. Metal oxide bearing materials for mineral carbonation. It recaptures carbon from the atmosphere. And it was supposed to save us." He turned away, gazing at the front window where the fog rolled and slid over the glass like smoke. "The salt is a byproduct, we accounted for it. But this isn't right."

"The salt did this?" Emily asked. She aced chemistry class and knew there was a lot more to salt than the kind to season food. "It isn't just salt, is it?"

"The brine. The machines perform electrolysis. But it's on a scale never attempted before." That wasn't an answer; Emily glared, urging him. He quickly shook his head. "Diatomic anion. It's hydroxide."

"Along with salt." Emily put the words together, asking, "You mean the machines are making sodium hydroxide?"

"It's a byproduct, like with chlorine production. But it's so much stronger than it's supposed to be." Worry returned to her father's face; his gaze fixed on her burns. He looked at the walls next, the way they were groaning.

"How long?" Emily asked. "How long do we have?" Her father closed his eyes. His lips danced without a sound. He was thinking. Calculating. It's how he worked. She liked to tease him about it sometimes but didn't feel the urge to do so now. He shook his head, the cramped expression returning.

"I'm going to stop it!" he blurted and pulled her into his arms without warning. "I need to get to the machine."

"What's going on?" a small voice chirped from behind. Sammi stared up at them, bleary-eyed, her security blanket in tow, the bottom tattered from being dragged. "Daddy, I'm itchy in my eyeballs and mouth—yuk."

"Come here," Emily said and knelt, running her fingers up the long sleeves of Sammi's pajamas to check her sister's arms. There were welts. They were safe, for now, inside the house. But for how long?

"Sammi, listen to me," their father said, knees popping as he joined his daughters on the floor. It spurred a short giggle, but her sister's smile disappeared when she saw his face. "Sammi, I need to go to work today, and while I'm gone, you've got to listen to your mom and sister. Understand?" A hesitant nod, Sammi squirmed and swiped at her arms.

"But I... I always listen," she answered, jumping into her father's arms. "Daddy, I heard something. I don't know, but I think I heard something bad."

"Don't you worry about what you heard. Don't you listen to anything except what your mom and sister tell you. Can you run upstairs and get dressed for me?"

Sammi's feet were moving before they hit the floor, footed pajamas thumping on the stairs.

"Is Sammi getting ready?" her mom asked, eyes puffy and red. "I've packed all the food and water that we can carry. The batteries, the radio, and the flashlight are in the car too."

"Dad, how safe is the car?" Emily asked, the walls groaning louder. "I mean, if the house—"

"The cars will last longer than wood, maybe even brick," he answered. "Wood is porous, and this stuff is like a super paint thinner. It'll eat through it fast."

"But not the metal?" she asked, confused.

"Metal too, but slower," he answered. "It's the motors, though. They need air."

With his words sprang new alarm. "You mean the engine won't run?"

Hands on her shoulders, he assured her, "It'll run long enough to get you to the mall. That's where you have to go." He turned to her mom, asking, "Barbara, you went into the garage? How was it?"

"The smell is stronger. I can taste it," she answered him and shook her head. "I can feel it too. But I think it'll be okay."

"Good," he said to himself. "And I've already got stuff in my car too."

"Wait, Phil! We're not going together?" her mom questioned with disapproval.

Emily's father shook his head, resolute. "Barbara, I've got to fix this."

An explosion rumbled overhead, dust shimmering and falling like snow. It wasn't the roof, though. Whatever it was came from outside. An aftershock? "What was that?"

"It's happening so fast," her father mumbled. His gaze stayed on the ceiling as if waiting for it to squash them. "The house isn't going to last as long as I'd hoped."

"What does that mean?" Emily asked, voice breaking, wood splintering behind the walls.

"The rafters are coming apart. Basic structure, it won't be long before the roof collapses." His answer was clinical like a morbid diagnosis, and she felt hurt that he could sound so callous about the only home she'd ever known. He looked at their faces. "We're out of time."

"Phil, you're going with us!" her mom insisted.

"Listen to me, Barb. I'm taking my car. You and the kids go in your car." He nodded his head encouragingly. "Get to the mall like we did during the last hurricane. The building is close and it's safe."

"But how safe is the machine?" Emily asked. When she saw her father's expression change, a terrible intuition struck her. It wasn't safe. None of this was safe. Chin trembling, she grabbed his arm. "Daddy, no! Don't go. You gotta come with us!"

He looked to her then and the desperate fear in his eyes took her breath away. Voice sharp, he said, "It's the reactor, down deep inside the heart of the machine. It has to be stopped before it's too late."

"How much time?" her mom asked. "How much time before it won't make a difference what you try to do?"

He pinched the bridge of his nose, and his lips began to move again. Counting. Revising a calculation. "An hour. Maybe two at most," he answered. "But I have to get inside."

"But if you're inside...?" Emily started to ask, emotion

making her voice quiver. Her father took hold, pulling them into his arms, her mother's breath shuddering. Emily dug her fingers into his shirt, holding onto him, knowing he might not make it back.

"I'm going to make this right!" he said, and then was suddenly gone.

TWO

The engine turned once and then sputtered. Emily tensed, knuckles white, hands clutched together. Another try and the car came to life with a lurching shake. It choked then and died. Was it too late? Muffled cries and curse words filled the small space, her mom thumping the steering wheel. She tried to mask the fear with a forced smile, glancing at the rearview mirror as Sammi stirred in the back seat. Emily watched her mom pump the gas pedal, turning the key again and holding it. The motor grunted, its internals grinding. It kicked over, coughing and spitting, and roared to life.

"Oh my God—thank you," her mom sighed, leaning in to kiss the steering wheel. "I don't know what we would have done."

"Call Dad!" Sammi answered from the back seat. Emily turned out of habit, checking her little sister, making sure she was tucked into the booster seat. Sammi raised a blanket just beneath her chin and shoved a thumb into her mouth. Emily wiggled her own thumb and kept it there until Sammi saw it. Her little sister's expression changed, shame filling her eyes. A distant crash jerked Emily's attention. When she looked back, her sister had already popped her thumb back in and turned her face to avoid eye contact.

Can't hurt her now, Emily thought sadly. Sammi had no idea what was on the other side of the garage door. *None of us do.*

"Emily," her mom interrupted. "Does your phone work?"

"Four bars," she answered, relieved. There were zero texts waiting, the relief brief. But it was early, her friends surely asleep, their parents unaware? These were questions and assumptions that were impossible to know. The simplest explanation would be that they were all already dead. She decided not to share that part. "Good service and a full battery."

"It's something. The power is still bouncing, though," her mom said, ducking to look at the side mirror. Gray daylight slipped into the garage as the door rose, the rollers clanking. "They won't last much longer."

"That fog?" Emily craned her neck, searching outside. Gray mist silently rolled upward like it had against the bedroom window. Had she ever seen a fog so thick, blinding even? They were safe. But for how long? She heard another crash inside the home. A wall or ceiling collapsing perhaps. Sammi sat quietly, intent on thumb-sucking the time away, oblivious to what was going on. "Mom, how do we get to the mall? We can't drive in that?"

"I don't—" her mom began to answer and hunched over the steering wheel.

"Do it like Daddy did," Sammi answered, words wet and matter-of-fact. "Daddy said he going to his work."

"Right. But I can't see anything. How did he drive in this?" her mom asked, thinking out loud and running her fingers over the steering wheel. Locks of her straight red hair draped loose in front of her eyes. She hit the dash's console, the pixels on its screen coming alive. A left-side sensor glowed bright yellow, teetering on red. "We'll use the car's sensors. They show where the other cars are. The curbs too."

Catching on, Emily opened the GPS app, the map appearing with their house and street address. She panned right and up and dropped a pin on the mall's location. "This'll give us a turn by turn. We can follow it like breadcrumbs."

"Like breadcrumbs," her mom agreed, a cautious smile flashing.

"Breadcrumbs?" Sammi asked through sucking sounds.

"Starting route to—" the GPS began to say.

"What is that?" her mom interrupted, lowering her head and focusing on the windshield. Emily followed her mom's gaze as a cloud of chalky debris ticked off the glass.

"It's the ceiling," Emily answered, a chunk of plaster dropping onto the car's roof, plunking like an acorn. That's when she saw the dust coating the hood, undisturbed like freshly fallen snow. It meant the garage was already collapsing, their time shorter than expected. The wall in front of them moved, the center of it bulging as if blowing a dying breath. Large cracks opened at the center, spidering in every direction. Emily glanced up just as the ceiling broke, its insides spilling. "Mom! We gotta move. NOW!"

"What is that?"

"Hit the gas, Mom!" Emily screamed as the bones of the house began collapsing, the walls crumbling, the roof caving. "Go now, Mom! Go!"

"Hold on tight!" her mom screamed, fright evolving into raw panic. She stomped the gas pedal, a blast shaking the car. Wood splintered and tumbled as they shot backward into the gray mist. Emily turned in time to see Sammi's eyes narrow and her face cramping, turning bright red as her body pressed tight against the safety belts.

"What's happening?" Sammi cried.

"It's okay, baby girl, we're leaving!" their mom answered, another explosion thundering from above them.

"It's the attic and roof!" Emily shouted, thinking of what her father said. The house fell in pieces, the wood tearing like paper with insulation and drywall flying loose around the car like confetti.

"Our home!" her mom cried, launching backward, the calamity deafening with the roar of a thousand campfires. Breathing hard, sweat teeming across her face, Emily's mom stared straight ahead while the charcoal mist covered the windows. Thunder shook the car; her mom, weeping, said, "It's going. It's really going."

"Move back some more," Emily told her and shrank into her seat. Motor revving, the car rolling until the lip of the driveway and street passed beneath the tires. A thunderous boom rushed toward them, spraying debris onto the car like a hailstorm. The brakes squealed, the death cry forcing her mom to turn away. Emily reached over and took her hand. She felt the bite of tears while their home died in front of them. Now wasn't the time to mourn, though. The car was engulfed by a billowing gust, leaving them blind and vulnerable to its dangers. "Come on, Mom. There's nothing we can do."

"I know," her mom said and stared hard at the map. "I'll need help watching the sensors and the screen. You call out the directions."

"Go left out of here." The car jerked forward when the shifter slid into drive. But almost at once, they stopped with a squishing thump. Her mom cringed, easing up on the gas pedal.

"Don't stop, Mom!" Emily demanded, heart tightening. Instinctively, she shoved a foot into the floorboard. "If you stop, you might get the car stuck on it."

"Oh God! I think it's one of the neighbors," her mom cried, standing on the gas pedal, tires spinning, the car rising and falling over the body.

Silence descended between them, save for the wet kisses from Sammi's thumb-sucking. "Straight now," Emily finally said, becoming aware that she was panting.

"Let's hope there isn't more," her mom said. "When we reach the highway, we'll be able to move faster soon."

A buzz erupted, phone vibrating in Emily's pocket. It was a new message. Excited, she grabbed it. "I got a text!"

"The phones are up?" her mom asked. She didn't wait, asking, "Is it your dad?"

"*Are you guys okay?*" Emily read aloud. "Yeah, it's from Dad!"

"Tell him we're on our way to the mall," her mom said, tears glistening. Her voice broke, "And ask him how he's doing."

"I am..." Emily typed, thumbing the screen, shortening the words to a few letters. She hit send, the car jerking and jarring her neck, the right sensor flashing red. "Move left. I think that was the curb. How fast are we going?"

"I'm staying below ten. Not too fast, you know, in case we hit something."

"Yeah, but what if someone hits us!" Emily answered, a sharp intuition telling her they had to move faster. Her mom regarded the danger, raising a brow, phone buzzing twice more.

"Dad says that he's nearly there. And that he loves—" she stopped, voice choked "—loves us very much."

"Call him," her mom demanded, looking over, cheeks tear-stained and ruddy. Emily didn't hesitate and made the call. She put the phone on speaker, the unanswered rings echoing in the car, tensions mounting. The call was answered, a mechanical voice saying, "*All circuits are busy. Please try again.*"

"Can't do this now," her mom said, muttering the words. She stopped and swiped her eyes. "He should've come with us, should have! But he made his choice."

"Mom," Emily said with a bite in her voice. "Dad's trying to stop this."

Her mom glared, her expression filled with disappointment. "Your dad can't stop it! He *knows* he can't stop it!"

"What do you mean?" Emily asked, regretting her words.

"The planet isn't something you can tinker with. It's too big!" she answered, voice growing. "He should be with his family. You tell him that!"

Dad, we love you too, Emily typed. These were her words. Not her mom's. Maybe she was right. But her father was one to fix things. He'd have to do something if there was a need for it. It was what made him *her* dad. She stared at her phone, the cursor blinking. *We'll see you at the mall.*

"Wait," her mom blurted. "Don't say that. Just say that we love him—" Emily hit send before her mom could finish.

"Already did," she answered. "And I told him that we'll see him at the mall." For a moment, her mom said nothing, only stared ahead.

"Exactly when did you get so smart?" her mom asked.

Emily's cheeks warmed. "I was *always* smart," she answered. "You're just starting to notice."

"Love you, girl," her mom said, stretching to rub her shoulder. "We'll get through this. Family."

"I think it's safe to go faster," Emily said, studying the screen. The windows were gray, the visibility less than a few feet. It was the sensors that told her they could move. There was nothing blocking them. No other cars. It was as if the road had been cleared. It hadn't of course, but a little wishful thinking and a little more speed would get them there sooner. "If Dad's already close to work, he's got to be moving faster: a lot faster."

"Hmm," her mom grunted and leaned into the steering wheel, a stare fixed on the windshield. The fog eased over the glass in an ethereal dance like thin fabric flowing. "I'll try to go faster but keep your eyes on the screen."

Emily watched the screen, a tiny triangle representing their car. It moved slowly along the highlighted path, passing intersections where she knew there were traffic lights. And with each, she cringed some, expecting to be sideswiped. Nothing happened, the map stayed unchanged, the course revealing a world they could no longer see. Hidden in the fog, there were roads and bridges. There were overpasses and buildings. And creeks and small ponds. All were showing up on the screen, but she could see none of them.

What the GPS couldn't show them was the debris, some of it thumping beneath the tires. Her mom eased off the gas, fingers tightening around the steering wheel. It was a new concern—not just about people, but there were stranded cars and wildlife killed by the fog. How many animals wandered blindly, collapsing onto the road's blacktop? There'd be squirrels, foxes, and skunks. There were opossums too, and deer big enough to destroy a car.

A blast of white exploded in her face, a stark light flashing bright like lightning. Her body drove forward, arms and legs jerked ahead, the seatbelt contracting. Her mom was gone then, the inside of the car disappearing into the safety of airbags. It was the accident she anticipated. They'd struck something. Tires chirped and the car skidded sideways, coming to a rest a moment later.

"Emily, honey?" Fingers crawled across her chest and neck, probing. The hand retreated, her mother asking, "You okay?"

"As good as I can be, I guess," she answered, pawing at the airbags, flattening them. "You?"

"I think I'm okay," her mom answered. She'd covered her face, blood seeping through her fingers.

"Mom, your face!" Emily yelled.

"It's my nose," she answered, wiping it. Her mom clutched her neck and dared to turn. "Your sister?"

Sammi whimpered, her thumb bloodied, the tip of it bitten.

"She'll be fine," Emily answered, wrapping fingers around

Sammi's hand. "Mom, how's your nose? Do you think it's broken?"

Blood trickled, bright red drops blooming on the center console. Her mom shook her head and yanked tissues from her handbag, wadding them before shoving each into her bloodied nostrils. "We weren't going that fast?"

"I know, we weren't," Emily replied, another concern rising as her gaze wandered about, searching for cracks and leaks, any kind of damage. "The cars. Dad said they wouldn't last."

Without hesitation, her mom turned the key. The motor turned over instantly. "Thank God it's still running!" Her voice was nasal and eyes puffy. "Sammi, you good, baby girl?"

"Good," Sammi grunted, the whites of her eyes big with her injured thumb already back in her mouth.

"Lemme help," Emily said, airbag powder shimmering in the overhead lights.

"Fingers crossed," her mom said and hit the gas pedal. The car lurched forward, motor running hard. The car didn't move. She hit the pedal again, a roar vibrating in their feet, the car barely moving. "Come on now!"

"Look at the driver-side sensors." The dash beamed red and yellow with whatever they'd struck. "What if you try turning the wheel the opposite way?"

"Yeah, let's try that," her mom grunted, hitting the gas and spinning the steering wheel. The car pushed a few inches but rocked back into place. Metal grated against the road, the front of the car bucking like a horse when they tried again. The driver-side tire was hung up. Baring her teeth, jaw clenched, her mom stomped the gas pedal again, the motor screaming. The car lunged upward, grinding and dragging whatever they'd hit.

"Mom, stop!" Emily ran her finger where the window met the door, the material damp with cracks. "We can't risk getting stuck."

"Then we've got a problem." Her mom threw the car into park and reached for the keys.

"No, don't!" she blurted, pulling her mom's arm. "Don't shut it off. We don't know if we'll be able to get it started again."

"Well, we're stuck on something," her mom said, looking uncertain. She tapped the dash where the sensors blinked steadily. "It's on my side."

"What if we try going in reverse?" Emily asked. "Like when we're stuck in the snow?"

Her mom regarded the idea, answering, "Worth a try." The car's motor pitched high again, rearing up, the front falling as they began to move. They drove in reverse, traveling blindly, dragging whatever it was they'd hit, broken glass tinkling, metal and plastic clashing.

"I think it's coming free!" her mom yelled with bright surprise.

"It is! Now, try going forward."

"Here goes!" she said, dropping the shifter into gear. The car lurched and then stopped hard. There was no give, nothing dragged. It was as if the front of the car was pinned against a wall.

"Mom!" Sammi shouted, her thumb raised again. Emily reached over and took hold of her sister's wet finger to try and rub away the sting. Sammi had a childlike wonder on her face, asking, "We going now?"

"You might just want to hold onto this," Emily answered, tucking Sammi's thumb close to her little body. "Keep it safe."

"Uh-huh," Sammi mumbled, wrapping her hand in a blanket. "We go see Daddy?"

A sudden sadness caught Emily, the surprise of it touching. Would they see their father again? Her stomach was in knots, the fog swarming around them. The unknown wasn't just what they couldn't see. It was inside them, their futures. She swiped the black screen on her phone, telling Sammi, "Daddy might be at work by now." It was the only thing she could think to say. "I'll tell Daddy you said you love him."

Sammi forced a smile. She was scared.

"It's no good," her mom barked, the engine idling. She patted her forehead, blood smearing in the sweat. "We're not going anywhere."

"What are we going to do?" Emily asked, pulse racing, the itch on her skin becoming intolerable.

"I dunno," her mom grunted, eyes bulged while looking around the car, searching the floors and glove compartment. She stopped when reaching the back seat, asking Sammi, "How's my baby girl doing?"

Sammi raised her hand. "Bit my thumb," she answered, voice like a mouse.

"Aw," her mom answered with quick kisses to make it all better. Sammi's smile returned. Plastic rustling, her mom threw a bag over Emily's shoulder. "We'll use these."

"Plastic bags?"

"Emily, help me collect them?" her mom asked. "Your dad said to pack every bag I could find."

"What are they for?" There were dozens bunched, her mom tossing them into the front seat.

"He said to use them when we got to the shopping mall," her mom continued, plastic crinkling. "For when we get out of the car."

"Outside?" Emily thought of Ms. Quigly's drowning voice and the old woman collapsing against the front door. She shut her eyes until it passed, reluctance building. "Mom, it can't be safe. Even with the bags?"

"Honey. Please, I need your help!" Her mom grabbed her hands, weaving their fingers together the way she used to before a swim meet. There was assurance and confidence in her eyes, the feeling of it strained. This wasn't a meet. It wasn't a race. This was life and death. A horribly tortured death. Her touch was warm, the sting of tears growing. To save them, her mom was going to go outside. "Emily, baby. I need you to keep moving."

"You can't go outside." The tears came as she turned her head away, hiding them from Sammi. "We'll try the car again, drive in reverse if that'll work."

"Emily! Look at me, girl! We can't do that. We've tried." Emily swiped a tear. "I need you to do what I say."

"Uh-huh," she agreed, knowing that nothing she said would make a difference. She climbed over the seats, the headrest digging into her ribs. Sammi stared, mouth puckered around a wrinkly thumb, and said nothing. Emily found the roll of large lawn bags, the cool plastic firm in her hand as she started unrolling it and covering her mom's arms. "How long will the plastic protect you?"

"Your dad said it'd be enough to get inside the mall," she answered, sleeving a bag onto her leg.

"You'll need eyes," Emily told her, digging a finger into the plastic sheet. Their gazes locked before Emily put the hood over her mom's head. *This can't be the last time*, Emily thought, the idea of it crazy. *This can't be the last time I see my mom.*

"What are you waiting—" her mom began to ask, breath shaky. She brushed her fingers across Emily's cheek, saying, "It'll be okay."

Emily's eyes darted to the shifter and gas pedal. "You sure this is the way?"

"I'm ready," her mom answered and motioned for her to come closer. She spoke quietly in her ear, a warm breath touching. "I don't want to put that bag on my head until I'm ready to open the door. It'll scare your sister."

"I understand," Emily nodded and moved back to her seat and tried blocking Sammi's view. The clack of metal came unexpectedly, the car door opening. She sucked in a breath, expecting a count or a wave of a hand, or even a goodbye. But before she could object, her mom wrapped herself in the plastic and was gone.

Sammi was the first to cough, choking on the fog, the mist's wispy vapors drifting around the opening. It clawed slowly in a come-hither motion, but most of it stayed outside like it had in the garage. The inside of Emily's nose burned from the smell, its stench toxic. Her mom disappeared into the gray fold, turning once while batting her arms. She vanished, the door shutting with a thud. An eerie quiet filled the car as the fog rolled across the windows, paying no mind to who was inside.

A sudden thwack rang out from beyond the hood. Emily jumped and took hold of Sammi, tiny fingers cradled in her palm. *Mom?* It sounded like an arm striking the car's hood. Another blow came, a hand appearing on the windshield. She glimpsed it for a second, but then it was gone. It was followed by the heavy thumping of fists and shoes, her mom feeling around the side of the car toward the front tire.

"Mom?"

A distant grunt. Barely detectible.

"Mommy outside?" Sammi asked.

"Shh," Emily scolded, trying to listen, an instant pout forming on Sammi's face. "Help me listen. Can you do that?"

"Uh-huh," Sammi answered, strands of strawberry hair between her fingers. Emily put on a mock smile, but the sour look remained.

When Sammi opened her mouth to speak again, Emily put a finger to her lips and quietly repeated, "Shh."

"Emmy," Sammi slowly whispered, thinking it'd help. It didn't. "Where Mom going?"

"Help me listen, okay?"

"But I wanna go outside too." A buckle unlatched, the sound of fabric sliding across the seat. Emily's heart shot into her throat. There was no mistaking what her sister was doing.

Emily twisted around to see Sammi's hands perched on the door handle, clutching it, pulling on it.

"No!" Emily yelled, Sammi's shirt sleeve an inch from the tips of her fingers. She never reached Sammi, though, the moment exploding with a booming force. It was surreal, a weightless surprise. Her body suddenly in flight. The direction was sharp with a clanging thunder of metal crunching and plastic crumpling. It filled her ears as she flew, the back of her head striking a headrest. Emily sensed they were spinning, the car tires chirping against the pavement.

When it was done, Emily came to rest against the windshield, the air squeezed violently from her lungs. Her vision turned dark with long-tailed stars circling the periphery. Agony urged her to scream like she'd never screamed before while everything around her dimmed and glass sprinkled onto the road like a distant wind chime. The inside of the car faded then, vanishing slowly until it was gone.

THREE

Eyelids fluttering, cloudy apparitions floated in and out of Emily's eyes. The taste of metal clawed the back of her throat. It was blood. She touched her mouth carefully to feel a cut on her lip. Not too deep. Superficial maybe. Her teeth and gums were sore, and there'd be some bruising like she'd been punched in the mouth. Throbbing in her dazed, the echo of a heartbeat was louder than she thought possible. Her arms and legs were heavy, the strength in them zapped. Her stomach rolled and threatened to spill. She gagged and resisted the urge to vomit. Pain rifled into her shoulder with a memory of what had happened. *They'd been hit by another car?*

"Sammi!" she called, finding her sister's empty booster seat. The ringing in her ears swallowed her voice, making it muffled and tinny. "Sammi, baby girl?"

Emily fell forward, a stifled scream slipping from her mouth. She sucked in a short breath, a burn pulsing in her side. Ribs? Bruised? It was familiar, a soccer injury from last season. She could breathe through it, though. That's what mattered. Her face was wet, stinging with sweat and whatever was in the fog. She froze and dared to look at the window and doors. They were still there, intact, the sight shocking.

Her heart raced, pounding; she could feel it clear down to her toes and into her fingers. She batted the mix of sweat and blood from her eyes, maneuvering her head and shoulders onto the seat. That's when she saw the crack in the windshield. A touch. Just one. The glass was cool, the edge of the break like a razor, but it was holding.

A car horn whittled past the ringing in her ears. Another car. Whoever was driving, were they dead? Was their body squashed against the steering wheel? The horn blared, its volume becoming unbearable, the noise unavoidable. She pressed against the floor, fingers splayed, a vibration rising into her arms. It was the engine. Their car was still running. She raised her head and faced the windshield, the blank eyes of a black plastic bag skittering over the car's hood.

"Mom!" she yelled, her mother's makeshift plastic hood drifting into the fog, dread rising from her gut. "Mom, can you hear me? Mom!"

"Where Mommy?" Sammi whimpered in a thin voice.

"Sammi?" It came from behind, Emily crawling over the seat, muscles quivering as she cautiously hovered. Sammi's tiny body was bundled in a knot, fitting snugly on the floor. The car door was shut, never opened. Surely if it had been, her sister would be dead. Whoever hit them may have saved Sammi's life. "Can you move?"

"Uh-huh," she answered groggily, wriggling, arms up, legs unfolding. Sammi's eyes were large like saucers, drippy with fright, filled with a crazed and confused look. She kept a thumb in her mouth, forehead scraped, a drop of blood beneath her nose, lips stuck in a pout.

"Come here," Emily said, choking back a sob, the sad sight of her sister putting a hard lump in her throat. Emily wrapped her arms around Sammi's trembling body and hoisted her back into the booster seat. There, they stayed a moment, sisters clinging, a tiny pocket of comfort in this cold new world.

"Too tight," Sammi said, squirming. "Emmy?"

"Sammi, I need you to help me, okay?" she said, asking while probing Sammi's sides and back and arms and legs, checking for injuries. She swept the long red hair out of Sammi's somber face, inspecting the small cuts, a lump beneath with a black and blue mark forming in the middle of it. If they were home, an ice pack would be on it. But they weren't home and there were concerns of a concussion. As for the rest of Sammi, being small for her age had an advantage. Sleeving the strap and buckle into place, Emily clicked it shut, warning her, "Don't undo it again!"

"I'm sorry, Emmy," Sammi told her, balling her hands to rub the tears. "I didn't mean it."

"Here," she said while painting a smile. Emily held up her sister's wrinkly thumb, the bite mark from earlier nearly gone. "You hold onto this for me."

Sammi didn't return a smile, dropping her hands onto her lap instead. "I want Mommy," she said, her stare falling to Emily's phone. "Call?"

"Right! My phone." Emily reached around to get it, a message showing. But it was older. Too old. Was she unconscious? How long? She touched the back of her head where there was a lump like her sister's. She winced, pressing the bruise, heart dropping at the idea of time lost. "How long were you on the floor?"

"I dunno," Sammi answered with a shrug.

"We got a text from Dad," she said, showing her.

Sammi's lips moved, spelling out D-A-D. "What's it say?" Her sister's spirits brighter.

"It says that he couldn't—" Emily stopped reading, her mouth going dry. "Dad didn't make it to work. He turned around to go to the mall."

"Dad at the mall?" Sammi asked, not understanding the magnitude of the first message, the magnitude of the machine still running.

"That's right, Sammi," she answered. "We'll see Dad at the mall!"

"What else?"

"Just those two," she told him. "No more messages. None for a while, now."

"Tell Daddy we see him at the mall." Sammi clapped with a toothy grin. She pointed at the windshield. "But gotta get Mom."

"Mom!" Emily shrieked when her mom's face swam out of the fog, blood streaking down it, her jaw broken. *Mom*, Emily mouthed, seeing horror and despair in her sunken eyes. In an instant, Emily saw all the gloom and death she'd ever need to see. "Sammi, cover your eyes!"

"But—"

"Cover them now!" Emily scolded, eyes stuck on her mom's face.

"Mommy!" Sammi screamed. "What happened to Mommy?"

"Sammi!" Emily snapped. "I told you to keep your eyes shut!"

"But why does she look like that?"

"Cover them up, Sammi."

"I'm covering them," she whimpered. "Not gonna look."

"That's a good girl."

Emily's mom fell, her body scraping against the car.

"Mom!?" Emily clutched the plastic bags, opening one. She could wrap herself, go outside and fix this. That's what her father would do. That's what he would say too. He'd fix this. But the door, it was pushed inwards like it had been struck by a giant hammer. Emily tried unlatching the door, but the handle wouldn't move. It wouldn't budge. When there was motion, she realized it wasn't just the damage, it was her mom holding the door. "Mom! You gotta let go of it."

"No!" her mom's muffled voice grunted. A thump struck the door panel, and Emily imagined her mother sitting on the road with her back against the car.

"Mom!" Emily screamed. She rapped her palm against the window, the strikes stinging. "Momma! You got to move away from the door!"

Two bangs returned, the door remaining.

"What?" Emily asked, voice broken. Sobs heavy. "Please, let me open the door."

Another knock, more distinct this time. There was scraping, too, like fingernails against metal.

"Momma!" Emily shoved her face against the window, glaring at the road, trying to see. The glass was cold, her breath fogging it. "Please, *please* let me open the door."

Two knocks, her mother objecting, Sammi whimpering.

"Please, Momma," Emily pleaded, tears dropping from her chin. The cries dried up when the car's engine sputtered. Instinct took over and Emily pressed her foot on the gas pedal, the engine revving. The orange needle shot around the dial, the RPMs nearly pegged. "Momma, we can't stay?"

Another knock, her mother's bloody hand appearing in the window. It moved across the glass, up and over, again and again, before falling out of sight. Emily leaned away from the door, trying to make out what was on the glass. Alone, at the top, was a heart which glowed against the gray fog. Beneath it, Emily read the one word. "GO!"

"Momma, no!" Emily cried, the engine sputtering again with a threat of dying. "I love you, Momma." She eased onto the gas pedal, forcing the engine to stay alive. She waited for a response, but there was nothing.

"You gonna get Momma?" Sammi asked tearfully.

"Can't—" Emily tried answering while shoving the car's

shifter. Her hands shook terribly, and she fumbled with the button.

"The mall?" Sammi said, a cry gaining. "Momma?"

"The mall, baby girl." Choking painfully on the heartbreak. Whatever it was that had hung up the front wheel before was gone, the tires moving without issue. Emily drove. The few driving lessons would have to be enough as she managed to move the car around until the GPS triangle on the screen appeared with them pointing in the right direction.

The GPS triangle continued on the blue navigation path. Emily used the blaring horn, the constant noise growing distant, telling her they were heading away from the accident. When the GPS said it was time to turn, she rolled the wheel, carefully monitoring the sensors to stay clear of other cars and bodies, animal or otherwise.

They drove steadily, the car pitching and wobbly at times, but staying on the road. She followed the GPS path and listened to the horn's death wail, thinking they'd probably hear it all the way to the mall.

"But Momma?" Sammi repeated, crying louder. Emily had to ignore her little sister. The mall was all that she could think about now.

FOUR

"Two more turns," Emily said, tracing her finger along the screen's blue path. The fog blotted out the sun, leaving behind the gray daylight showing only a foot of visibility. Her foot cramped from working the gas pedal, stopping and starting—over and over. The point on the GPS where they'd crashed was far behind them already, far enough to silence the other car's horn. They'd driven far, slow and steady, the blaring noise gone. By now, Emily thought her mother was dead, the idea heavy in her heart. There was the urge to grieve, but she couldn't. Not until they were safe.

Sammi stayed quiet as the miles passed beneath them. There were the occasional bumps, Sammi's crying out scaring them both. Emily lulled Sammi with her voice, hiding the dangers while soothing her sister at the same time. Sammi didn't understand what had happened. Couldn't understand it. And thankfully, she was too young to mourn. Emily wasn't, though. And more than once, she thought she'd have to pull over. She held the course, though, telling herself one more mile again and again until she knew there was only the one remaining. They were almost there.

Not too soon either. Drops of poison formed on the windshield, beading where the glass was cracked. Emily caught herself staring at it hard. The outside slipping into the car a drop at a time. Worry mounting, she felt the need to move faster, to press her foot harder on the accelerator. The fog rolled over them and passed by the windows. There were bodies in the road along with animals and cars to maneuver around, the last of the miles becoming an obstacle course. That's when she understood, they weren't the only ones going to the mall.

Mom's dead, she heard in her head, spinning the wheel, changing course when needed. *What do I tell Dad?* She saw his eyes whenever she checked Sammi in the rearview mirror.

"How do I tell him that I killed Mom?"

"What about Mommy?" Sammi asked, hearing the mumbles.

"Nothing, baby girl," she answered. "We're just about there. Dad will be there too."

"Daddy will be there," Sammi said, eyes lazily wandering.

More drops formed, a streak running down the glass, leaving a smokey trail where it touched the console. Emily dared a touch, finger hovering above the largest crack. The fog was coming in faster, condensing more on the inside. A burn rested on her fingertips, and she quickly snuffed it, picking up the plastic bags and hanging the roll over her shoulder.

"Sammi?" she called with a lift in her voice. "It's time to get ready, girl."

"Huh?"

"Come on, Sammi!"

A groan.

"Costumes, Sammi," she told her sister. "Remember when we made them for Halloween?"

Silence.

"Sammi, you'll help?" Waiting for a sound. "Costumes and then it's time to see Daddy."

But it was too quiet. A lump rose in her throat as she searched the rearview mirror. She looked for the bloom of red hair, the freckles that were like hers. Sammi's reflection came into view, her image fractured by cracks and missing glass. When Emily saw her little sister, she gasped, her mouth falling open. Sammi was deathly pale, and her lips were almost white. Call it a familial drive, whatever it was that sprang to life, it had Emily slamming the brakes.

"Wake up, Sammi! Girl! I need you to wake up, now!"

Sammi stirred. She lifted a hand to the cut on her forehead.

"Yes. That's right. You bumped your head," Emily reminded her while opening a bottle of water, the plastic snapping with a pop. "You gotta stay awake now. You hear me? We're almost there."

"Wha—" Sammi began. Emily tipped the bottle, pouring it over her sister's head. At once, Sammi's eyelids peeled open, lips parting with a shout. She tried waving and shooing at the water. Emily splashed her sister again, Sammi's hands swiping furiously, mouth gasping as though she'd been thrown into a pool. "Emmy! What you doing?"

"It's time to put on the costumes," Emily answered, handing her the bags. "We're going to see Daddy in a minute."

Sammi took the roll, eyes bulging while pinching the plastic. The moment went quiet, save for the bags crinkling, Sammi's expression registering where they were.

"Blood, Emmy," she said, pointing back at Emily. "Bleeding."

Emily covered the cut on her mouth, a heartbeat throbbing in her swollen lip. Sammi didn't need to see any more than she had. Emily winced from the pain in her side, bruises aching. She'd hide that too.

"I know, Sammi. I'll be okay." Her voice wavered with uncertainty. "Another turn and we'll be at the mall. Understand?"

Sammi nodded. Her color was returning. The freckles too. It was better.

"Costume?" she heard Sammi ask, continuing the drive.

"You work on a costume." Rustling plastic filled the car. "Cover your arms and legs. I'll help you cover your head."

The last mile seemed the longest. Emotion and pain taking hold. Emily followed the blue line until she hit a parked car, bouncing off it and continuing forward. She eased off the gas pedal, slowing before bumping into another parked car and then a third, the hits insignificant. When she hit another, it reminded her of the vacuums that run on their own. That's what this felt like. From the back seat, Sammi worked the bags, voice becoming livelier, laughing at how comical she looked when wrapped in plastic.

"Daddy never does that," she quipped, the car rubbing a curb. "Again, again, again!"

"Not now. Not on purpose, anyway," Emily said, growing tired. "Got all your plastic on?"

"Uh-huh," she answered, holding up a bag. "But my eyes?"

"Push your finger through the plastic." Plastic stretched and popped, the car hitting something again. And this time it was the last time. From the GPS map, there was only one thing in front of them, the concrete curb separating the asphalt from the mall's entrance. They'd made it. All at once, Emily began crying. Some of it was for her mother. Some relief. She swiped at her runny nose and turned off the car.

"We here, Emmy?" Sammi asked, waving the plastic hood like a flag.

"Just a hundred steps," she answered. It was a small fact she'd learned only because she and her girlfriends had counted them one afternoon when they'd grown bored of the mall. "A hundred steps to the doors."

"Hundred steps," Sammi repeated. "Whadda 'bout your costume, Emmy?"

Emily stopped and thought maybe she could drive over the curb and onto the sidewalk. She could drive them right up to the doors then. *The bollards*, she remembered. Stumpy concrete legs sprouting up through the pavement like guardian statues. They'd been installed after Ms. Quigly's husband ran into the doors. He wasn't supposed to be driving and mistook the gas for the brakes. She couldn't see the bollards, but knew they were there.

"Are you ready, Sammi?"

"I'm ready," she answered, tossing the roll of plastic bags over the seat. "Make your costume."

"Get ready." Emily stretched a sheet over her left arm, grimacing when the bruises yawned with a stretch. She sleeved her other arm and punched a hole for her hand. Her thoughts stalled, head cloudy as though she was going to pass out. She cradled her head to arrest a spin, their time short.

"Emmy?" Sammi's voice asked distantly. "Let's go, Emmy. I wanna see Daddy."

"The water," she said, thinking it'd help. "Sammi, cover your head with the plastic. All the way, okay."

"Uh-huh," Sammi returned while Emily cracked open a bottle and dumped it over her head. The cold water woke her up with a snap, hair falling flat against her face.

"Sammi, hold your breath on three. Three, two... one."

"Three!" Sammi yelled, playing along like it was a game.

"Take a breath and hold it as long as you can." The car door swung open, Emily pushing her feet outside, the salty fog capturing her lungs instantly. Condensation from the car's handle burned too, but she ignored it and opened Sammi's door.

"Hold it?" Sammi asked through a cough.

"Holding your breath, okay," Emily demanded.

"But I'm scared," Sammi returned, fog threatening.

"I am too," Emily struggled to say. "Daddy will be inside there."

Sammi reached up, clutching her sister's neck. Emily counted each step, walking briskly toward the mall's tall glass doors. This was one walk she could do with her eyes shut. A straight shot. One hundred steps from the curb to the doors.

By the twentieth step, the caustic air leached through her wet hair and burned her scalp. Spider legs, she thought wildly. The burn felt like spiders crawling around in her hair, their feet electric. She pushed forward, stretching her gait, her eyes watering uncontrollably while trying to wash the poison from them. Sammi's hands loosened, falling away from her.

"Hold on," Emily coughed, raspy mucous rattling deep in her throat.

"Trying, Emmy," Sammi answered, shoring her grip.

By the sixtieth step, wooziness set in, and Emily's head felt like it weighed a thousand pounds. Her legs were failing, knees weak, her feet heavy. She gripped her sister, clutching the plastic Sammi had put on, her arms and legs wrapping around her tighter.

"I got you, baby girl," Emily said, her voice sounding oddly like her mother's, the term endearing.

"It hurts to breathe, Emmy," Sammi complained in her ear.

Before she could answer, a flash of light filled her eyes. They'd crashed into the tall doors, bouncing backward. A sudden warmth spread over her middle and dripped down her arms. It was liquid and runny and turned cold almost at once. The heavy flow continued, and she thought that she'd started bleeding, or maybe that Sammi must be bleeding. "Sammi?"

"I'm sorry, Emmy," she cried, squirming. Her sister had peed.

"It's okay, Sammi. We're here, anyway," she croaked, thinking the pee was soothing the burns on her arm. Emily grabbed a metal handle, the door swinging open, the light inside reaching past the plastic. Sammi pulled off the plastic bag, grabbing at the back of her head. Emily did the same and saw that her sister's face was swollen and red, small blisters forming like she had the chicken pox. "We're inside."

"Emmy?" she said, staring at her with terror. How bad did she look? Emily turned away, glancing around the inside of the mall, a dozen faces staring back at them. Some familiar, some not. But all of them wearing the same empty, unexpressive faces—the ones she'd often seen on television after a disaster.

"Emily!" a woman's voice called. Ms. Newl, her ninth-grade science teacher, ran toward them. It had been a few years, but the woman looked the same. Even the clothes struck a few memories—the paisley-patterned rayon blouse and the grass-green pants, along with her chunky bangle bracelets and knobby earrings. Beneath a crop of straight gray hair, the linen-white foundation was blotchy, tear stains beneath her puffy eyes. She had pink lipstick, which was smudged, and her eyelids were brushed faintly with a sparkly blue, an indigo blue, she'd once told her. "Honey, you two got burned. Come on, we've got some help set up in the food court."

"Are there a lot of people?"

"Some," she answered, searching past her as though expecting Emily's mom. Instinctively, her teacher primped her hair, saying, "I've been here since yesterday. Got stuck here with a few others."

"How about my dad?" Emily asked, setting Sammi down. But she couldn't stand and fell to her knees, vomiting. "Oh my God! I'm so sorry."

"You need help, child," Ms. Newl said, gingerly dabbing gauze on their cuts and bruises.

"We were in a car accident," she was able to say before another wave of nausea hit her. She wiped her mouth with the back of her hand and looked at the group of faces. Her father wasn't there. "My dad? Is he here?"

"Phone, Emmy!" Sammi said, a vibration rising from

Emily's pocket. Her phone buzzed and it wasn't just a text message. It was actually ringing.

"Hello?"

"Emily, honey?"

"Daddy!" she nearly screamed. "We made it, Daddy! We made it to the mall." The faces around them grew serious with curiosity. Her father's voice began to break up as people offered to help. She waved them off, intent on listening.

"Sammi, and your mom?" her father asked. "I can't reach your mom's phone!"

"Sammi is here with me," Emily answered, beginning to blubber. She bit her lip when her mother's face flashed like a horror show. She couldn't bring herself to tell him what happened. Not over the phone. "You can see us when you get here!"

"Emily, I'm so sorry," he told her, his voice going in and out. "I'm so sorry this happened. It was all my fault. All of it." She held the phone away from her head, trying to understand what he was saying.

"I don't understand. The fog was an accident. Right, Daddy?" A moment of confusion and doubt snapped at her heart.

"I love you, guys. Always remember that. Okay, Emily?" Her father's voice went quiet, her ear filling with his sobbing. Had she ever heard him cry? Had she ever heard anything so sorrowful?

"Dad?" she asked, hearing something in the background, something that stabbed her soul. It was a car horn. A horn that was stuck, blaring. Instantly, her heart went still. *The accident. We were struck. Was it Dad's car?* "What's that sound? Dad... where are you?"

"Emily, I love you." The horn wailed, mixing with her father's words as curious faces began to spin around her. "I'm not going to make it to the mall."

"Why?" she yelled at him. "Why aren't you coming?"

"I hit something. It's bad, honey. It's got me trapped inside. I love you, guys—"

The phone cut out a final time.

The view in front of her turned over as she heaved. She was vaguely aware of being lifted, her breathing painful. She was succumbing to the damage from the fog. The faces that had stared were now carrying her, saving the daughter of the man who'd released a poison monster upon the world. If she died in this moment, her father's secret would safely die with her. Comfort came when she heard Sammi's voice, encouraging her to stay awake like she'd done with her earlier. Emily's arm fell, and she felt Sammi's tiny fingers wrap around hers, tugging on them.

"Daddy will be here soon, Emmy," Sammi told her. "Daddy will be coming, just like you said." And in that moment, before losing consciousness, Emily decided to never tell anyone what her father had done. She'd never say a word about the catastrophe he'd caused. Instead, the story she'd tell would be about the tragedy of two lovers, dying together, yet separated by a disaster. And she'd tell of the great accident, and how sisters fought and survived the day when the skies fell.

FIVE

Emily's last memory was the taste of metal, like a penny. Blood? A cut on her mouth? There was the bitterness in the back of her throat. And a sting creeping from deep in her lungs too. The fog. It bit her? It was poison, wasn't it? The warm touch of Sammi's hand. Her little sister's voice whispering in her ear, chirping like a sparrow in the yard. There was the sense of being lifted when they'd reached the mall, her body carried like a leaf in the breeze. All of it paled, though, the memory stirring around a horrible pain, a terrible heartbreak. It was the hissing phone static that came after her father's last words. Emily wasn't in her memory anymore.

"Shh, girl."

Mom's voice?

"You'll be okay."

"Mom?" Eyelids clamped, Mom and Dad were on the road. Dying.

"You're safe now."

"Safe?" A stir, drifting forward. "Dad?"

"Isla. My name is Isla."

"Isla?" Eyes swimming in the dark. Head spinning.

"It's Spanish." The touch of a damp cloth. "It means island."

"Isla," Emily said, a woman's face coming into view. Emily licked her lips. Dry and split. More alert to the salty air. "The mall?"

"The mall, yes," she answered. The woman with the Spanish name dabbed a cloth to Emily's forehead. Pretty, her skin like cinnamon, her eyes the same, warm and without threat. She had bangs of chestnut-colored hair that draped in front of her face. Isla swept them to the side, lifting a bottle of water. "Drink. It'll help."

"My sis—" Emily tried to say, a harsh rasp stinging her throat. She pawed at her neck, an ache throbbing deep in her arm.

"It's the poison," Isla said, sweeping a twisty lock behind her ears. A woman in her mid-twenties or early thirties perhaps; she was older than Emily. Not that age mattered. Not here. Emily took the water, the first sip turning into a gulp. The cold touch wasn't enough, and she tipped the bottle. "Whoa, easy. I don't want you getting sick."

"There's lights," Emily managed to say, eyeing the power in the mall's courtyard. They were surrounded by stacked, reddish-brown pavers that made up a circular wall. She recognized the place from the Friday nights of her freshman and sophomore years. It was where she spent hours with her girlfriends while the older boys hung around the arcade. Where were they now? She didn't recognize any of the faces. Nobody she knew. Instead, it was like a scene of a horror movie. A living nightmare. She turned away, breathing heavy. "Isla, how... how many made it here?"

"A few dozen is all. So far. But there might be more coming," she answered, brow rising with hope as she faced the triage area, the bodies lying head to toe, some covered in blankets, others with their clothes removed, their burns exposed.

The fog didn't know age. It didn't know race. It didn't know the rich or the poor. It only knew one thing. It knew how to burn. Emily forced herself to look, to see what her father's machine brought them.

Most of the triage was the consoling, the mending of burns and tending to crying children, and deep discussions around the loss of homes and loved ones. And then there were those writhing in pain, their lives teetering, their bodies cordoned off in a nearby section where a man and woman darted around like hummingbirds feeding.

Isla shook her head, adding, "We don't have much to help any of them. Just a few things we were able to scrounge before it got bad."

"My little sister?" Emily asked with a worried bite. "She was with me when we got here."

A smile formed on Isla's face, the suddenness of it a warm surprise. "That kid is a real character."

"Sammi? Is she okay?" she asked, emotion stinging her eyes. She considered sharing about the accident with her father, his car crashing into them. It might raise questions, though, and her only concern had to be for Sammi right now. "She had a bad bump on her head."

"She did. We took care of her." A chuckle, Isla adding, "Give that little sister of yours a few days and she'll be running this place." She stood up, a hand extended. Emily took hold, legs weak and feeling rubbery.

"Where is she?" Emily asked, searching.

"Sammi is with the kids near the food court, playing."

"Right, I forgot that there's a kids' play area by the merry-go-round."

"Listen," Isla told her, cupping her ear. Emily did the same, and beneath the cries and woes of the triage, there was the distant laughter and squeals of happy children. Like Sammi, the children were too young to understand what was happening.

They were too young to mourn what was lost. A spin wiped the grin from her mouth. "I need a sec—"

"Gotcha!" The voice of a man startled her. Emily glanced up cautiously, his face unfamiliar. He had bright red hair like hers, his skin fair as well. His blue eyes were inviting and without danger, the sincerity of his voice telling her that he wanted to help. He was older with only the slightest show of age around his eyes. Emily clutched his arm, the sleeve patterned with army fatigues that showed he was military. He offered a smile, dimples appearing like charms, her weight shifting to his hands. "We don't want you breaking anything."

"Who are you?" was all she managed to say, his hands large, supporting her easily.

"He's with me," Isla answered and helped take hold to lower her. "Nolan, this is Emmy, Sammi's sister."

"The firecracker?" he asked, brow raised. "Great kid."

"Emily," she corrected them. Sammi was the only one who ever called her Emmy. When they traded a look, she added, "But, I don't mind Emmy."

"Emily," he said with a grin as he helped her to sit, cold rushing into her bottom, the stout brick wall as she remembered it. She shivered and kept hold of his hand to offer a handshake, his grip swallowing her fingers. "Nice to meet you. I'm Isla's fiancé, Nolan."

"Under the circumstances," Isla added, frowning.

"Yes, of course!" Embarrassment washed over his face with a boyish quality. "Under the circumstances."

"He's a bit uncouth," Isla snickered and playfully jabbed him with an elbow. "I'm still training him."

"You're military?" Emily asked, the humor brief. She glanced beyond the couple with hopes of seeing more like him. More men and women wearing fatigues. There were none. "Are you alone?"

"I'm army, but I'm on leave," Nolan answered, dimples

disappearing, a sharp jawline and narrow chin in place. "We were headed up to New York to see the waterfalls and stopped here for a bite."

"We were beat from the drive," Isla continued, their words overlapping, speaking together the way couples do. "The security guard took pity on us and let us hang out for a bit after the place closed."

"That's when we saw the fog coming." Nolan's expression changed with troubling fear. Emily rubbed her arms, the blisters mended with gauze. "It didn't look right at all."

"The security guard went outside to investigate," Isla added. She raised her hands like she was driving a motorcycle. "He was on one of those Segway things and drove into it."

"We heard him. We heard what happened to him," Nolan said, his attention waning as a few men entered the courtyard. "The guard never came back."

"That's when we decided to stay inside," Isla said, finishing their story, her eyes glassy.

"It's good that you did," Emily said, commenting while tugging on her hair. Nolan gave her a slow nod as she continued, "Our being ginger and all, it burns instantly."

"We can't have that," Isla said, pulling herself closer to Nolan. Her focus returning, she asked, "Sammi said you guys drove here?"

"We... I mean, my mom did first. She used the GPS to give us a map and guide us. Our car has all these sensors, too, which helped keep us on the road."

"That's a smart way to do it," Nolan commented, fingers on his chin while watching the men. There was caution in his eyes, the type that told her to be concerned. His focus returned, a consoling look on his face. "Sammi told us about your mom. That she went outside."

"Uh-huh," Emily answered, emotion returning. She blew

out her lungs, trying not to choke up. "I can't talk about... not yet."

"I'm sorry," Isla said, mouth turned down. "I'm afraid we're going to see a lot of it."

"Speaking of," Nolan said, motioning to an elderly couple entering from the department store. In the dim light, Emily saw the way their skin glistened, the woman's screams harrowing.

"We could use the help?" Isla asked, voice rising, matching the urgency.

Emily hung her thumb over her shoulder, asking, "My little sister? You're sure she's okay?"

"Yeah, she'll be fine," Nolan answered, a dimple appearing.

Emily dipped her chin, unsure of what to do or how she could help. But she followed. If for no other reason than to undo some of what the machines had done. She matched their steps, Nolan's stride longer, his height taller. Isla was on the shorter side, but she moved swiftly as they traveled a makeshift path between the victims. When they reached the arcade, Emily stopped, her legs frozen. This wasn't just the place where they triaged victims, it was where they kept the dead.

SIX

In real life, the dead aren't at all like you see in the movies. Emily moved numbly, covering her mouth, fingers shoved against her lips. Her stomach flipped; the air ripe with decomposing bodies. Sallow faces were frozen in terror, eyelids peeled back, a hazy film clouding their eyes. Her throat closed around a gag when seeing the thick ribbons of black and blue, the blood gone still. When Isla and Nolan told her a few dozen had made it to the mall, they didn't mention the number who'd died after they'd gotten there. They didn't mention the number of dead.

Footsteps echoing like a light applause, Nolan reached the old couple first. The woman was hunched over and gasping, her husband gawking. Emily couldn't move. Try as she might, it was as if her feet had sprouted roots into the tiled floor. It was the dead that had her attention, the bodies cordoned off, placed out of sight. No sound. No movement. Dead was dead.

A shuddering breath. *Turn away*, she demanded, and shut her eyes.

The touch of a hand, gentle. "Emily, it's okay if you need to go back," Isla said, having returned.

"I'll be fine, thanks." But it was a lie, her voice trapped in a sob. "I was thinking of my parents."

"Lots of us lost their people," a man commented gruffly. Emily noticed the smell of cigarettes following him. The words jarred her, but it was the look of him that put a fright in her. He had a desiccated face with bandages wrapped around his head, the gauze stained and weepy, scraggly brown hair sprouting beneath. His clothes were torn and dirtied, forearms burned like hers, each wrapped with what looked like paper towels and blue tape. The man glared over his shoulder, unflinching. "Ain't nobody getting out of this nightmare."

"That's Jeter. Don't mind him," Isla said, her grip urging her to turn away. "That guy came in with some family, a brother and a couple of his boys. They barely made it, and one of them died. I think it was his brother—"

"It burns!" A bellowing scream cut Isla's words, the cries coming from the old woman. Nolan worked what looked like a bottle of milk, dousing her face, the woman's fingers splayed and rubbing it in. "Oh God, make it stop!"

"Go, I'll be fine," Emily said. Isla ran to the woman, shoes squelching, her warm touch fading. Emily was alone again as one of the dead stared absently, their cloudy eyes giving her a shiver. She knew the face, the name a memory that was hard to call back. Knowing made it worse. Knowing told her there'd be more. How many more? She eyed the windows, heavy fog rolling silently. There'd be countless by now. Wouldn't there? There'd be dead all around them. Her father, her mother, were a few she knew. What about aunts and uncles? Or her cousins and second cousins? How many had come to their last family picnic? More than a hundred?

Her gaze followed the cigarette man as he joined up with some others. He was still watching her as if there was a plan in his head. What was in his eyes made her skin crawl, and it made her turn away, instinctively sensing danger. If her mom was here, she'd warn about men like him, warn about the look on his face. Or was it something else? Did they know who her father was? Her palms turned itchy with nerves. What if they knew more? Did he tell them everything?

"Make it stop!" the old woman hollered, her screams becoming unbearable. Emily covered her ears, the cries seeping through. She pressed hard enough to make it hurt. It didn't, though. Blood drained from her face, and she stopped bracing. How do you silence guilt? The old woman was one more person dying from the *poison* her father's machine released upon the world. "Please!" The woman's plea a drowning one, she flopped onto the floor, her head striking the hard tile with a hollow thwack. Emily turned away then, the tone of Isla and Nolan's voices carrying unmistakable dread. They couldn't do anything more for the woman.

Emily returned to the dead man's face, the memory of him ticking like a dying spark. He was older, youthful streaks of color mixed with his silver hair. His front was soiled with sweat stains and blood that had dried stiff. How long did he live after reaching the safety of the mall? How long before he died?

"Mr. Rainer?" Emily exclaimed, the name finally reaching her numb brain. She dared to move closer as if to offer condolences. Behind the dead film in his lifeless eyes, she saw the baby blues of her school's vice principal who'd greeted her every school morning. She tried another step but recoiled from the smell. It wasn't just death that covered Mr. Rainer. It was his clothes. They held onto the poison like a sponge, the stench toxic. Although the dead can't hear and Nolan was out of earshot, Emily spoke softly to him. "I'm sorry, Mr. Rainer. I'm sorry for whatever it is my father did."

A jarring crash erupted distantly, the scatter of metal clamoring. Emily searched the stores, the dark openings, some still gated. A pair of survivors emerged from the kitchenette store, arms filled from scavenging. Emily faced the remaining survivors and their small camp of tents and sleeping bags. That's when it hit her. She was alone. It was her and Sammi. *Mom and Dad aren't coming.* She had to do something. Anything. She ran her hands over her front, the thought of food and clean clothes and somewhere to rest. A steel griddle fell and bounced, a woman cursing it. They had the right idea, and it wouldn't be long before the stores were picked clean.

"We're alive," she murmured, a growl rising in her stomach, the dead behind her as she walked to the food court. Twenty or more tents had sprung up, unnoticed until now, their tops like a colorful field of wildflowers. A woman sat cross-legged picking through a bag of hamburger buns, two children next to her with their palms raised. It was food from the foot court, but how much was there? A teen ran past, arms hidden beneath a pile of bags; potato chips and pretzels, a flash of red which could have been Doritos, her favorite. The better question was, how much food was left?

The food court was closed, the counters empty, save for empty cartons and piles of condiments. The Subway shop and Sal's Pizza Shop looked orphaned in the pale light. She imagined a few friendly faces beneath uniformed caps, standing behind the counters, smiling and waiting for her order. Emily blinked the image away and went to her two favorite haunts, a Starbucks and Dairy Queen. A boy and a girl were tucked behind the counter of the ice-cream shop, faces grimy with food coloring, spent cans of whipped cream and an open jar of maraschino cherries between them.

The tables and chairs where she'd eaten a hundred meals before stood quietly, unused and undisturbed. There were a few people at one of the tables, their heads down. One woman glanced at her, chin in a palm, eyes half-lidded, a bottle of wine in the other. Silver light beamed down from the skylights, dust shimmering in the bands. Across the food court, in the furthest corner, she made out the red letters of an emergency exit sign.

Beneath it, a barricade of chairs and tables were perched high, guarding anyone against accidentally going outside.

"Thought you were dead." Emily flinched, a voice suddenly behind her. It was a young man dragging a bedsheet with Mr. Rainer's body, the scene of it unexpected, unimaginable. It also came with a sense of relief. It meant they weren't leaving the bodies to decompose out in the open. Someone had taken charge, the others cooperating. He dropped the cloth to wring out his hands, fingers and palms red from the strain. A mess of sandy-brown hair flopped in front of his face. He puffed at it, blond highlights catching the gray light. Next to her fair complexion, he was tan like a lifeguard, the contrast making her feel self-conscious. She'd always felt that way, having grown up with every red-head and freckled-face joke there was.

"I know you from my school?" Emily blurted, speaking before her mind could catch up. She'd blame her skipping heart, realizing who he was. Beneath his strong features, there was a beautiful boy she knew once. Thoughts of him sprang from an old memory, an attractive notion. Buried in the rubble of her house, tucked between the mattress and box-spring, there was a black and white copybook. And inside the cover was a single heart shape which was penned in purple ink, the name Peter Wilkes in the middle. Nobody forgets their first crush.

Shooing the hair from his face and squinting, he answered, "Right, you were a couple years behind me." He motioned to Mr. Rainer's body, adding, "Ya know, I wasn't kidding, it really was a good thing I saw you move. Could've mistaken you for one of them."

"Cordwood," she commented grimly. "They looked like cordwood to me."

"Yeah, they do." From above a tidy patch of sun freckles, his green eyes quickly looked her up and down. A sudden shyness fell over her, and she bashfully covered her front. His look was caring, though, and she sensed gentleness and concern. He wasn't ogling like the older man had earlier. He was making sure that she was okay. He held out a hand, offering it, "Peter—"

"Wilkes," she interrupted and took hold, touching him briefly before shying away. She matched his smile, a light flutter in her belly. "Yeah, like you said, it's a good thing I moved."

"Emily?" he asked, focus narrowing. "Is it?"

Ears perked with hearing her name. "Emily Stark."

"I thought that was it," he said, glancing at her hair. His head dipped to look at their vice principal, and then to a few people who were wandering aimlessly. With a heaviness in his voice, "I guess... I suppose that it's good to see you here?"

"We're alive," was all she could think to say. "Me and my sister, we made it. But my mom and dad didn't, though—" She lowered her head, unable to finish.

"I'm sorry, Emily," he said, clumsily touching her arm. The moment was awkward, but she welcomed it. When she looked up, he said, "I haven't seen my mom yet, but she said she was coming."

"You made it here!" she said, wanting to offer encouragement. "Your mom would want that."

"I was lucky. Had a night shift to cover. I work the beaches by day and the mall at night." His eyes glistened and he hastily swiped his face, annoyed by the sentiment. "Listen, Isla and Nolan asked me to check on you."

"I was going to check on my sister, Sammi," she answered, seeking out her face amidst the group of kids playing duck-duck-goose.

"Sammi?" he asked. She raised her chin. "She was pretty shaken up at first but was fine once she got to playing with the other kids."

"There she is." As if on cue, Sammi was up and playing chase, tagged by a boy wearing an eyepatch, the two running around the circle of children. In the middle was Ms. Newl, looking haggard but playing the part of schoolteacher, a tablet in hand, pencil in the other while taking notes. Sammi stopped mid-run, and waved, the eyepatch boy stomping a foot, demanding Sammi continue. "It's like none of this is even happening?"

"Your sister's young, is all," Peter said, offering an explanation. He nudged his chin toward a couple walking by, saying, "I don't think any of this has really set in yet."

"No, I guess it hasn't," she agreed. She glanced at their vice principal, asking, "Where are you taking him?"

"Rainer?" Peter pulled up again on the sheet, Mr. Rainer's joints sounding an objection with a rapid *pop-pop-pop*. Emily jumped, the rigor mortis catching her off-guard. "There's a spot in the back we started to use. It's where I've been putting them."

"Them?"

"The ones that didn't make it."

"Makes sense," she nodded in understanding, a spin dizzying her suddenly.

"Whoa!" he said, taking hold of her shoulders. His hands were gentle yet strong. "Maybe you should go back and lie down?"

"I think I need to eat," she answered and shook her head. She straightened herself, the dizziness pressing. Before she could stop it, a throaty gush spilled between them.

"There it is," Peter said, jumping out of the way, his feet dodging the splatter. "Was wondering if you'd done that yet."

"I am so sorry." *Oh my God, I just threw up on Peter Wilkes.* Mortified, she groaned as another wave came, pain gnawing in her side. The watery sight of the mall floor was a puddle of vomit, long red locks hanging down. Peter did something then that surprised her. He pulled her hair back, tucking it safely behind. "I can't believe that just happened."

"Emily, listen," Peter said in a steady voice. "Look at me."

She couldn't, though, the shame of it too much. His hand

appeared with a tissue between his fingers. Without hesitation, he wiped her chin.

"You don't have to do that," she said, taking it.

His eyes found hers, the boy she'd once crushed on was trying to help. "Emily, everyone here has gotten sick. We don't know why, but you'll start to feel better now."

"They got sick?" she asked, returning his gaze, a water bottle now in his hand.

"It's not cold," he shrugged. "But it'll help some."

"Thank you," she said, hurrying a sip, soothing the scratchy burn in her throat. Water spilled around her mouth and dripped down her shirt. She didn't care. It felt good.

"Take it easy," he warned. "You'll get sick again for sure." But she couldn't get enough and drank until she felt her stomach turn. "Breathe some."

"Thank you," Emily said, a burp escaping as she handed it back. There was a breath mint waiting in his other hand. She couldn't help but smile a little and take it. "Did Sammi get sick?"

"Everyone did," he assured her, waving a hand at the windows. "Isla believes it's our bodies reacting to whatever that is."

Dad would know, she thought but didn't dare say it. Sammi was sitting again, cross-legged as another girl with brown pigtails made her way around the duck-duck-goose circle, tapping the tops of the children's heads. "I guess cleaning supplies was one of the first to get raided."

"We found the janitor's closet really quick." Motioning to the pile, he added, "Don't worry about the floor, it'll get cleaned up."

"The fog. The poison in it," she managed to say, a heave rising. "It's good we're getting rid of it."

"Some like Mr. Rainer here, I think they took in too much and couldn't push it out."

Emily straightened up, quickly wiping her mouth. From her pocket, she held her phone. No signal. "Any service?"

"Not since whatever this is started." His voice was soft and quick, trying to cover up the concern. "I got my mom for a minute, but the call died. Nothing since."

"You've got a sister too?" Emily asked, remembering a younger girl, a few years behind her.

"Bug," he answered with a smile. "Christina, but I call her Bug."

"*Bug?*"

"Started when she was a baby. Ya know, when they're small and smelly and wrinkly, I thought she looked like a bug. The name took." A tear rolled down his cheek and was wiped away impatiently. "She's with my mom."

"I hope Bug is okay too," she added, hoping it helped. "Sorry, I gotta do this." She didn't know why, but her gaze kept falling to Mr. Rainer's bugging eyes. Without another thought, she reached down and pinched the dead man's eyelids, closing them. Peter jumped back, surprised. Maybe it was the exhaustion, or the poisons leaving her body. Whatever it was, it felt necessary, the move surprising her too.

"Do what you gotta do," he told her, clapping his hands lightly. "I could use the help if you can stomach it."

"I could try," she answered and rubbed the touch of death from her hands. Mr. Rainer's skin had felt like paper: dry and chalky. Emily shuddered, gooseflesh sprouting on her arms. "I gotta get some gloves first. A mask too."

"I can make that happen," Peter began, then stared at Mr. Rainer. "That dude always seemed to pick on me. I mean, the guy was such a hard-ass."

"It was his job," she answered, stomach dropping with the thought of what awaited her. Did she just volunteer to help move dead bodies? "What's next?"

"Let's get him to a spot in the back," he said, swinging a

thumb over his shoulder. From a back pocket, rubber flapped as he handed her a pair of gloves. "You can use these until we get more."

"There was no other place to store the bodies?"

"Well, outside would have been ideal," he began, eyes wide.

"Can't do that," she commented, understanding.

"We do remove the clothes, though. And then clean them."

"Clean them?" She slipped the pair of yellow rubber gloves onto her hands and imagined jugs of liquid soap and Mr. Rainer's naked body. She shuddered again. "What do you mean, clean them?"

"They were talking about removing the clothes and putting them in trash bags since they might keep us sick," he answered. Peter shook his head, staring absently at Mr. Rainer's body. "But really, none of us know for sure what we're supposed to do. For now, we're just putting them in the back."

"How many?" she asked but didn't want to hear the answer. "Wait." She waved her hand in front of her. "It doesn't matter."

"Sure?"

"I'm sure."

"Well then, Emily, welcome to the clean-up crew."

"Thank you?" she said, questioning the decision to help. "After Rainer, I want some time with my little sister."

A mechanical bang thumped the air and stole their attention, metal clanging. "I think that's the generators," he said, sweat glistening on his brow.

"There's power?" she asked. His face teemed with sweat. She eyed the sconces which glowed dimly. "Lights are on."

"Those are the emergency lights," he started to say, dabbing his forehead. Emily realized just how warm the food court felt. How stuffy it was. "The standby generator kicked in when we lost power. It has a battery bay that gets charged, so the generator isn't running all the time. There's not a lot of power, though."

"It smells different in here. Like it's old and musty." Maybe that was a good thing to keep the poison outside. "How long will the generator run?"

Peter shrugged his shoulders. "It's got a big propane tank," he answered, but she didn't understand. "Which is supposed to be full. But nobody here knows how long it'll last."

Death caught Emily's attention, the smell of it. "Let's get him moved."

"Grab that side," he instructed, handing her a corner of the sheet. "And lift."

She followed Peter, sipping the air, her head turned away. And though death was a part of every breath, she found what was hidden beneath it. It was the taste of salt, and she wondered how long they were safe from what was outside.

SEVEN

Muscles aching, they rested three times while carrying the body. The air muggy, a sheen on Peter's face, sweat raced down her back, triggering another stop. The sheet slipped through her fingers, the body flopping, arms and legs stiff like boards. Emily braced herself straining to stretch out her back. A hunger pang lurched in her belly, arguing with the deathly stench hovering between them.

"How much farther?" The tips of her fingers tingled, the circulation cut. She clapped her hands, wincing. "You said it was in the back?"

"Over there," he answered, breathless, hands on his knees. A moment passed, and he added, "We're almost there. Ready?"

"No, not really," she answered, but ignored what her body was telling her and wrapped her fingers around the sheet. Grunting with a lift, she commented, "Now I know what people mean when they say dead weight."

"Dead weight," Peter answered with a moan, muscles flexing as he took the heavier weight.

They passed a store with outdoor gear, couples inside

peeling clothes from the racks, another group hoisting tents and folded chairs. "I need some of that stuff."

"I grabbed a bunch last night," Peter said, gritting his teeth. "God, how much did this guy weigh?"

"Thanks," she said, bumping his shoulder, struggling to keep balanced. She bumped a pair of resin doors next, peering up at plastic windows near the top. In all the Friday nights and Saturday afternoons, she'd probably passed the doors a thousand times and never noticed. "This the place?"

"*Mall Personnel,*" Peter said, reading the words written across the front. "I guess that's us now."

They shoved the doors open, moving them while dragging Mr. Rainer, his body scraping. On the other side, the doors flapped shut and blasted a pistol shot that made Emily jump. "Now where?" she asked, arms hanging limp.

"A little farther," Peter told her, raising his hands and encouraging her to continue.

"Gosh," she said, eyes adjusting to see a million cables and pipes snaking around them. They ran along the ceiling and climbed the walls and stretched out in every direction. Tin-colored vents ran alongside them, the biggest of them large enough to crawl through. Most were rectangular, a few of them round. How far did the vents go? The food court perhaps? Farther?

Without even the emergency lighting, some of the back areas remained a mystery, the corners hidden in blackness. From where she stood, there was no telling how deep the space went. A creepy vibe making it feel like an old basement. It wasn't, though. It was newer, just dark, is all. Still, she couldn't be entirely convinced there wasn't a monster waiting to jump out and grab her. She scared herself into a jump, yelling, "Shit!"

"Hanging in there, Emily?" Peter asked.

"Kinda," she said. "Is it safe?"

"As far as I know." He didn't sound convincing. "I know it's dark, but there's nobody over there who's going to mind."

"I'll be fine," she said, chewing on her lip. It was a lie of course. Scared was scared, and given the circumstances, there was nothing wrong with being afraid of the dark. She dared another look but turned away, choosing to let Peter lead them. She wanted to be back at the food court where it was bright and open, and where monsters didn't lurk in the shadows or crawl along the ceilings. "Never been back here, is all."

"It was the only place we could think to put the dead," he said, and briefly looked at her.

One of the vents ticked, a control panel near her hummed softly. "I had no idea there was so much going on back here."

"Like the inside of your body? Bet that doesn't look as pretty as the outside either," he laughed, trying to make a comparison. He quieted when realizing what he'd said, embarrassed flush on his cheeks.

"I get what you mean," Emily said, easing his mind. "But thanks for the compliment... I think."

"No problem." A light chuckle this time, a bit more nervously as they turned another corner.

There was a smell in the hidden guts of the mall. It was mechanical, the kind she'd smelled before at the auto garage where her father took the cars to get fixed. She'd always liked that smell. The tires, the fuel, and oil. Something about it was rugged, and she found herself liking it even more now since it helped cover up the salt in the air. Only, when they turned to enter an empty space, a pungent smell hit her like a slap in the face. It explained why this place was selected.

"Here is good," Peter told her, four bodies sitting like matchsticks. Mr. Rainer making number five.

"Uhh, is there enough space?" she asked, sizing up the area with the bodies still to be moved.

"Dunno," he answered, heaving Mr. Rainer's torso alongside the other bodies. Emily did the same, lining his legs. He saw that she covered her mouth and nose. "Now you know why we picked another spot. Can you imagine what the food court would smell like?"

"I get it," she said, stopping short when noticing the lines, the blood vessels thick like a roadmap had been drawn on the dead. She took hold of some loose cardboard and placed it over Mr. Rainer's face, seeing that Peter had done the same for the others. "Let's get out of here."

"Let's hope we won't have to move them again for a while."

"Does the mall have a doctor's office or a nurse's room?" she asked, thinking ahead of what to collect. There was no knowing how long they'd be at the mall. "We should grab any supplies on the way back. Save us a trip."

"I picked up one first thing from the security office. Isla had me bring it to her." He followed the path back to the part of the mall she knew, another body waiting at the department store. "You have time to help with another?"

Stomach grumbling, she pushed through the resin doors. "I need to check on Sammi and find food first."

"We'll grab a bite too," he offered, leading the way. "I'll show you where there are some protein bars too."

"You don't mind?" she asked, stopping as the doors shut behind them. Concern weighed on her thoughts, the colors in the mall changing. "What's going on?"

Peter walked into a band of light and stared into the overhead windows, cocking his head. "It's got to be the sunset. Right?"

"Sunset?" Emily asked, alarmed. Was it that late already? "How long was I sleeping?"

The whites of his eyes flashed. "All day." He was quick to follow, "But you needed it."

"That can't be," she said, shocked. To her, it seemed like the first of the poison was just a few hours ago. "I only got here this morning."

Peter shook his head, and she bit her lip. "That was almost eighteen hours ago," he said. "You slept straight through the day."

"Sammi," she mumbled while listening. She reached for her side, feeling the outline of heavy tape over her injured ribs. An awful thought occurred to her then. "You mean, Sammi has been alone all this time?"

"I wouldn't say alone," Peter answered. He put his hand to his ear, the children's playful laughter continuing. "Everyone is pulling together and helping."

"Food too?" she asked with a terrible thought that Sammi had gone hungry.

"Of course," he answered with a smirk. His brow rose with concern. "You've got to be hungry—"

"Food? I should have been there for her," she said, speaking over Peter as images of her mother and father flashed with an undercurrent of guilt. The tears came, her voice unsteady. "Sammi is only three and sometimes she forgets where her shoes are."

"Hey there," Peter said, taking one of her hands. She didn't know why she mentioned Sammi's shoes. It was such a random thing and had nothing to do with the mall. Her mind was suddenly flooded with concerns about her little sister. With her parents dead, Sammi's well-being was her responsibility.

"I'm sorry," she said, snot running. She swiped her face, a hot flush on her neck and cheeks. "I just don't know what to do next."

"I'll take you to her," Peter answered, his hand gently gripping her arm. She moved closer to him, a subtle and unintentional reaction. "Aside from Isla and Nolan's help, we also have Miss Foster from the elementary school. They've been here since the clouds fell."

Emily nodded, unsure if she could say anything else without bursting into tears. "Clouds fell?" His choice of words put a pin in the moment. "You mean the fog?"

He nudged his chin toward the dead. "That's what one of them said when he got here." His face twisted, disturbed. "I never saw anything like it. We found him near the entrance you came in. Other than his shirt and pants, he didn't have anything else on him."

"Go back to the first part, the clouds falling part."

"That's what he called this." Peter raised his hands up, motioning to everything around them. "He said the clouds fell. And then, before dying, he said that it'd be forever."

"Forever?"

"But I didn't tell anyone about that part." Peter hesitated, his voice sounded anxious, scared even. "He was saying something else about the machines—I dunno—the guy was really losing it before he died."

"The machines?" she asked, glancing around to see if they were alone. It pained her to think it and she tried desperately to recall what her mother said to her father. *Tell me you didn't do this, please, Phil! Tell me!*

"Emily?"

"Huh?" She looked up, eyes locked with his. And in that moment, she thought she'd tell her first crush everything. She thought she'd blurt the secret that changed the lives of everyone in the mall, possibly the world.

"You mumbled, *Tell me*," he said, brow furrowed. "Tell you what?"

"I wonder who he was?" she asked, avoiding the question with a question Peter couldn't answer. But she did have an idea. Didn't her father say something about the clouds too? What if this stranger worked at the machine and knew what caused the accident? "Did he have anything on him?"

"Uh-uh," Peter answered, brow staying firm. His expression

changed with a question in it. "Wait a second. He had clothes on—"

"What is it?" But Peter was gone, reversing course and returning to the inner workings of the mall. Emily tried to keep up, shoes slapping the concrete until they were out of breath and standing over the bodies. As expected, they hadn't moved, the matchsticks remaining. "What?"

"It's this guy, the first one."

Emily stepped around the bodies to the man and lifted a layer of cardboard, a sheet of bubble wrap drifting. The man's hair was fire-red like hers, and his skin was still fair as though he'd died mysteriously in his sleep. To Emily, he didn't look dead at all, and she thought to poke him with a stick and see if his pudgy skin would pink up. His eyes were green and still seemed to be alive. There was no hazy film buildup in them yet like the others. Emily readied her fingers to pinch his eyelids close, but then hesitated.

"Peter. Look at this!"

"What?" Peter gave a reluctant look, lasting only a second. "It's the burns, right?"

"They're missing!"

"That's why I came back," he said, stretching his neck. "I didn't realize it at first."

"How is that possible?"

Peter slid back onto his haunches. He blinked, refocusing his attention on what she'd said.

"If you were outside, the burns were unavoidable." Emily pulled her hair back, showing off the splotchy red around her neck and cheeks.

"But I'm not burned," he told her. "Isla and Nolan were fine too."

"You were all in the mall already. Right?" Emily began to nod, encouraging him to agree. "Did anyone else come in without burns?"

Peter shook his head. "Nope. They all had burns. But what if this guy was just covered better than you were?"

"Or maybe he wasn't outside at all," she answered, mind racing. Was what she proposed even possible? She dug through the man's clothes, noticing it was a lab coat, but said nothing. "Where did you say you found him?"

"At the entrance you and your sister came in."

Emily regarded the entrance, her mom's car stuck on the sidewalk. "Did you see him come in from the outside?" Peter didn't answer. "Did you?"

"I didn't see where he came from." He motioned to the body. "Do his clothes smell?"

"Huh?"

"His clothes," Peter repeated. "Do they feel like Mr. Rainer's or any of the others?"

Emily understood then: her clothes had been covered in plastic, but Mr. Rainer's clothes stank of the fog. She sniffed the air, fighting to smell past the death. She patted the stranger's chest and arms next, half expecting the dead man to jump up laughing as though she'd been tickling him. He stayed dead, though, his clothes dry and without anything resembling the foggy smell. If none of the poison had touched him, then he hadn't died from being outside. She shook her head. "Peter, I don't think this guy was outside at all."

"We have to tell someone," he said. "Cover him back up, the assembly is coming up in a few minutes."

"An assembly?" she asked. Before applying the bubble wrap and cardboard, Emily closed the stranger's eyes. His skin was cold like the concrete floor, dead for sure. But he just didn't feel the same as the others. "I'm almost done." When Peter turned away, she shoved her fingers into the dead man's clothes, rummaging through the stranger's pockets, looking for anything that might lend a clue.

"You won't find anything," Peter said, turning to wait for

her. "We already searched him. If there was anything to find, we would have found it."

"What about this assembly?"

"We're gathering in the main court at the Starbucks by the escalators." The thought of coffee, or even a frap, reminded her that she'd been hungry earlier. And as they left to return, the nagging question followed. What did the man know about the clouds falling? More than that, if he wasn't outside, then what killed him?

EIGHT

Emily wiped the sweat and grime from her face. Humid air carried from what she called "the guts", the mall's internals where the bodies were stored. It was Sammi whom she wanted to see most, the play area looking a little different than her Friday and Saturday night romps at the mall. There were children here. More than she expected. Six or seven at least along with Sammi.

"You hanging in there?" She eyed Sammi from head to toe and tugged on a department store tag that hung from farm-styled dungarees, the pants long, the bottoms rolled up.

"Emmy? Where d'ya go?" Sammi asked and put on a frown, her mouth stuck in a pout.

Emily waved Peter over, looking up briefly. He knelt next to them, saying, "Hey Sammi. Was it okay if your big sister helped me?"

Sammi seemed to consider the question, thumbs hooked from the denim straps. "Well, s'pose it okay... dude." She followed up with a crisp nod, saying, "I got new clothes. But they're kinda for boys."

"I see that," Emily said while primping and propping out of habit. "Did you eat?"

Sammi's eyelids rose and she leaned in as if telling a secret. "Ice cream. But it was kinda melty."

"Oh no," Emily said, adding worry to her voice. "Did you eat a lot?"

Sammi began to nod, but it faded, and she rubbed her middle, tiny hand making circles. "My tummy hurted after."

"I bet it did," Peter commented with a chuckle. He made a gurgling sound which made Sammi laugh.

"Can you stay here with the other kids a bit longer?" Emily asked, glancing at the stores. "I need to get some things for us."

"We gonna get a tent like we camping?" Sammi asked and ran fingers through her hair, a tangle forming. She winced and leaned in again to tell another secret. "Emmy, can we get a toothy brush too?"

"I'll find you a big pink one," she answered her. "And other stuff too."

"Okay," Sammi said, jumping on the balls of her feet before racing off to join in the playing.

"That was easy," Emily said, having thought her sister would have questions. "She didn't ask about my dad?"

"Could be shock. Lots of people still in shock." Peter stood and offered a hand. "I can help get you set up. Like I said, I stashed a bunch of supplies."

"That'd help," she answered and turned around slowly to find the stores that she'd never been inside. On the top level, she immediately recognized two girls her age. Twins from her high school, and the smartest in the class. One of the girls saw her and waved.

"You know them?"

"Kinda," she answered and waved back. "I just can't remember who is who... Jin and Fen, or Fin and Jen?"

Peter smiled. "They came in before you, along with their father and mother," he started, and nudged his shoulder, motioning behind them. "But their mom, she didn't make it." Emily peered at the olive-green doors and wished Peter hadn't told her that. She didn't need to be any more familiar with the matchsticks than she already was. If she didn't distance herself from it now, she'd surely suffocate by the time the dead were all moved.

"By the way, who put this shirt and jacket on me?" Emily asked, forcing a change of topic. She showed Peter the store tags, gray daylight shining on the name of a popular clothing store. She liked the colors and the fit, but these were not her clothes, not the ones she was wearing when they ran from their house.

Reluctantly, he raised his hand. "It was just your top. What you had on smelled like pee," he answered, squeezing his nose and mouth. A warm flush rose on her neck. Peter laughingly waved his hands. "Sammi told us what happened, that she'd had an accident. Isla said that the urine might have even helped cool the burns on your arms."

"Right, I remember that. But you didn't answer my question."

"Which part?"

"Who changed my clothes?" Peter sneered wickedly, his smile stretching wide. Emily covered her front bashfully. "U-uh! No, you didn't... Did you?"

"Nah. Don't worry." He laughed. "Isla had me pick something out for you. She changed you."

A stir of excitement tickled deep inside, the idea of him seeing her intriguing. But the relief of knowing Isla changed her was better, settling.

"You did good," she told him, fingertips running along a sleeve. "These aren't bad."

"I grabbed them from that Abercrombie place. It's about the only store that doesn't smell like the clouds," he said, jangling a large ring of keys from his hip. "Name the store, I'll get us inside."

"Thanks," she said, emotion catching her off-guard. Her nose stung, eyes tearing, grateful that her father was right. The mall was the place for them to go. "I did have some clothes, my mom had me pack a few things. They're still in the car."

"Forget about those," Peter said, stepping toward the center of the mall, arms rising with a wave. "We've got every kind of clothing you could want."

"If only we could eat clothes," she added. "Have you guys talked about food?"

His smile was gone, and Emily could see from the look on his face that food was discussed. "The food and water are only going to last a couple days." He mocked a smile and laughed. "But at least we'll be dressed for it."

"What about the food court?" Emily got up onto her toes to see it. From where they stood, there were the Candy Jar and Pretzel Factory. Next to them, the Smoothie Shack and Burgers and Buns place sat in the dark. Her gaze wandered, understanding. "It's the power. Anything refrigerated is going to spoil."

"Or is already spoiled," he clarified.

"Already?" she asked, thinking back to the last hurricane. "Stuff in the fridge should stay good a while."

"I think it's got something to do with the fog," he answered with uncertainty. "I marked whatever refrigerators and freezers I could find. Taped them off so nobody opens them."

"The fog?" she asked and thought of some of what she'd spoken to her father about. Glancing at the vents and skylights, she wondered if the sodium hydroxide, or the chlorine or whatever else was in the fog, was leaching into the mall. "Glad you saved some of it."

"Nolan thinks the stuff in the refrigerators that wasn't in a container is already gone. But there's still some milk and yogurt and stuff. No eggs, or any of the meats."

Rubbing her belly, the circumstance sounding dire. "Could be that anything frozen will last a little longer."

"The assembly. Part of the agenda is to talk about cooking what we can." A grumble. Peter handed her a candy bar. "The dry food is almost gone too."

She bit into the nougaty bar, teeth ringing from the sweetness. There were at least twenty tents standing, another five or so being erected. "People are hoarding?"

"That's what Isla thinks too," he agreed. "It's also on the list."

"The assembly? Ask everyone to give up whatever food they've stashed?" she asked, understanding the need. He nudged his chin, the lack of enthusiasm felt. Nobody was going to give up what they'd taken. Not under these circumstances. Long term, they'd have to find another source of food. "How many people did you say?"

Peter looked over the tents as he began counting, his lips moving. The moment caught her, made her do a double take; her father always counted that way. She supposed a lot of people did, though, and forced the warm memory away. But he'd caught her stare and asked, "What are you gawking at?"

"How many?" she repeated, ignoring his question.

Her response was met with a slight eyeroll as he resumed the count, answering, "Looks to be over two dozen now. People are still trickling in, so I'd say we'll be near forty soon."

"Forty mouths," she said, the direness growing. "Peter, they'll need to start rationing right away."

"Or find another food source," he said. "But nobody is thinking about rationing yet. They're all trying to figure out what happened."

"It was an accident," she offered and immediately bit her lips, guilt gnawing as a look of surprise showed on his face. She knew in her heart that her father's intentions were true. They were good. But she had no proof of what actually happened.

Emily heard her mother yelling about his *precious machines*, asking him if they were responsible for this. What would happen to her and Sammi if anyone found out the truth, and who they were? "Or maybe it was a storm, carried in from overseas?"

"Yeah, it's a storm all right. Just nothing anyone has ever seen before," he answered, the surprise on his face ebbing. "There's a few who think this is some kind of attack. They think the attackers put poison in the tropical storm that was forecast to run up the coast."

"How would they do that?" Her question was asked with genuine curiosity, the theory not well thought-out.

"Some other guys are insisting it's those carbon scrubbing machines." Emily stopped breathing and didn't move a muscle. Peter shrugged and his mouth twisted as he added, "Who knows what really happened."

"We got to concentrate on what to do now," Emily said, steering the conversation away from the machines. Only, there was a tropical storm forecast and she couldn't help but point at the mall's roof and walls, the large windows. "Peter, that tropical storm. It's coming."

"I know," he said as he swung the bundle of keys from his hip. "They were forecasting high winds and heavy rains. Who knows what's going to happen when that hits."

Rain. Heavy rain. Did her father say anything about the machines and what'd happen in a tropical rainstorm? A shudder raced down her spine as Peter unlocked the security gate in front of a small store. It was the newsstand she'd passed a million times without ever giving it a second thought. She glanced up at the blue *News & Stuff* sign as the security gate crawled into the wall and ripped the quiet with clanking metal.

"Hungry for something other than that candy bar?" Peter asked.

"Yeah, sure," she answered, setting the candy bar aside.

"Let's see what we have in here. It's about the only place I haven't investigated yet."

"A mystery," she said, trying to sound positive. She passed a rack of magazines, the covers of glamor and fame seeming distant and unimportant. Next to it was a shelf of paperback books, the names of famous authors also less important to her somehow. "Peter!"

"Jackpot," he said, his shoulder bumping hers as they stood in front of a refrigerator. "Untouched."

Emily placed her hand against the glass, and to her delight, it was still cold. "I think whatever is in here might still be good."

"Grab what we can—" he began, fingers wrapping around the handle. She clutched his hand, the touch warm. "—What? What is it?"

"Not yet," she told him, wanting to preserve the cold while they continued to explore the store.

He licked his lips like a dog waiting for kibble. "I'm kinda thirsty."

"And I'm hungry," she argued. Her hands went to his, urging him to turn around. "We can make a meal of it."

"Now you're talking." A pale orange counter carried an old cash register, a row of round metal stools sprouting from the floor. Emily kept hold of Peter's hands, pinching his fingers as she led him to a carousel of soft pretzels. She counted five of them hanging from thin metal posts, still golden-brown, and waiting to be picked like ripe fruit from a tree. That was two-and-a-half in a fair split, her stomach growling. "I love soft pretzels."

"And we can have these for dessert." She slid a basket of cellophane-wrapped muffins in front of them. "I'm going to take a few to Sammi too."

"Strawberry?" Peter asked, returning from the refrigerator. He sat on the stool next to her and plopped two strawberry milks in front of them. "They've still got a chill. Not a lot. But some."

Emily braced one of the bottles, condensation forming. "Yeah, it stayed cold," she said, a mouth stuffed with pretzel, a banana muffin in her other hand.

Silence descended between them as they ate. Nuisance noises rising, the sound a particular annoyance any other time. Not today, though. Not now. There was desperation in her appetite which had come back like a punishment. And as she ate faster, there was a frightening moment when she thought they'd run out of food. She tore the cellophane off another muffin, chewing half of it down, wincing at the pain in her throat. She ignored it, a fleeting sense of normalcy returning.

"I can't believe how hungry I am," she mumbled, muffin crumbs spilling.

"That refrigerator stayed cold longer than the others," Peter said, making small talk before chugging the bottle.

"I never knew there was food in here," she commented, belly turning while she searched the store. There was something cozy about the place, something special. She motioned to Peter's keys. "I'm glad nobody else been in here."

"We're the first. I missed it when we made our way around the food court." Sated, he spun the carousel, the remaining pretzel spinning into a golden blur. "Spoiled food and dead bodies are all we're going to have soon."

"That's why we need another source," she said, gathering muffins for Sammi. "It'll be first on the agenda?"

"Probably," he answered, leaning closer to gently wipe a crumb from her cheek. The gesture was small. Innocent even.

A bashful smile took hold but disappeared when a vibration rifled into the stools. "Did you feel that?"

"Uh-huh," he said cautiously, dust falling from the ceiling. "What is—"

"Peter!" she yelled and raised her hands, the counter shaking, a thought of her garage coming to mind. Surely the mall was safe. It was made of thick concrete and brick and mortar. A rumble sounded, distant and guttural, its vibration reverberating through flesh and bone. "What is that?"

"I don't know," Peter shouted, his voice cracking as he tried to balance.

"Hold on!" Emily yelled, the odd vibration erupting into a steady shake that rocked them up and down.

"I think it's an earthquake," he shouted, bracing.

"We don't get earthquakes," she hollered back as the pretzel carousel shook erratically, teetering on the counter lip before falling over. The commotion grew into a tornado as a mechanical song filled her ears with a noise she'd never heard before. She covered her ears, screaming, "It hurts!"

"Emily!" Peter's face was beet-red, shaking like the store around them, his nose gushing, his hands pressed against his ears.

"Peter, hold on!" There was a rhythm in the quake, and it put into motion what was never meant to move. The small store shook to pieces, its contents dancing around them while she tried to grab hold of Peter's arms. The counter toppled, the stools fell over, the walls cracked, wood splintering. Their screams were spent without a voice, any sense of hearing gone. She locked eyes with Peter's, the sight making her sad. Had she ever seen such fright in a person's face before? Instincts took over and she clutched his body, her chest against his, fingers on his face, holding their eye contact while she mouthed, "We have to get out of here."

A strong jolt jarred the mall, tossing the shelves with the cans and bottles. She lost her grip, lost Peter, his face flying sideways. She tried bracing herself against the remains of a stool but landed awkwardly, her bruised ribs crying out and stealing the breath from her lungs. Peter landed with a harsh thump, his pupils enormous, eyes darting and blinking furiously. That's when she saw the gash, his skin torn raggedly across his hairline.

Emily took a firm hold of his arms, glass bottles shattering, liquids spilling, muscles in her legs pumping to get them standing. She held his arms tight, squeezing like she'd never squeezed, and shoved their way through the mess until they were out of the store. At once, Peter motioned to the skylights, the earthquake teasing the roof with chunks of rock plummeting. He shielded her, arms covering like an umbrella when a larger chunk struck. It crashed next to them, blooming like powdery, brick-colored blossom. And then, in a single, swift motion, every sound was suddenly sucked out of the mall like a giant breath. And with it, the stale, salty air was gone. Or, at least the most potent of it.

"What was that?" she asked, feeling the urge to cry, blood rushing with a toxic level of adrenaline. Blood poured from the gash on Peter's head, his fingers coated from swiping at it. She cracked open a napkin dispenser and handed him a stack, instructing, "Press it against the cut."

"I guess we *do* get earthquakes," he said with a noticeable calm. The tone was a lie, though; she could see the hysteria dancing in his bulging eyes.

"This first," she said, sucking in a quick breath while taking hold of his shirt. When he pulled away, she reassured him with her focus, the shirt already torn. She replaced the napkins with fabric, pressing until he reared back. "This will do for now."

"Hear that?" he asked, the echo of distant cries, the sound haunting.

"I see Sammi," she said, up righting a chair to stand on, the distance to the play area close enough. Relief came then, her little sister waving to them. "She's okay." Emily covered her ears, the hairs standing on the back of her neck. Whatever was happening, wasn't over. Beneath the sounds of crumpling brick and stone, there was a tone. Not just a tone, though. It was a pressure like her ears were popping in an airplane.

"What is that?" Peter said, fingers shoved into his ears.

"Are your ears popping?" she yelled with a throaty rasp, her voice absent.

"What?" he hollered, the pressure punching the air. Peter's lips moved furiously, screaming words she couldn't hear.

"Take my hands," she mouthed, toes and fingers tingling, her body vibrating. It was as if they were being assaulted by the sound. *A shockwave?* What if it wasn't an earthquake? What if they'd been struck by an explosion? A huge explosion, and this was the aftermath of it. With her hands, she motioned an explosion, and then mouthed the word. "I think it was an explosion!"

"Yeah!" Peter nodded. He was holding her again, his body trembling, his gaze fixed on the ceiling. Would it hold?

"Peter?" Wet kisses touched the inside of her ears, a drop of blood shining bright on the tip of her finger. "I think it's over. We can move now."

"Thanks. What the—" he started to say, but his voice faded, their fingers woven tight, he let go and brushed the dust and pieces of ceiling from her shirt and hair.

"How's your head?" she asked, picking debris from his hair. The bleeding from the gash was slowing, red trails between his eyes drying.

"I've never heard anything like that before," he said, opening and closing his mouth like a fish. "Can't pop my ears."

"They'll come back," her voice sounding thin like she was talking into a tin can. "Must've been an explosion. A real close one."

"A gas station?" he asked, the question more of a comment. "Definitely going to talk about this at the meeting."

"Come on," Emily said, leading him back to the play area. "I want to see Sammi."

"Yeah. I know how much it scared me." His voice sullen, his gaze unfocused. "Can't imagine how frightening it was for her."

"I can."

NINE

Emily knew her little sister's hugs. She knew them all. The one Sammi gave her now spoke of fright and worry. The trembling that followed said that she was terrified. Her cheeks were a candy-apple-red, hot and stained with tears. Her sobs were hitched, chest shuddering, arms and legs tight around Emily with fingers clutching onto her shirt. Emily shh'd her sister, rocking softly to console. It didn't work, though, and she sat with her back against the stone wall and held onto her sister the way she'd seen her mother do.

"It's okay, baby girl," she whispered, trying to sound like their mom.

"I want Daddy and Mommy," she replied. Her words seized Emily's breath. She couldn't bring herself to tell her the truth. "Mommy hurted. Is Daddy all right?"

Hushed murmurs. Sammi's body shaking. "Sammi, Daddy isn't coming," Emily finally said, rocking gently.

"Emmy, Daddy said the mall." Sammi pushed herself up, red hair clinging to her damp face.

"I know what he said." There was frustration in her voice.

She kissed Sammi's forehead, and met her little sister's eyes. "Daddy would be here if he could."

With that, Sammi seemed to understand. Or was too tired to argue. She collapsed against Emily, heartbeat racing. While the play area was covered in toys, block houses destroyed, plastic bowling pins scattered, the indoor playground equipment had fared better than other parts of the mall. Perhaps it was the foundation, made sturdy, secured with iron inside of thick concrete. Beyond it though, broken glass littered the floors, display signs were toppled, chairs turned over, chunks of plaster sprinkled across the dark tiled floors. A few survivors were already cleaning up, a younger couple tending to a nearby trashcan, its guts spilling over.

"Emmy," Sammi sniffed, voice snotted. She looked at her face to face, a drop of blood on the side of her round cheek. "That sound hurted my ears."

"Yeah, that *hurted* me too," Emily said, turning enough for Sammi to see. She poked Emily's neck and picked at the bloody dry patch as a fresh shudder took her tiny body. "A lot of us got hurt by it. But it's over now, okay girl."

"There gonna be more?" Sammi asked through a sniff.

"I don't know," Emily answered, wondering the same and wiping Sammi's runny nose. How many things were still running? Wasn't there a couple of power plants nearby? What happened when all that stuff got left alone, left without a crew to maintain them? *They're like babies*, Emily decided. *Babies crying for attention.* A scary notion seized her. *What happens when one of them has a tantrum?* "It's quiet now. That's what matters."

"I like it better this way," Sammi said, shoving a thumb in her mouth.

"Me too." Isla sat alongside them, her bronze skin shiny, looking flushed. The mall's temperature was rising, but Isla looked almost feverish. "You okay there, Sammi?" she asked, hand over her mouth. Nolan knelt beside her, eyes red-rimmed and bloodshot. To Emily, it looked as if he hadn't rested since this started. Neither of them had.

"Hi Isla. I be okay." Sammi tried smiling. "Hi Nolan."

"Hey there, Firecracker," Nolan said, the space cramped, he shifted to see beyond them. "I'm making the rounds to check on you guys before I go help."

"We're good," Emily said, focus drawn to the racket at the Smoothie Shack, thick plastic snapping with a thwack, fiberglass splintering. Two men were removing the giant milkshake and straw from above her favorite store. In the mini-earthquake, or whatever it was, the sign had broken loose and hung precariously, even derelict with the threat of squashing anyone beneath. Peter circled around the men, a rope in hand, the other end tied off while he directed the activity. He stopped once to press a finger into his ear and wiggle it. Her hearing was the same, clogged and muffled. "Thank you, Nolan. Thanks for checking."

Nolan was about to stand but must have sensed she had questions. He shook his head, answering, "I've been asking around. Nobody knows what that was."

"Daddy would know," Sammi said suddenly. Emily shifted uncomfortably, jostling her sister as Nolan and Isla traded a look. Before she could explain, Sammi continued, "Right, Emmy? Daddy knows—"

"Might have. Our dad was an engineer," Emily said, speaking over her sister. She brushed Sammi's hair back, driving a fingertip through one of the tangles. Sammi winced. "Dad knew a lot of things."

"He sounds like a very smart guy," Isla said, tone meant for Sammi. Her focus returned, asking, "Peter mentioned the meeting to you?"

"Assembly," Nolan corrected her.

An eyeroll. "Meeting. Assembly, same difference."

"He did," Emily answered, fine debris falling around them like snowflakes. She raised her palm which quickly filled. Only, it wasn't white like snow, it was tinged yellow, made of paper and insulation and other building materials like the kind she'd seen before her garage collapsed. "I'll be there."

"We might have to get masks," Nolan said, pinching the material, pawing at his face, irritated. "Don't want to be breathing this shit if it continues falling."

"Babe, your eyes," Isla said and motioned to her face. "Maybe go wash it out."

"I'll do that." Hands raised, he made like he was going to scratch them out of his skull. "Irritated."

"There's a drugstore. They might have some masks and eyedrops," Emily offered. One by one they looked up, the ceiling cracks seeming superficial. Her gaze moved to where Peter was, the space between them hazy like a skyline blanketed by a light smog. "Pieces of the ceiling. The dust. It's in the air."

"Shit, it is," Nolan said, agitation growing. "I'll get us some masks and eyedrops."

"Can you get one for Peter?" Emily asked. The corner of Isla's mouth rose with a smirk. Emily realized how it sounded. "What?"

"And Nolan, babe, make sure you tell Peter that it's from Emmy," Isla instructed, smirk growing.

"Hey," Emily said, chuckling when Isla laughed.

"It's good to get to know people," Isla said, turning serious. "We're going to be here a while. We're going to need each other."

"Everyone okay over there?" a voice yelled from the other side of the food court. The small figure of a man was clouded by the dust too. Isla waved a hand, pitching a thumb over her head.

"Sammi, you want to go help?" Emily asked, thinking her sister might do better if she was involved. Other children were already picking up toys. Sammi stared on cautiously, the heavy sobs eased. "They look like they need an extra pair of hands. What do you say?"

"I can do that," Sammi answered and jumped down, running ahead without looking back.

Emily pinched her top, the fabric damp and clinging. "Is it me or is it getting hot?"

"That's on our list to discuss too. We must figure out what we do about the air," Isla said, catching some of the debris. "Especially if this shit is in it."

Emily shook her head, having no idea. "Air and food and water," she said, thinking of the priorities.

"That's a start," Isla warned. Emily frowned, mind juggling a half dozen other things to add. "We've still got the bathrooms and running water. But what do we do when that stops? What happens to the sewage?"

"Oh God! I don't even want to think about that." Emily looked on to see Sammi plop down in front of a pile of oversized Lego bricks, her legs folding beneath. "That's not exactly the cleaning up I had in mind, but it'll keep her busy."

"For now," Isla sighed. Her eyelids fluttered as she held back a cough, saying, "There's so much to get done if we're going to be stuck here."

A brown and white blur caught Emily's eyes, the sight seeming impossible. "Isla, look up there!" She pointed to the skylights where a group of birds flitted from beam to beam. Another pair joined them, their chirps barely registering. "They must have been inside the mall when this happened."

"Wow," Isla said, surprised. The excitement drained from her eyes, her stare blank. "They might be the last birds we'll ever see."

"Gosh, I hope not." Emily frowned briefly, the comment edging on a hard truth. "Maybe we could feed—"

A cough led to two and then three, Isla covering it and wheezing. "The dust must be getting to me," she gagged.

"Here, drink some of my water." Emily handed her the bottle, the clap of footsteps approaching. Nolan raised his arm, black and white masks in hand. "Those will help."

"I got you," he said. He tended to Isla, the motions without thought, seeming rehearsed. It was the look on his face that told Emily there was more going on. He lowered his head, looking her in the eyes. "In and out. In and out."

"Can I get you something?" Emily asked, concern growing.

"My bag," Isla told Nolan. He was up and running, leaving without another word.

"Are you okay?" Isla didn't answer, turning, the front of her shirt opening enough for Emily to see a medical port. "I... I didn't know."

Isla covered her chest, forcing a smile, eyelids batting. "It's not that bad really."

"Do you mind if I ask what it is?" Emily said. "I might be a bit uncouth too."

With that, Isla let out a soft giggle, nerves easing. "You can be as uncouth as you want," she replied, lowering her hand, the dressing around the medical port shiny. "It's called a chemo port."

"Cancer?" Emily asked. Though she only just met the woman, the news struck her painfully hard. "Is it bad? I mean, they're all bad and all."

"It's not good?" Isla replied light-heartedly, forcing a smile through a cough. "In my lungs. Never smoked a day in my life either. Not even once."

"I'm so sorry," Emily told her as footsteps ascended again, Nolan's large boots clopping heavily.

He was wheezing badly when he dropped to his bum and

opened Isla's brown leather bag, her initials stitched in gold cursive writing. "It's in here somewhere," he said, rooting through it. His hand appeared then, shaking a bottle of pills, his expression like a magician's, "Gotcha!"

"I don't even know if these cough suppressants work anymore," Isla complained, fishing for a pill at the bottom of the bottle. "Better than nothing."

"How's your throat?" Nolan asked, concern creasing lines between his eyebrows.

"Same." Isla shrugged.

"Let's see what—" His hand returned to the bag, rustling through it. "You've got some hard candies and there's also some of your special gummies."

"Special gummies?" Emily found herself asking, unsure what that meant.

A smile flashed, Isla snatching them. "Special gummies for sure!"

"Oh. Now I get it."

Laughter. "It's about the only thing that helps me get through the day," Isla said, chewing fast.

"If there's anything I can do to help," Emily offered, searching Isla's face. "Anything at all."

A hand. Isla's warm touch on hers. "I appreciate it."

Fiberglass tore with a jolting crash, the sound ripping through the courtyard. Emily bolted up, a hard look fixed on where Sammi was. She sighed, seeing her playing. Noise continued to ricochet, bouncing around as the Shake Shack was dismantled, Peter wrangling a large part of it. He drove the remains of the sign into a rolling garbage bin, the milkshake straw jutting out of the top. When he saw them watching, gauzy bandage on his head hanging loose, he waved, "Sorry. We're almost done."

"Help me!" a bone-chilling scream echoed.

"Did you hear that?" Emily asked, prodding her ears.

Isla nodded slowly. Another cry yelled, "Please, someone! Anyone!"

Her feet were in motion, the response near immediate, the first steps behind Peter who ran ahead. Emily had nothing in hand, no first-aid, no bandages, no anything. But she ran, the cries gaining.

"Behind you," she heard Nolan shout. A moment later, he passed, a whiff of sweat chasing.

Breathing fast, they reached the double doors leading to the bodies. But it wasn't one of the dead screaming. One of the twins had fallen from the second level.

"Shit, shit," Nolan said, sliding to his knees, arms stretched guarding. Emily dropped next to the girl, Nolan asking, "Check for vitals."

"Vitals. Right."

The twin was flat on her back; one of her arms pinned beneath as if it never existed. Her legs were spread apart, a bone poking through the skin beneath the knee. It was mendable, but it was the ring of blood around the twin's head that brought immediate concern. Isla looked at them, wide-eyed, hands pressed against the floor. Emily touched two fingers to the side of the girl's neck, hopeful she'd get a pulse. There was none.

"I tried to hold her, but she slipped," the girl's twin told them. "Is she... is she dead?" No movement and no pulse, the twin was completely still.

"This girl needs a hospital," Isla said, whispering.

"What do we do?" Emily asked.

"I'm not sure—" Peter replied. "Check her pulse again!"

Emily did as asked, fingers applied again. *No thumb and just a soft touch*, she recalled, hunting for a pulse. A bump. It was there. Barely. Emily's heart rocketed into her throat, asking, "Someone check for me, I think I felt something."

"Here, let me try," Isla said, her hand shaky. It steadied when she pressed her fingers to the girl's neck.

"Anything?" Nolan asked.

"Shh!" Isla glared as everyone held their breath. A slow nod. "I got a pulse."

"That's what I felt." Emily's heart leaped.

"There's another one," Isla said, confidence building. "It's faint, but she's alive."

"Alive!" Peter exclaimed. Emily brushed the hair from the girl's face.

Above, the other sister shrieked and took off running for the stairs, shoes clapping. When she arrived, she asked, "Can you help her?"

Peter shook his head, saying, "Maybe the older guy who came in with his wife? He's a doctor?"

"Well, we can't leave her here," Emily said, assessing the girl's leg. "We've got to move her."

"I can do it," Nolan told them, inching closer, assessing her weight.

"What if we dragged her?" Emily asked before Nolan lifted. "You know, in case there's some injury to the neck or spine?"

"I know what to do," Peter began, stopping abruptly. He raced to the nearest store, the front window shattered, a bushel of comforters and sheets on display. On his return, he whipped one of the sheets, air cracking with a snap, and spread it across the floor. "Help me get her on here. She'll slide across the floor like it was ice."

Four sets of hands eased the girl carefully onto her side, the girl's sister stuffing the sheet beneath. "And the same on the other side," Emily said, the motion repeated.

"We've got her on a stretcher," Nolan huffed, corners of the sheet bunched in his hand. "Let's hurry and hope someone can help."

"Where's the doctor?" the other twin asked.

Isla focused past Nolan, Emily asking them, "Has anyone seen him?"

"Still over there with his wife." Nolan stopped and looked over his shoulder, adding, "She didn't make it."

By the time the food court was in sight, the twin on the sheet had gone gray, the color on her face and hands gone. Were they too late? Emily checked for a pulse, sweat stinging the back of her neck. Nerves racing when there was no pulse to be found.

"Is she dead!?" the twin sister cried, her father joining. His face was frozen with concern while he looked to his daughter for answers.

"I dunno!" Emily returned, hands trembling while she hunted for a pulse in the girl's wrists but only felt the cold. "I'm not getting anything."

"Who's that?" Sammi asked, her sister's voice surprising Emily. "Is she dead too?"

"No! She's not dead," the twin snapped, eyes filled with doubt, darting around and seeking support. When there was none to be had, her gaze fell to her gray sister. For a moment, Emily thought the girl would break down and cry right there. "She's hurt, is all." And then she did cry, crumpling to the floor in a heap.

"What do we have here?" the old man asked, Nolan by his side. His silver hair was flat against his scalp, his middle round and doughy. There were blistery pink burns with coin-sized welts across his neck and hands and arms. In a gentle lean, he placed a hand on Nolan's shoulder and lowered himself to the dying twin. One by one, he shined a penlight into the girl's pupils, a frown narrowing as the beam passed over her black eyes. "Pupils are dilated and fixed."

"What's that mean?" the girl's sister asked. "You can save her?"

"We can make her comfortable," the old doctor told her. Shaking his head, he added, "But, given the circumstances, I'm afraid that's about all we can do."

All we can do, Emily heard, the sheet slipping from between her fingers. She backed away from the scene, the image of it surreal, the reality of it like some kind of nightmare she couldn't escape. This was another death that hadn't been caused by the storm. It was a death inside the mall, like the man they'd carted to the rear of the mall earlier. How many more? How many would die senselessly?

TEN

People were still dying. They weren't just dying outside, they were dying inside too. Emily realized that the mall was just a mall. There were no guarantees for safety or refuge. There was no guaranteeing anything. She wanted to be back in her bed where she could tuck herself beneath thick blankets to hide in a bubble of heat, legs balled up to her chest and her headphones drowning out all other sounds. But that wasn't going to happen. She stood next to Peter while Nolan and Isla took to standing at the center of the courtyard. Footsteps shuffled slowly, the mall survivors gathering, the crowd humming with soft conversation.

Sammi sobbed lightly into her shirt, the fabric damp with tears. She was asking about their mom and dad again. She'd seen what happened to their mom but didn't understand that their dad was with her, that he was stuck in the other car. Emily ran a hand through her sister's hair to comfort her, but there wasn't anything she could do or say except to be there.

Laughter rang out from behind them, the abrupt interruption turning heads. Emily's insides shrank when seeing who it was, a stare fixed on her from the one who was gawking earlier. It was the old man, Jeter. The cigarette man who'd spoken to her earlier. His eyes were dark, almost black, and he found her immediately and leveled a stare. Behind him was a group of men, one tipping a bottle and then passing it around. They strolled into the courtyard like they were entering a bar. Jeter surprised her then, telling the others to ditch the bottle while he took to the wall and sat, arms crossed, his attention waiting.

A maternal instinct clicked in Emily. It was a sense that made her nervous for Sammi—nervous for them—protective and guarding. Emily turned to face Nolan and Isla and ignored the jeering and snickering and noises. A thought surfaced in her mind: those gathering would surely want to know the truth of what had happened. For her sake, and for Sammi's, they'd say nothing to anyone about their father's work with the machines.

Emily nudged Sammi's chin, urging her to look at her. When she did, Emily held a finger to her lips, saying, "We'll need to be quiet."

"Okay," Sammi answered, eyes swimming, the day growing long. She grinned weakly, but it lasted only a second before she tucked her face into the crook of Emily's neck.

"Probably past your bedtime, isn't it?" Emily told her sister, planting a kiss on top of her head.

"I can take her?" Ms. Newl offered, arms extended, bangle bracelets clanking. "We were able to find some apple slices and crackers." She cocked her head, speaking away from the children, "They're pre-packed. You know, preservatives."

"Could be safer that way," Emily said, adjusting Sammi's weight, warming to the idea of putting her down. "You sure?"

"Of course. Snacks and naps." Ms. Newl smiled. "We've got some volunteers to help out." From over her shoulder, Emily saw a few girls helping, including the twin whose sister had fallen. "Sammi is our champion at duck-duck-goose."

Peter leaned close, saying, "It's probably better if she's not here for the discussion."

Sammi tightened her hold.

"It's okay, girl, do you want some fruit?"

Sammi looked at Ms. Newl, caution wavering in her gaze.

"Sammi, there's story-time too," Ms. Newl offered, holding up a children's book.

"Emmy, you'll still be here?" Sammi asked.

The question pained her, but Emily lowered Sammi, answering, "Of course, I'll be right over there. Grown-ups just need to talk for a bit."

"But, but Emmy, you not growed-up," Sammi said with all the sincerity of an adult.

"I won't tell if you don't," Peter said, chuckling and ruffling Sammi's hair. He turned serious as he bent over and pointed toward Isla and Nolan. "We'll be right over there."

"Not too far," Sammi instructed, pointing a finger. She let go then and turned to run.

"Wait," Emily called after her, grabbing once more with a squeeze. "Now you can go." Sammi darted off with the other children.

Peter's fingers brushed Emily's hand, the group growing. There were more survivors now. A lot more since they'd arrived at the mall. More meant they'd need supplies sooner. A balding man walked in front of them while picking at a gauze bandage taped to the crown of his head. It was yellow and red at the center, a blooming ooze drying. His arms were burned like Emily's, the bandages needing to be changed. The sight made her skin itch, but she fought the urge. Medical supplies. They'd already run through whatever could be found and needed more. The list in her head grew, the thought of it overwhelming.

Cautiously appearing from behind the man, she saw the eyes of a little girl. Saucer-round and dusky blue, the girl searched them up and down while clutching onto a faded family photograph. The girl was alone with her father, a sorrowful twinge reminding Emily of who was missing. The girl's father got onto his toes, his expression desperate as he looked over the crowd. When he lowered his face, defeated, Emily knew it was loss. She could have died a thousand times in that moment.

The man's little girl reappeared, running ahead when seeing Sammi and the other children. Skin like alabaster, her hair was a familiar color, a shiny auburn that looked like the girl's father's. It was badly tangled with stringy pigtails which hung lopsided and uneven. Even her shirt was out of sorts, having been put on inside out.

Emily approached, telling him, "The kids have snacks and there's a schoolteacher watching them."

"They won't mind one more?" he asked, hands on his hips.

"Not at all," Peter assured him.

"Go on now," he told his daughter. Like Sammi, the girl was reluctant at first. It was the laughter that did it, the children young, caught up in the playful happiness. The girl ran, her shoes mismatched, different colors, but at least on the right feet. When she reached the kids, she tucked the photograph into a pocket, missing once, but then safely put it away before saying hello to Sammi.

Nolan raised his hand to quiet the chatter. Across the group, there were enough people to fill a small auditorium. Many were dressed in new clothes, taken from the stores, the tags and antitheft devices dangling. With slumped shoulders, dull eyes, and blank features, Emily felt the tragedy and saw it in the way they carried the remains of their spirit.

Something familiar caught her eye. Hidden in the recess of a dark corner, Ms. Quigly stood watching as Nolan and Isla worked to get everyone's attention. *That's impossible!* Her heart jumped. *Ms. Quigly?* She blinked away the mirage, seeing it for what it was, guilt playing with her mind. It was a small decorative tree. Without thinking, she reached behind her and took Peter's hand, squeezing his fingers until he did the same. The guilt that came with Ms. Quigly's death shrank away—just a little, though.

The skylights had grown darker, fog swirling and stealing the light. Still, the mall stayed warm and had grown muggier, uncomfortable even. Beads of sweat glistened on Nolan's head, a ring of grime circling his neck and collar. He'd opened his army fatigues, which surely broke with any military regulations, but there was nobody here to care. In the tight gathering, sweat's sour smell was strong, and she supposed it'd get worse. How long before the shelves in the pharmacy emptied, the antiperspirant and deodorants becoming a memory of what was once before?

"Thank you for joining," Isla began, her voice rough. "We've got a lot to discuss so if you'll all be patient with questions."

A low murmur, someone behind them asking, "Are they in charge?"

"Nobody is in charge," Isla replied. "This isn't a committee. Nothing like that."

"We just thought it best to call an assembly and discuss what's next," Nolan said, voice booming. He leaped onto the short wall in a swift motion. "Come and get closer if you can't hear me."

"What was that shake?" a woman asked, rising from the back of the group. "We don't get earthquakes around here."

"That was no earthquake," a voice cracked. It was the old man. Jeter continued, "That was an aftershock."

"An aftershock? From what?"

"From an explosion!" he hissed.

"Please," Isla said, voice rising over the chatter. "Nobody knows what that was and we have other pressing—"

"It was probably that machine on the beach," the voice replied, ignoring Isla's plea.

Emily's insides tightened, anxiety building. She crossed her arms, the nerves raw. "What about water and food and other supplies?" she called out, hoping to steer the conversation.

"Exactly. Yes," Nolan replied. "Let's discuss next steps, like supplies."

"It was that damn machine!" Jeter said, raising his voice, his stare remaining. He wore the same clothes as before and his face was pocked with red welts, the blisters torn open. And though he was tall and seemed feeble, skin hanging loose, the man frightened her.

"Jeter, that machine is a couple miles away," someone rebutted.

"You don't have to tell me that! I fucking know where it is!" Jeter snapped. "I live by it. Monstrous big that machine. Empire State Building big but tipped on its side and sitting on the edge of the ocean. Damn thing is like a beached whale, its body half in and out of the surf with nowhere to go. Tell ya'll another thing too. They say it ain't done being built, but I know it's running! I heard it. And I've seen things too... vomits poison from them tall stacks right into the sky. Been doing it for weeks! Just need to find someone who's been working there—"

Does he know? Emily's throat closed around the thought. *Was that why he was staring at me?*

As if to emphasize Jeter's last point, an explosion boomed, a distant roar expanding like thunder during a springtime storm. The crowd ducked, but Jeter didn't move. He stood like a statue, pinching two fingers as if rubbing a cigarette between them. Another rumble lasted a few seconds: smaller and more distant than the first. Peter reached for Emily's arm, and she found herself leaning into him, huddling toward the security of another.

"Everyone okay?" Nolan asked, eyes huge, a hard line creasing his forehead. "So much for hoping we'd felt the last of them."

"Was that the machine too?" a voice near the edge of the crowd asked. "Jeter? What are you thinking?"

"I don't think it was," Jeter began to say, words riding on a whistle. "It might have been something closer, though. Probably a power transformer?"

"We still got the generator running, which we'll talk more about in a minute." Nolan wiped the sweat from his brow again, Isla handing him a sheet of yellow paper. "I asked for help earlier, can we get a quick status? How about communications first?"

"That one was mine. I'm Jerry to anyone who don't know me," a slender man answered with a slight drawl. He cleared his throat and flipped the cover of spiral tablet, paper rustling. "Cellphones are down as everybody already knows. We were able to get into the computer and electronics hobby shop and found some CB radio equipment like the truck drivers use. Got an antenna mounted and the radio running on twelve volts from a bunch of batteries we wired to it."

"And? Anyone on the other end?" Nolan asked, his words leading. Jerry looked on reluctantly, lips tight. "Jerry, have you heard anything? Anything at all?"

Jerry slumped forward and shook his head. He hung a thumb over his shoulder, adding, "But I got Tom back there scanning all the channels. He's sending messages on channels 9 and 19 where people should be listening. We did hear an emergency recording, but it stopped after that earthquake or explosion, or whatever that was."

"What about the antenna?" Ms. Newl asked, voice rising from the edge of the play area. She had one eye on the kids, another on the meeting, and cleared her throat, asking, "Are the antennas the right type? How about size or direction?"

"I mean, the radios are inside, and the antennas are inside, but maybe we need bigger—something with more reach?" Jerry asked. He shook his head. "I'm more of a computer guy. Networks and printers, that sort of thing."

Heads turned in unison, the back and forth like a tennis match. "Antenna selection and setup is crucial for proper transmitting and receiving." Ms. Newl's tone was the same used when she'd given the class instructions on dissecting a frog. She relaxed some, voice softer, "Maybe I could take a look?"

"That'd be swell," Jerry said, the southern twang stronger.

"Communications, Ms. Newl, you'll help," Nolan instructed. "Jerry, you mentioned batteries?"

Jerry nodded, a thin smile appearing. "No shortage of batteries. The store is full of them," he answered. "All kinds too, which we'll need once the generator dies."

"Speaking of which," Nolan said, turning to face a middle-aged couple standing near the front.

"Guess that'd be me. I'm Dolores. Dolores Shelbourn," the woman began. She wiped her hands on the front of her pants before continuing. "Power situation is that we're still near full on the propane tank." A small sigh lifted from the group. "Only using the generator for emergency power which I recommend we continue."

"What about running a power line to the CB radio?" Peter asked. Emily felt his hand leave hers as he got onto his toes, asking, "That'd give Jerry some plug-in power? Could do more?"

"That's a far better use," Ms. Newl agreed. "We could bump the transmit and receive power with the right equipment and power. Save on batteries too."

"Can we make that happen?" Nolan asked.

"Yes, technically," Dolores answered. She raised her hands up then, brow raised with a whoa. "However, is that the best use of the propane we have?"

"There could be other people. Other survivors," Emily

abruptly said, surprising herself. She rose onto the balls of her feet; feeling compelled, she added, "Like our relatives."

With that word, there came a gush of agreement, someone saying, "I need to know if my husband is out there. And our kids!"

"And what about the Internet?" another voice said. "If we get power to the CB radio, we can set up the Internet?"

"I can do that! For sure. That's my thing," Jerry answered, hopping with excitement. "The mall has a router and Wi-Fi. As long as the other end is online, we'll be online."

"Sounds like there's multiple opportunities to expand on communications," Isla said, justifying the request. Nolan put up a hand, voting without calling for one. "It might tell us if this is only local or not."

"Yeah, turn the Internet back on," a few others said, hands raised.

Emily raised hers too, saying, "Internet. Run a line for Jerry to use."

"I want to see *the* Facebook again," an older man said. "My daughter is on there. She's in Seattle."

"Dolores, you good?" Nolan asked, raising his voice over the crowd as talk of the Internet grew. Isla joined him with both hands raised, signaling to quiet down.

"I'll get power to them." Dolores sought out Jerry, saying, "Catch up with you after the meeting."

"That's power, but no promises it'll work," Isla told the crowd. They talked over her, the excitement building.

"People! Please, listen up!" Nolan shouted. "We've got a hundred other things to get done. Jerry, you're good?"

Jerry bobbed his head, a hard frown forming. "But like you said, there's no promises. We might have Wi-Fi but can't say what else will be online."

"We should be trying everything, anyway," Nolan

commented. As she watched the proceedings, Emily realized Nolan was a natural at this. "So, how are we on food and water?"

A smaller woman raised a hand, face pinched, hair pinned in a tight bun. She stood, a pair of canary-yellow pants bright in the dim light, and answered, "Water is still running clean. We've got no reports of issues."

"No contamination?" Isla asked. Emily thought of the earlier comments, the bathrooms and sewage. She shook, goose-bumps rising.

The woman pursed her lips and shrugged. "Well, I mean, there's no way to know for sure. The recommendation is to only drink the bottled water."

"The running water should be fine for cooking," Isla said, hand catching a cough that pulled Nolan's attention. "We've found some camping gear and can boil what we need."

"That's a good segue to ask about our food situation." Nolan marked the yellow sheet. "How are we doing on supplies?"

Emily saw wariness, the crowd moving in unison, heads turning. The woman with the canary-yellow pants bit her lip, turned to the food court and back. "There's a day, maybe. But it's mostly junk food," she answered. "There was a limited supply to begin with and we burned through it already."

"What about the Food-Mart next to the mall?" Jeter said, hand raised, voice whistling. He groaned when he stood, a younger man next to him taking a hand. "It'd mean going outside, though. If that's even possible."

Images of the mall's inner workings came to mind. The cabling and duct work which was big enough to crawl through. Before she knew what she was doing, Emily raised her hand. Peter glanced at her with surprise, Nolan motioning to her. "There are service tunnels, right? For the utilities. If there is one, then we could go beneath the fog?"

A low hum, voices questioning, Nolan asked, "Does anyone know if this building connects to the Food-Mart?"

"She's right," someone answered from the back. "There are service tunnels all around this complex."

"Service tunnels?" Nolan asked, then added, "Makes sense. Utilities like the plumbing and electrical and whatever else comes from the town."

"Sounds about right," Jeter spoke up, supporting the idea.

Keys jingled loudly, the suddenness of it alarming. Peter held them above his head, shaking them like a noise maker until the crowd went quiet. "I think I saw a map of the mall with the service tunnel beneath."

The body. No burns, Emily thought. *Was that how the man got to the mall? A service tunnel?*

"If we can find access," Peter began to say. Nolan penciled some words, nodding as he wrote. "Then Emily and I can bring back food and medicine."

"Huh?" Emily asked, heart tightening. The thought of leaving the mall terrified her. But the thought of Sammi starving to death was worse. "Yeah, we can try."

"Say you find access to the service tunnels," someone started. "What do you do if the fog is in them?"

"Scuba gear?" Peter answered, tone questioning. "There's a shop with wetsuits, all kinds of scuba gear."

Reading back what he'd written down, Nolan spoke up, "You and Emily will look for access, a service map, service tunnels if they're here." Sweat rolled down the side of his face. The air felt heavier, thicker since they'd started the meeting.

As Nolan continued reading, Peter leaned in. "I don't think the scuba gear will work, anyway."

"Why? I used plastic trash bags and those held." Emily met his eyes and saw rigid concern.

"That part would work. Protection from the burning." He pointed to her face and then his. "It's the blindness. There's gotta be multiple tunnels. If there's fog, I've no idea how we'd find the Food-Mart."

"We have to find the right service tunnel," she exclaimed. "And it has to be passable."

"But what if it isn't?" Peter asked. "Or the fog is there?"

She looked at him, blood running cold. "Then we all die."

ELEVEN

Then we all die. Emily didn't regret saying those words. She didn't regret the looks she got from a few nearby who'd overheard the conversation. It was the truth. They were going to die if they didn't find food and water. What she regretted was the look on Peter's face, his color like ash, his eyes wide in a terrified stare. It was the kind of fright that'd haunt her long after the moment passed. It put a hard knot in her gut.

There had to be a service tunnel. Her dad would know where it was too. And knowing he'd know made her miss him even more. Emily scanned the glares, the look of questions. If he were here now, what would her father ask? He'd start with power and water. It came from somewhere and she'd never seen anything overhead. Not once in all the years of coming to the mall. There were manhole covers in the parking lot and in the streets. She'd seen them along the outer perimeter when she and Clara Williams were memorizing the number of steps to the mall doors. That meant there had to be access inside—access big enough to stand in and walk.

"In the back," she blurted in Peter's ear. He looked at her, questioning. He needed more. "Where the bodies are. All those pipes and wires. That's gotta be it."

"We—" he began, a cry interrupting. She shut her eyes, recognizing the voice, and recognizing the anguish too. It was the twin, Jin. Emily craned her neck to see the old doctor standing over the fallen sister, his face dipped as he delivered bad news. With a sullen look, Peter continued, "I guess Fen didn't make it."

Emily faced the front where Isla and Nolan continued running the meeting. They stood like statues, Jin's cries carrying. In death, the meeting's urgency was forgotten. Emily clutched her chest, the sorrow setting like a stone. How many more before she became callous to it, the pit of gloom more distant with each? As if feeling the same, nobody got up. Nobody questioned. Instead, they went about their assignments, the assembly breaking.

"Let's move her, okay?" Peter asked, extending his hand. She took hold with a squeeze and went to Fen's body. The girl's skin was gray, her eyes like coal. Emily watched as Peter tried consoling Fen's sister but didn't think the twin was hearing him. The old doctor noticed it too, and, with Isla's help, they escorted Jin away. Peter got on one side and Emily mirrored his moves, a hundred eyes seeming to be watching. "We'll make this quick."

"Quick," she agreed, bunching the sheet in her hand until her knuckles turned white. They barely made a sound, the body sliding. Emily said nothing as thoughts of the service tunnel returned. What if access to it was in the same place as the makeshift morgue? What then? The number of sick and injured was apt to climb, the body count too. It was a morbid thought, but these were some of the things that had to be discussed. In a way, it was how the dead spoke. It was their presence, their existence. And the mall didn't have enough room for them.

The resin doors clapped shut, Emily sucking in a breath, desperate to stall the rotting smell. Her gaze found the darkest corners, that place where shadows couldn't live. As a child, it was where dangerous things lurked. The back of a closet. Beneath the bed or bedroom door. In the dark and hidden from sight, an arm's reach from being seen. But what if there was a miracle waiting in them, like an access panel that had been overlooked?

Her phone had no cell service, but the light still worked. She shined it into the corners, Fen's body dragging behind, muscles in Emily's arm straining. Peter caught on and began flashing a beam of light too, following the pipes which sprouted out of the concrete. She ran her phone's light along the wires crawling up the walls and across the ceilings, the mall's arteries and veins going in every direction.

They placed Fen's body alongside the others. "I can't tell what's what!" Emily confessed, the snaking pipes and wires too many to follow. "I mean, these have got to be coming in from somewhere. Right?"

"That they must," Peter said, a beam of light jumping to symbols and markings along the wall, trying to make sense of them. He shrugged his shoulders, just as confused. "These might as well be in another language."

Daring a touch, Emily draped her fingers on one of the conduits and expected to feel it vibrate or hear it hum. It was cold, though. Lifeless. The end of it entering the concrete and disappearing. "You don't think there's just pipes in and out of the mall? You know, instead of a service tunnel."

Eyes down, Peter let out a sigh, the flashlight shining beneath his chin. "Shit, I hope not. Things will get stupid desperate if we can't get food." He put a finger to a pipe, the surface glistening. "This must be cold water. But be careful. There's no telling if there's anything that'll shock you."

"Peter!" Emily said with a trace of relief. Her knees went weak finding what they needed. A door. She was right, after all. Sometimes there were secrets hidden in the shadows. This one was hidden in the floor opposite of their makeshift morgue. "Peter, a door."

"God, I hope it's what we're looking for," he said, crouching as their lights converged on the surface, metal gleaming. It was painted yellow which had faded, the edge closest to her bumpy and pitted with rust. "That's gotta go somewhere."

"Feels cold." Fingers steadying, she breathed out slowly and held her hand against the surface. "A little damp too."

"It's condensation," Peter said, swiping his hand and rubbing fingers together.

"Might be colder behind the door," she added, voice high with excitement. She grabbed the handle, the metal knurled with a diamond pattern which was worn smooth.

"Wait!" Peter said, alarmed. She felt it then, a slight vibration buzzing in her fingers. There was life coming up through the service panel, something mechanical and distant. "Might be the generator I feel."

"If it's coming through here, then it should make it easier to get a line to the electronics shop." Emily pitched her phone's light toward the ceiling, electrical cables spewing from a giant panel. "I'm sure they've got tools to figure out which cable it is."

"They can take care of it," Peter said, squatting next to the door.

"Let's see what's in there," she said, squeezing the handle.

"Hold your breath," he warned, taking hold and jerking the handle. Without thought, she held her breath, pressing her lips tight. There was no telling what they'd find. Peter did the same, his cheeks puffing. The hinges creaked, the metal clanked and banged with mechanical protests as they hoisted it open and rested it against the wall.

Chilly air blew from the cavity as if the tunnel were letting out a long breath. She eased her eyelids closed, the touch of air cool and soothing. There was no burning. No sting from it either. Emily dared a tiny sip, sucking in as Peter looked on with red, ballooning cheeks. It was fresh, and she breathed deeper, the taste like a damp cellar.

"The air is okay," she told him.

"It doesn't smell bad either," he said with a sniff. He peered into the black opening, his pupils wildly huge, starved for light. "It's nothing like from outside."

"There's no smell to it," she said, eyes adjusting. "Maybe because it's below the ground. What do you think?"

"We're a couple miles from the beach, below sea level, I think?" Peter said, asking. His face turned bright with an idea. "What if whatever is going on outside only hits above sea level?"

"That might be—" Emily began, stopping when strands of red hair gently waved. "Look Peter! It's like a breeze."

"But where is it coming from?" He touched the strands of long hair, pondering. "Has to be the market."

"We've got breathable air and light," Emily began, intent on going.

"You first," he said, biting the side of his mouth.

She searched the inside enough to see the first steps of a ladder, and then stopped, throat dry and scratchy. How far did it go? How deep? The light only went so far, the bottom hidden. "We'll... we'll have to go slow."

"Are you up for this?" he asked, head tilted.

He must've heard the hesitancy. She was sure of it. "I'll be fine," she answered, trying to sound convincing. Her Chuck Taylor sneakers were stuck to the floor. They were her favorite shoes, but despite willing them as she was, the thick soles weren't budging. Her feet were frozen, and her insides trembled. "Peter, I know I can do this."

"It's good, Emily," Peter said and began shimmying through the door. "I'll go."

"Let me help you," she said, insisting and taking hold of his arms. He backed into the opening, the floor swallowing him whole, the ladder rungs chiming like distant bells.

He shook, exaggerating the motion, his sandy-brown hair flopping from side to side. "Damn! It's gotta be twenty degrees colder in here."

"That explains the condensation." She tapped his arms when a low whirring sound rose from below him. "You hear that?"

"Fans?" he asked restlessly, lowering himself until only his head and neck were showing. "I'm not sure what it is."

"Whatever it is, it sounds far away," she said as darkness spilled over the rest of her first crush. In harsh contrast of her phone's light, he could have been lowering himself into a pool of black goo, the image unsettling. When there was only a tangle of hair at the surface, she asked, "Is it deep?"

"There's a platform here," he said, shaking off another shiver. His arm appeared, waving her to join. "One step at a time?"

Emily smiled into the hole begrudgingly. "One step at a time."

"I'm down," he yelled, his shoes striking a walkway, ringing on the metal and seeming to echo forever. "I'm glad I had this light."

"How far can you see?" Emily asked, body turned around, the position awkward, feeling like a crab crawling backward into a hole. Her right sneaker touched first, and then the left. A steady breath of cold raising goosebumps across her body. "Peter, how far is it?"

"Come on down and see," he answered. She peered down in time to see his hand grip her shoe, guiding. "I can see a faint light a hundred yards from here. Might be less."

"That's good—" Her foot slipped on the rung, rubber screeching, stomach lurching the way it does when in a fall.

"I got you," Peter said suddenly, catching hold of her legs.

"Shit!" she said rather breathlessly. Warm embarrassment on her cheeks, she tried to sound coy, "Who's got you?"

"Being tall has its advantages," he answered while easing her down the rest of the ladder. He turned, fanning his arms, and said, "I give you, the service tunnel."

"It does exist!" Words couldn't express the relief, but the sting in her nose and eyes was there. "That means, we've got a chance."

"We do," he agreed, sweeping his hand through his hair. He pointed at the distant light which was a mere speck like a starlight. "If the market is there."

"It has to be there." She didn't look at him when she spoke. Instead, she searched the tunnel, the beam from her phone's light darting from the ceiling to the diamond-plated walkway, the tunnel turning out to be more square than round. The walls carried a new collection of pipes which stretched beyond anything she could see.

"Follow the pipes?" she asked, waving her phone.

"Yeah, but which way is the market?" Peter answered and made his way around her, the space tight. He motioned behind the ladder, the tunnel continuing. "I'm all turned around."

"Let me think?" she questioned, shutting her eyes to get a sense of direction.

"I mean, it could be that way—"

"Peter!" she belted, voice bouncing. Hands raised, she said, "I'm good at this."

"Sorry," he said, backing off, pitching his toe against the walkway.

"It's that way," she answered finally, certain of the turns they made in the mall and where she'd entered. "It has to be that way."

"I trust you," Peter said, aiming his flashlight behind them. "I think you're right. Look."

She followed the light behind the ladder as far as she could see, the darkness keeping most of the path hidden. "There's no pipes or electrical or anything that way."

"Right," he said. "Seems all the pipes come up through here."

"If I'm right, that direction leads to the ocean," Emily commented and shined the phone's light beneath the walkway. It was wet, a small trickle of water. "Maybe this is a storm overflow too?"

"Who knows what they use these tunnels for," he said, annoyance in his voice. "Let's get moving."

"Should we close the hatch?" Emily asked, eyeing the opening, the emergency lights shining through. "Or maybe we leave it. You know, so we can see it?"

"I like that idea, keep it open so we can see," Peter added. She felt his hand near hers again, fingers brushing until he took hold. "Ready?"

A nod. It came with anxiety creeping up alongside a mounting excitement that fluttered in her belly. There were lives depending on the outcome. They had to find something. Peter's skin felt clammy, and she turned an ear toward what was behind them. If she tried hard enough, could she hear the ocean?

She heard something, but it wasn't the waves or gulls or anything natural. It was the faint whirring she'd heard earlier. Emily gripped Peter's hand tighter, her heart racing to catch up with an idea of how the man without any burns had gotten inside the mall. He'd come from the tunnel. He'd come from what was making that sound. It was the machine. And it was still running.

"I'm ready."

TWELVE

Every footstep echoed. Every word they spoke bounced. If there was anyone else in the service tunnel with them, they'd know it. There wasn't. *But we'll stay quiet,* Emily decided. Which was the safest thing to do. They weren't as alone as she'd thought, though, a squeak coming from the front, a second behind them. Her muscles tensed when tiny claws skittered in the darkness, nails scratching metal, a chill rifling down her spine.

"Did you hear that?" Peter said, flashlight beaming onto a pair of beady eyes, black pearls shining. "Shit, we're not alone."

"That was a lot bigger than a mouse," she said, exaggerating a shake as if bothered by it.

"There!" he said, pivoting, his voice abrupt.

"Another?" She followed the band of light, a snaky tail vanishing beneath the walkway grate. "Peter, I think those are rats."

"Why did it have to be rats," he grumbled. "Let's hope they don't start to nibble on things."

"Nibble?" Emily cringed, the skittering continuing. "Let's hope."

"Might just be a few." His tone was sharp as he swung the

flashlight like a pendulum. The blade caught gray blurs grouped and spreading, more of them disappearing behind a pipe, another slinking around it. "Oh shit."

"It's the pipes," she began, shining the phone's light above them. "It's like their own private highway."

"They probably ran from the fog too," Peter commented, hand warm in hers. "Let's just keep moving."

"They won't bite?" she asked, the question unanswered. Peter motioned to their left, Emily glimpsing a fleshy tail as it dashed into the dark. She sucked in a breath, a deeper fear seeding with what the rats did next. A row of them sat perched on a fat pipe and stared as though waiting for them to pass. "Look at that."

"They've got nowhere else to go," he whispered.

"Like us," she returned. And the rats did watch them, her earlier thought wildly validated by the fixed stares they were getting. More of them lined up and waited, her mind thinking crazily about a carnival game she'd played once—*three balls, three throws, knock one down and win a prize.* They seemed to watch with a kind of fascination that filled her with frightful dread. "You don't think they see us as food, do you?"

"Food? Could be."

At once, her knees jellied, muscles turning weak from the fear. "Uh-uh," she growled and reacted, kicking, the tip of her shoe striking the walkway grate. The rats didn't move. Frustrated, she looked for something to throw, but the service tunnel was surprisingly clean.

"Let's keep moving," Peter told her and pointed the flashlight toward the distant light. "I don't want to be down here any longer than we have to be."

"Me neither."

"And we don't want to give them rats anything to think about." He laughed nervously.

"That's not at all funny, Peter!" she said, vaguely aware she was squeezing his hand. She shivered, the motion sudden. "It got cold."

"It did," he said, putting his arm around her. She fit in the crook of his body, the warmth inviting. She wrapped her arm around his middle, steps matching. "Is that better?"

"It is," she answered, the shyness melting. Time passed, their words replaced by the tempo of their breathing and the echo of their footsteps.

"Can I tell you something?" he asked, slowing. Emily didn't answer but stopped with him. He surprised her with the tip of his finger touching her chin, easing her face up until she only saw his eyes. In the darkness and isolation of the tunnel, she was lost in them, unable to look away. She melted a little inside. She was sure of it. "I think I'm probably never going to see my family again and that hurts. It hurts a lot."

Emily pressed her hand against his heart, the loss familiar. "I'm sorry. Sorry for all of us."

He struggled a moment as if finding the words, and finally said, "I just wanted you to know that I'm glad you're here. You and your sister."

"I'm glad you're here too," she said, daring to move a little closer. He didn't back away. He didn't look away either. For the tiniest instance, the moment immeasurably small, Emily thought Peter was going to kiss her. But it went to that place where unfilled moments go, a dreamy *what if*, the moment stolen by claws scampering, the rats following. "We should hurry some?"

"Yeah, I'd say maybe hurry a lot." He laughed.

Emily pointed her light, the beam from Peter's flashlight following. New feelings stirred, her heart warming to his words. Was it okay to feel this way? Was it okay to feel something new? For him? Now wasn't the time to regard a concern. There were priorities. Food and medicine and staying ahead of the rat parade that was following. She wove her fingers with his, holding his hand tight, and continued forward. They were closer to the light. But not close enough to feel safe yet.

The rats remained close to them. Not so close as to be a danger, though. Still, with every squeak and chirp and hiss they made, the hairs on Emily's arms sprang. It wasn't that she didn't like rats or mice. It was because she couldn't shake the sense that the rats were watching them, watching her. A hundred beady eyes. Thousands perhaps. The idea of it making her stomach squeeze tight.

"That's it," she said, voice shaky from the cold. Sneakers squelching, a rat returning the call, they stood next to a ladder, another hatch door above them. With a heavy sigh, the door unremarkable, Emily added, "Let's hope the thing opens."

"That would be good," Peter replied, his jaw clenched and chattering. Without another word, he was close, nose to nose, his arms wrapping around her and running his hand up and down her back. "It'll be warmer up there."

"You think so?" she asked, leaning into him. He didn't back away, his hands moving faster.

"I hope so," he returned with unsureness in his voice. When he let go, the cold rushed in like a strong wind and replaced where his body had been. He pointed at the wall and the source of light they'd been following. It wasn't at all like the emergency lights in the mall. It was the kind with a heavy glass jar and a small metal cage to protect it. The bulb was made of clear glass, a white-hot curly filament burning hot. Emily looked away, an afterimage floating in the dark, gaze falling to the ladder beneath it.

"Do you think anyone will be in the Food-Mart?" she asked. When he didn't answer immediately, Emily confessed the question that was bothering her. "Do you think it'll be safe?"

He shook his head. "I don't know." Peter took hold of the ladder and jerked on the rung, the posts in the concrete jostling. "Who knows, someone up there might have already come down here? They saw the rats and went back up."

"Maybe," she commented while shining the phone's light on the pipes, tracing them until they vanished, the tunnel turning inky-black. In the dark, she heard a small commotion. It was distant but there. "I think I heard something."

Peter stopped on the first ladder rung. "Huh?"

"Do you hear it?" Emily asked. Gripping her phone, hand trembling.

Peter cupped an ear and leaned forward. "I hear something. But to me, it sounds like water." To Emily, he didn't sound convincing. "We're fine. If anything, I'm surprised that we haven't heard more."

She shined her light on the door, urging him, "You lead, I'm right behind you."

His shoes were old and worn, each of his steps ringing out on the metal rungs. When he reached the top, he knocked the metal plate with the heel of his hand. "No answer."

"Tap it with your flashlight?" she suggested. "Metal on metal and all that."

The light danced above her head, door clinking. The sound rang truer and easier to hear. They waited. An awful thought occurred to her. What if the hatch was locked? Or stuck? A minute passed before Peter knocked again. Nothing.

"Nobody is home," he said, handing down the flashlight. "I'm going to try and push it open."

"Keep the light on it?" she asked. The question went unanswered. He grunted, straining to push. Nerves flitted like sparks jumping. She held the light steady, a sweaty sheen on his face. When it didn't budge, he backed away a moment before lunging upward, arms and legs shaking. "Do you think it could be locked?"

"Nope, I don't think it's locked," he answered while poking around the lip where the door met the concrete. "I think locked would feel different, like there'd be some give to it."

"Stuck?" she asked, voice quieting with an interruption from the tunnel. She swung the flashlight, the beam striking whiskered faces. It wasn't the rats she'd heard. It was something else. "Peter?"

"The light?" he demanded. She beamed it straight up, the beam striking his face, wispy steam rising off it. "I bet that quake or aftershock we felt earlier knocked over a shelf and it landed on the door."

"You think it's weighing it down?" A nod. She climbed, feet and hands small enough to grip the side of the rungs.

"What are you doing?" he asked, objecting.

"We can both fit," she assured him and pushed one leg behind a ladder rung, freeing her hands. "An extra hand. Muscle it. You and me together, pushing the door."

Legs woven together and face to face, he said, "Just hope this ladder holds."

"It'll hold," Emily said, tone filled with a confidence she seemed to muster out of thin air. There was no knowing what would happen, the concrete loose on one rung, and another sagging. "Push!"

Peter pushed with her and at once the hatch began to lift, a sliver of light appearing on his face. "That's it," he yelled with a grunt. "It's moving!"

The door was opened enough to see clothes. A shirt perhaps. The color a dungaree-blue, the kind she'd seen the market's employees wearing. "I... I think it's a body."

All strength was zapped, the hatch door shutting with a thwack as Peter reeled backward. "A body?"

"That's why it's heavy. The extra weight," she explained. There was a time before the clouds fell when she would have run from such a thing. But now, it was just another obstacle, a thing for them to overcome. Peter's face was stark white, and she gently touched his chin like he had her own earlier, coaxing him to look at her. When he did, she told him, "We can do this. Together."

"Together," he repeated. "Together, we can push the body off the door."

"Right. Push!" she demanded, and didn't wait, shoving her shoulder into the door. Peter followed her lead, panting heavily, the muscles in his arms corded like sinew. There was motion, Emily yelling in the small space, "It's moving!"

Peter's eyes bulged. "It is!" And as the door lifted, the sickening sound of a body flopping filled their ears, an arm falling from the opening. It hung between them like a curtain, the skin mottled and thick, scaled with dry blood. Without thought, Emily shoved it aside. It was covered with patches of brown and gray hair, a tattoo in the shape of an ancient scroll, the age stealing its clarity and turning the letters blotchy. "Uhm. Definitely dead."

Emily tucked the flashlight into her waistband, the butt of it digging into her side. Reluctant, she clutched the thickest part of the arm and shoved it up and back, demanding, "Push the door!"

"Now!" Peter replied, heaving until a thump came from above them, the hatch door flinging open.

She let go, climbing up and out, covering her nose and mouth immediately. "The smell, it's awful."

Peter followed, climbing out, a cupped hand over his mouth, gagging. "God! That's awful—" he started to say and gagged hard, mouth thinning into pale lines.

"What is it?" Emily managed to say with a cough.

"Rotting meat. A lot of it, I think," Peter answered, kicking his feet as he finished climbing.

"Where do we go?" she asked, stepping over the body and

hoping the rest of the store didn't smell as bad. There'd be no way to breathe if that were the case.

"Let's go to the front," he answered, dry-heaving, his cheeks puffed like small balloons.

"The rats," she said, lifting the hatch door. It shut with a thump, the force reverberating into her shoes.

"Good thinking." Peter heaved, a fresh gag taking his breath away. He stared at the dead man whose mouth was open, a string of what looked like drool dangling motionless from the corner. The man wore a butcher's apron which was stained bloody, the color a dark brown, the smell of rotten meat explaining what part of the market they'd entered.

"My hand," she urged him, eyes focusing. His fingers found hers, the touch becoming familiar as he followed her footsteps, matching where she placed her feet as she navigated them into the main area. Emily squeezed, jerking slightly to get his attention. He turned away from the dead butcher, wiping spittle from his chin, his eyes bloodshot and watery. "Peter, we made it."

"We made it to the market," he replied. His gaze returned to the dead butcher and the hatch door. "Let's hope we can make it back."

THIRTEEN

Yellow emergency lights were bright on the walls, mounted high and staining the ceiling tiles yellow. Were they powered by the same generator? How many days remained? Or was it hours? The front of the market was mostly glass, gray daylight offering light, the rear of the market stuck in a deep shadow. They passed the butcher where rows of meat sat untouched, their red color gone, the food spoiling. "None of those are salvageable."

"It went fast? Like too fast." Pinching her nose, Emily commented, "Might be like you said, something to do with the fog."

Peter glanced at the windows, the fog silently batting the glass. Even now, she could feel it stinging her bare skin, warning her they were too close. "Maybe whatever is in the fog is causing the meats to rot faster."

"That could be," she said, moving away, thinking of what foods would still be safe. The blade of a chef's knife gleamed yellow light. She yanked it from the shelf, breaking the hanging tab with one quick snap. Peter stopped when seeing her, eyes round as he raised his hands up in front of him.

"What are you doing with that?"

Emily realized how she must have looked and lowered the blade.

"For protection from the rats," she answered. Heat rose from beneath her collar, the market's air stuffy like the mall.

"Protection from the rats?" he asked. She saw the disbelief. Heard it too.

"Did you see the dead man? He died inside. We don't know how." Peter shook his head and dropped his arms. She lowered her voice. "We don't know if we're alone."

"Emily, it could've been the explosion. I mean, look around, half the shelves in the store are toppled." Emily regarded the explosion but kept the knife. A sudden thump from the aisle over gave them both a start. Peter didn't argue with her and took a meat tenderizer from the shelf. He wagged it in the air like a hammer, satisfied. "For protection. Like you said."

"It was probably canned fruit or something," she admitted. "Rolled off the shelf."

"Let's do this right," he said, pulling a leather strap from the shelf and working it around her middle. Nerves fluttered unexpectedly when he stooped in front of Emily, her fingers digging into his shoulders. Looking up, he said, "This will hold your knife so you don't cut yourself."

"You're making me a scabbard," she called it, having learned the word recently. Peter continued working the strap through a belt loop, pulling her closer.

"Yeah, kinda. I know it's not the best material, but it'll work until we find you something better."

"Thank you," she breathed. Face flushed as he stood, hands wandering down his tight arms. She reached his hands with the other piece of leather. "Here, let me," she offered, tying a piece of the leather into a loop around his belt, a perfect fit for the tenderizer handle to slide through.

"Emily, if we do run into anyone, you can't hesitate." Peter looked down at her gravely, glancing at the knife. "There's no telling what people—well, men, I mean—will want to do."

A terrible foreboding struck, and she clutched the knife's handle. Her mom had warned about what some men want and what they can do. "Honestly, I don't even know how to use this." Her voice shook and she hated that it did. Had she ever felt this vulnerable? He must have seen the expression and held her.

"I'm sorry," he tried to say, her body tensing. What he said had terrified her. "Just be ready."

"I will," she told him. The Food-Mart whispered to them, her ears perking, finding the sound coming from the front. Emily wiped her cheek with the heel of her hand, and Peter affectionately wiped the other. Bringing his face close, kissing distance close, he pressed his finger to the dent in her upper lip, leaving it there. She nodded, understanding.

"Somebody is up there," he mouthed. She raised her knife, following, silently. Sweat beaded on the back of his neck with blotchy red patches on his face.

"Anything?" she asked, the hairs on her arms and neck standing on end while they stepped around toppled dry goods. He stopped abruptly and faced her. He shook his head and tried to speak, but the words were slow to come out. "What is it?"

"We should leave," he said solemnly. His hands trembled and he flinched, dread filling his face. "Emily, let's get what we came for and go back."

"What is it!" she repeated, unable to see beyond his square shoulders. She glimpsed a cash register, and a conveyor belt that was still filled with a shopper's emptied cart. And she could see more of the glass windows, the fog swelling and shifting and dancing to cover all of them. "The fog? Yeah, so what!"

"It's bad," he tried warning, Emily pushing past him.

"Oh my God!" she muttered, her stomach in her throat. In

that moment, she wished she had listened to Peter. There was nothing good that could have come from seeing the front of the market. "Oh Peter!"

It had been a stampede. That was the closest thing she could think of to describe what created the scene beyond the Food-Mart's entrance. There were bodies stacked on top of bodies, some still upright, legs and arms curled and broken, crushed. *Cordwood,* she recalled. But this was worse. It was impossible to count them, but all had tried to get inside at the same time, death inching over them one by one, the pile growing until it formed a flesh and bone blockade.

Beneath the fog there were hands and feet. Young and old, they ran. They all ran, leaving their food carts and open trunks to squeeze through the Food-Mart's doors at the same time. But the poison was faster than they were. How many made it inside before the hole was plugged, before every square-inch of space in that opening sealed the store from the outside? The survivors inside the market weren't as lucky as the ones at the mall. For the few reaching the store, the fog had gotten them. There were bodies face down across the floors and filling the check-out registers, puddles near their faces, eyes stuck wide open.

"They tried to come through the windows," Emily said with a shudder. A woman had run headlong into the heavy glass. She held two young toddlers—one under each arm—the remains of her children hanging limp in clothes that could have come from the mall's OshKosh B'gosh outlet store. Dozens more were piled up behind the mother and her children, an avalanche of bodies squashed against the window. "Peter, what happened to everyone else?"

"Everyone else?" he asked, confused. He followed her gaze to those who made it inside. "They died."

"It should have been safe," Emily said, dread filling her with a familiar horror. She raised her arm to show him a pair of welts.

They were new, the sacs filling. "Peter, the poison. It breached the Food-Mart and it killed anyone inside."

"I can taste it like before." He exited the aisle. She followed and flashed a look at the metal rafters and then back to the large plates of glass front. "But it's not as strong."

Thumbing a blister, it burst, the liquid queasily warm. She clutched her chest, breathing faster and harder. How dangerous was it in here? "Peter, do you think we're safe?"

"Safer than they were," Peter answered, nudging his head toward the front. The question she posed had him looking around. "I'm thinking that sound we heard blow through the mall, it did the same here."

"Yeah, must have. But I don't want to stay any longer than we have to." A girder high above them whined as though twisted by some alien force, the metal screaming in pain. "Peter, the fog! I think it's eating the building like it ate my house."

"Eating!?" he asked, gripping the meat tenderizer as if it would help. "What does that mean?"

Emily motioned to his neck when he scratched at the welts, a sac bursting. She looked past the ceiling tiles to the rafters and exposed roof which had been torn open like a sardine can. "That aftershock. It opened the roof."

"Or it was the roof—" he stuttered, gawking at the opening, fog hovering. "Let's get what we need and go back to the mall." Small bulbous welts sprouted on Peter's face. The burns beneath his chin like a rash.

"It's not just the aftershock, this building was built differently."

"Your house was probably plasterboard and wood like mine. The mall is stone and brick and concrete," he explained, searching the rafters above like she had earlier. "The wood is no match for whatever this stuff is. The metal girders? I don't know how long they'd last." A pang of guilt ticked inside her. Her father knew. He knew what would protect them.

A deafening crash came from the opposite side of the market, shelves collapsing. Emily dropped to a squat, instincts making her duck. The floor shook, jars and boxes rattled, but it was unlike the earlier explosion, this one was inside. Above them, the rafters moved, shaking like the end of a ruler when snapped against the edge of a desk. It was the building. It was moving.

"Food and medicine. Grab what we can!" she screamed, but Peter was drawn away, curious, standing, raising a hand. "The roof! It's the roof, and it isn't going to stay up there!"

"What if that's what shook the mall?" he started to ask, an explosion interrupting him. Metal tore from metal, a rafter collapsing onto concrete. The sudden hit vibrated through them, Emily staring at the roof, waiting for the rest of it to fall. Peter dipped his head and waited too. When it didn't, he continued, "What about all this food?" There were boxes and canned goods littered across the floor as if someone had run through the aisle and swept the shelves.

"Get what we can," she answered shortly, snatching a roll of plastic trash bags and handing them over. "Not too heavy."

"Not too heavy," he returned, voice frenzied.

She couldn't break her hard stare at the rafters, eyeballs stinging. "The rest are going to fail," she warned. "They'll collapse faster and faster too. Just like at my house."

"One filled," Peter said while staring up and filling a second plastic bag.

"Hurry," she cried. The fog had reached her hands, the blisters swelling and breaking. Peter was suffering the same, pawing at his face and neck. She blindly grabbed boxes and canned goods, fruit juices and more, until the bag was almost too heavy to lift. "Pharmacy!"

"This way," Peter said, taking the lead. The run to the pharmacy went slower than hoped. The bags scraping, dragged behind them as if they were Santa's little helpers with sacks full of holiday joy. Only, there was no joy here. It was survival. "Which medicine?"

"Do you know where the pills are?" Another rafter ripped from its support column. She waited for the market's roof to squash them like bugs. It shifted with a heavy groan until settling. "I grabbed more bags, just start filling them." Emily threw Peter an empty trash bag and cleared the shelves of bottles. A hundred pharmacy bottles went into the bag, but when she reached a locked cabinet, she knew that the drugs they needed were inside. She jammed the kitchen knife between the doors, jimmying the lock, feeling the metal ridges on the inside and trying to shake the lock free. It wouldn't move.

"Here let me try," Peter said. Stepping up next to her, swinging wildly, the meat tenderizer breaking through the glass. Splintered shards fell like confetti, clinking as they fell onto the pharmacy floor. "Just don't cut yourself, okay?"

She cocked her head to the side, saying, "Get it all!" And as she went about taking the locked medications, a storm of glass shattered. The sound came from the front of the store, the ceiling's bowing too much for the front windows. She thought of the mother and her two babies, and wondered if that was the section of glass to give first. Something wet crept down her leg. Slippery and warm. Alarmed, she thought for a moment that she'd peed. She pushed her hand over her thigh, bringing up a palm of bright red. The knife! In all the rush, she'd cut open her leg on the chef's knife, after all. There was no pain when it happened, but now there was a low throb. Blood dripped from the cuff of her pant leg, crimson splatters like raindrops appearing on floor tiles. *It's not that bad*, she told herself. Emily pulled the makeshift belt. The motion drew Peter's attention, and at once, he was at Emily's side, kneeling to see how bad the cut was.

"I'm sorry," was all she could think to say. A rafter from the other side of the Food-Mart plummeted with a booming sound. "I didn't even know I cut myself."

"You put the blade in backward," he answered and then looked at her with sympathy. "It doesn't look life-threatening—yet, but you'll need a butterfly stitch or two. We better grab plenty of antibiotics."

"I'm sorry," she said again. "It was an accident." Peter picked up the leather strap and tied it around her leg.

"My fault," he answered, hand on his heart.

Emily pushed against the throb in her leg, adding more pharmacy bottles to the trash bag. She'd moved on to bandages and antibiotic creams when the last of the front windows crumpled. It was joined by metal thumping and grinding, welds that should have never failed were being torn apart. Debris flew around them, some of it seeming to come from the floor, the tiles cracking and splintering. They'd stayed too long, and Emily pulled Peter close, screaming, "We're done here!"

"Come on!" Peter took her hand, bags in tow, a peculiar expression on his face. As they ran, Emily glanced toward the front to see that the store was already changing. The roof had dropped, leaning precariously to the right as though suspended by invisible cables. She heard a mix of terror and excitement in Peter's voice, yelling words she couldn't understand. A large silver streak came down from the ceiling, stopping them from taking another step. Another streak, and then a thud of something heavy landed next to her. The collapse pushed her hair up in a rapid waft. She cringed, fearful, and tried to move, but her legs stayed frozen in place.

"What was that?"

"Holy shit!" Peter screamed, staring hard at what had fallen. She peered around to see a bell-shaped light lying on its side, spent like a child's toy top. "One more step and—"

"—Yeah, I know," Emily gasped, her voice choked. Her legs were wobbly, but she was up and running behind Peter when another of the lights crashed. She peered up to see the rest of them leaning derelict, threatening to fall like ornaments from a Christmas tree. Two more dropped, punching the air with hollow thuds. They were all going to fall, bells of aluminum and glass threatening them like bombs.

"The whole place is coming down!" Peter shouted. His voice straining, the giant trash bags slowing him.

"There!" she said, seeing the hatch door ahead, the tattoo man's feet sitting motionless alongside it.

"The air feels so much worse over here," Peter shouted, his words drowning in a dry heave, the decaying meat powerfully bad. "Why is that?"

"I don't know." Could it be that the air grew more toxic as it consumed the raw meat? Did it produce a byproduct which made the poison worse? What happened when the burns ate someone's flesh? She glanced at tattoo man to see burns around his neck that hadn't been there before. Would the bodies decompose rapidly? The thoughts spun in her mind and sickened her. Her father knew and his involvement deepened the mystery of the machines. *Just get back to Sammi.* She shook it off, leaving the questions in the market.

Peter was right, it was worse around the meats, fat sacs bursting on her skin. The stinging in her eyes became too much, watering them profusely, twisting the view of Peter until she only saw the faint shape of him. She squeezed them dry, cheeks wet, tears soothing the itch and burn. He struggled too, gagging, coughing and spitting, desperately trying to clear his view. Her nose and throat tightened, lungs squeezing. And somewhere deep inside, a fire had started.

The air sizzled as though lightning had seared it. *A storm?* She expected to see a blinding flash. She expected to hear a bellowing rumble follow. But the thunder never came. Something was going to fall, and anxiety had them both looking high and low. Emily held her breath, insides strung tighter than an instrument. She didn't wait to see what was happening, the rubber of her sneakers stopping at the hatch door. The entire building let out a monstrous groan as if a giant was breathing its last breath. Twisting metal rang through her like fingernails on a chalkboard, the girders crashing like a child's toy blocks. The ground shook and threatened to collapse the service tunnel entrance, Peter stopping midway as he snaked through the opening.

"Peter!" she screamed when he dropped from sight. Gunshots rang out, more girders pulling apart from each other. She looked down and saw the alarm on his face but motioned to the bags. "Catch!" she yelled, shuffling the bags through the hatch door.

"Keep them coming," he shouted, debris rifling past her. Air rushed over the back of her neck, lifting her up as the floor pitched briefly beneath her. The front half of the roof collapsed, crushing a row of food aisles, sending a wave of debris. Flat cans flew past her like hockey pucks, splashing against the brick wall. *Canned pet food*, Emily thought, oddly distracted by the blurred labels. Peter's hand jutted from the opening, reaching for her, clutching the air. Another food can whistled by, feathering the side of her head like a breezy kiss. One step to the right and it would have squashed her skull.

Her feet were in the hatch opening, hurriedly slipping from one rung to the next. She descended without a care or worry of falling. When her fingers closed around the top rung, she let herself fall. Peter's arms were around her, his body catching hers. She spun around and fell into him, breath hot and rapid, his heart pounding against her breast. She could have stayed like that—in his arms and face to face—but the sounds from above told her they had to run.

She cupped his face between her hands, screaming, "Run!"

"This way!" Peter screamed. In the dim light, the veins on his neck popped as he strained to speak. The service tunnel shook before they moved, the hatch door disappeared, throwing them into a black abyss. The sound that came next was like a thousand freight trains, deafening and terrifying, and Emily found herself clutching onto Peter, screaming as loud as she could, pleading for it to stop. For a long time, they held onto one another, waiting for the world to collapse and grind them into nothingness.

She was still screaming when she finally heard herself and heard Peter talking into her ear, telling her that they were safe and that they'd be okay. But they weren't safe. The service tunnel was in complete darkness.

FOURTEEN

Had it ever been so dark? Dread swallowed her pounding heart as she stared blankly ahead. Emily saw nothing, every muscle paralyzed while the market's destruction continued above. The service tunnel's cold fingers poked and prodded, touching every part of her body, the chill soothing the burns. She was vaguely aware of Peter speaking, his voice muffled, blocked by the high-pitched ringing. She was sure her eardrums had burst, the noise punching through them like icepicks.

"I think I see you," she said, the words barely registering. Gray light emerged to show the fuzzy outline of Peter's body. Arms stretched out, Emily found his face and neck, clutching and kissing him hard on the mouth. She was trembling all over. Peter was too. He returned the gesture, lips wet and soft, his chest beating wildly. "Thank you."

"I got you," Peter said, speaking softly as she buried her face against his neck. Her body shuddered with each breath. *It's the adrenaline,* her mother or father had told her once. *It makes your body tremble after an accident.* His hand was on the small of her back, pulling her closer, turning them away from the hatch door. She fell against him with a lean into the wall, the ruckus quieting until there was only their fast breathing and heartbeats thrumming. In the strange silence, there was a comfort she'd never experienced before: the feeling intense.

"We won't be going back up there any time soon," Emily said, the pupils of Peter's eyes huge, their noses nearly touching. She remembered her phone and found it in her back pocket. The light still worked, and she turned it on briefly, seeing they were alone. "The rats. I think the noise scared them."

"I think the noise scared everyone," he said, his voice hoarse. He bumped one of the bags, adding, "The rats will be back. Especially for these."

"Do you have your flashlight?" Emily asked. Her heart sank when he searched around his middle and shook his head. The emergency light near the ladder was gone and there was nothing between them and the mall's door. "My phone's battery is going to die any minute. Is it in one of the bags?"

"I'm looking," Peter answered, his voice filling with concern. "How much battery?"

"Not much. Not enough." Squinting, she tried to make out the end of the service tunnel where they'd left the door open. A dim gray reflection shined from the ceiling. "My eyes might be playing tricks, but I think I can see the mall?"

Peter turned, squinting just as she had. "I think that's it." His hands were in the trash bags, pushing through the food and the medications, jerkily searching, frustrated.

"You're not afraid of the dark?" she teased, fingers on his arm, following an instinct that was new to her. He didn't return the laugh. "Forget about it. We'll be fine. There's only one direction to go." Emily nudged his arm, eager to get back to the mall.

"Hold on," he said, picking up a can of baked beans. Before she could object, he climbed the ladder and shoved the hatch door open. Debris rained down. "You think that can will hold?"

"Sure it will. It's all we got," he answered, looking doubtfully at the can. He propped the door, the stink of rotten meat swimming around them. Peter dropped with a thump and lifted the bags, saying, "We've got a guide light behind us. Let's just hope the mall door is still open. Otherwise, we'll walk right past the ladder."

"What if we stay close to the wall?" she asked, her head spinning, stomach turning. It was stink mixing with the bite of adrenaline, the effects of it. A crash above gave her a start, the question going unanswered. She clutched the trash bags and forced a step, telling him, "Let's go."

Peter didn't object, but mumbled something to himself before saying, "Yes ma'am."

"Now!" she said, half kidding, trash bag crinkling as he joined her side.

"You're right about the wall," he commented, hoisting a bag over his shoulder. The air brushed by her with a whoosh, stinking of the market. Her gut pinched and rolled, but she pushed forward, not risking a stop. "Staying close to it."

For a hundred or so yards, they said nothing, the service tunnel disappearing around them. Darkness swallowed everything. It was penetrating, unrelenting, almost malevolent in its appetite for the light. If not for the muffled sounds of Peter's breathing, she would have thought she was alone. She kept her eye on the prize, the faint sliver of daylight where the mall was expected to be. But with each step, there came the ponderous thoughts of *what if*. What if that wasn't the door? What if it was the end of the tunnel, the beach and the machine her father worked? What if it was the fog lying in wait like a criminal ready to pounce?

Emily forced the questions from her mind, the stew of ideas turning toxic. She thought of summer nights, the solitude of her bedroom, a breeze from an open window, the rustling of tree branches and crickets chirping. She stayed in the memory as long as possible, but the seed of a new hurt had planted inside her. She was homesick and missed her mom and dad.

"Did you say something?" she asked suddenly. The echo sounded tinny and whiny.

"Uh-uh," Peter answered, their arms bumping. "I didn't say—"

"That! Did you hear it?" she interrupted. A clink like a footstep came from ahead. It wasn't like before. Not a rat or a mouse scurrying. She stopped dead and grabbed Peter, insisting they wait. "Listen."

"Hear what?" he asked after a moment passed. "Maybe you're hearing our feet, the echoing."

"No. It's not that." Her palms tingled and itched, blood rushing in a hot spin. "There was something else."

"Probably the rats?" She heard Peter's foot skid against the walkway, rubber striking the metal treads.

A gasp slipped from her lips as claws skittered over the pipes. Surprise mixed with relief, a rodent screeching. "Damn little shits are brave!" She struck the grate hard enough to hurt her foot. "Shoo!"

Emily looked hard at the Food-Mart's door behind them, the narrow opening Peter made barely visible. It was razor thin but enough to cut the darkness. It was their beacon, their guide telling her they were walking straight. If it was behind them, it meant they hadn't ventured into another service tunnel. Who knew how many offshoots there were. Before turning back, Emily saw the light flicker. She sucked in a breath, holding it as the thin sound of a footstep reached them. Jaw dropping, her tongue dry, she dared a whisper, "Peter?"

"What?" he replied, annoyed.

"Shh!"

"What is it?" he repeated in a rasp, turning to look.

"There," she pointed. Peter couldn't see her, but maybe he could see the light, see that someone was walking in and out of it. "Beneath the Food-Mart!"

"Who's there?" he yelled, his arm locking with hers. Silence filled the service tunnel, the market's light remaining steady as it jutted through the door. A shadow! A head and shoulders! Emily jumped, clutching Peter's arm, insides squeezing. A silhouetted figure bounced in and out of the light, winking, walking toward them. "We're armed!"

"Peter!" she screamed in a breathy squeal. "Run!"

"Who's there?" he continued, fright shaking his voice. Silence. Peter nervously clutched his hands, filling one with plastic trash bags, the other with the meat tenderizer. "I don't want to hurt you!"

The shadow figure continued forward, untroubled by Peter's remark. Emily could clearly make out the figure of a tall man with a slender build. He slowed a moment and then stopped entirely, breathing fast, air wheezing. He was coming again, head bobbing from side to side, peeking in and out of the light.

"Run!" Emily screamed, terror rippling through her. But in her haste, her foot slipped and one of the trash bags fell with a thump. She clawed at the darkness, chasing it while stumbling forward, momentum causing her to strike the walkway. Reaching, her fingers found Peter's shirt, pulling a wad of fabric, tethering herself to him, becoming one person.

"I can't see anything!" Peter cried out. She pushed against him with each hesitant step. Every cell of her body telling her to flee. This wasn't running. She didn't know what to call it. It was a blind leading the blind shuffle; movements hampered and crippled with terror.

"Just keep going—go faster!"

"I found it! I found—" he screamed, stopping abruptly when they struck metal. Emily clung to the ladder, her breath gushing.

"Hurry!" she begged, gasping. The black figure rocked back and forth, blinking like holiday lights. "Hurry, Peter!"

The footsteps were like a waking nightmare. They were

giant and thumped in her brain and stomped on her heart. In the mix of it, she heard Peter's shoes on the ladder, soles ringing out on the rungs. There'd never been a sweeter sound.

Light suddenly flooded the opening, bathing them in blinding brightness that spilled mercilessly into her eyes. Emily reared away, shielding her face from the glare. The suddenness of the mall's light blinded her to the approaching figure, his lowly stomps echoed like clapping hands.

"You're okay!" Nolan began to say, his face appearing. "We didn't know where you two—"

"Someone is chasing us!" Emily screamed, arms stretched, grasping for the ladder. The metal was wet, the warm air above touching the cool metal. "Hurry! Help us out of here!" Peter was out of sight, trash bags following.

"Grab my hand!" Nolan yelled, reaching shoulder-deep, forehead cracking against the hatch edge. His calloused grip squeezed her forearm, slipping on the blisters. Stinging pain rifled across her arm, a scream shooting from between clenched teeth. The stomping feet stifled the cry and she climbed.

Daylight. She was back in the daylight, her waist and legs dangling in the service tunnel hole, her heart beating faster and harder than she'd thought was possible. When a hand clapped onto her ankle and squeezed, she let out a blood-curdling scream, Nolan and Peter squeezing past her hips to fend off the attack.

"Who the—" Nolan's voice shouted, bouncing.

"He has me!" Emily cried, bucking her legs, missing and hitting and missing again. When the tip of her sneaker struck with a sickening thud, she was freed at once, the stranger scuttling backward with a pain-filled yell.

"Wait. Please, wait!" the stranger pleaded. "Emily! It's me!"

"What?" Emily asked, her arms falling limp and her jaw going slack. There was a moment and Nolan and Peter dragged her clear of the service tunnel, her bottom burning from the friction. "Wait!"

"Emily, please, it's me!" She knew the voice, but it was impossible. The fog's appetite was relentless, its hunger for human flesh insatiable. "Please."

Emily got to her knees, swiping the tears from her face, she inched forward enough to look into the service tunnel, to see who it was that chased them. His handsome face was deathly pale, beaten and bruised and stained with blood. But hidden beneath the carnage of their new world, she glimpsed a crooked smile she immediately recognized.

"Dad?"

FIFTEEN

Emily forgot about the bags of food and medicine. She forgot about the burns, the fog, and even forgot about the machines choking the world. From the service tunnel, her father's gaunt face appeared. Grimacing desperately, pupils shrinking, he squinted hard at the sudden brightness and shot a look at Nolan and Peter and then to Isla before his focus returned.

Emily shrank back from the impossible, believing he had to be a ghost. It was the only explanation. Mind grappling to understand, her thoughts teetered on collapse. A moment ago, her father had been dead. A moment ago, there was a stranger chasing them in the dark. But in this man's face, Emily saw her father. She saw that he was alive.

"Help him," Emily demanded. Peter was perched over the service tunnel, a leg raised, the bottom of his heel poised and ready to pummel the stranger's face. Her heart cramped, an unexpected scream rising that jarred their attention. "No, Peter! He's my father!"

"What!" Peter narrowed his eyes, confused as Isla shifted to guard the stranger.

Her father raised an arm, guarded, Emily yelling, "You're safe! They'll help."

"Sorry I thought—" Peter started withdrawing as Nolan secured the door, army cap flopping, a bush of bright red hair appearing. Nolan held out his hand, Isla joining as her father regarded the army fatigues. Phil Stark reached out of the darkness and climbed until he was standing in front of them, Emily wrapped her arms around his middle, squeezing, nose wrinkling at the stink of fog.

"It's okay, Em," he told her. But it wasn't okay. Nothing was okay anymore. "Sammi? You're okay?"

"We're good, Dad," she began, lost for words. She motioned to the tunnel, asking, "How?"

"I had no idea it was you. I heard a noise and followed the light."

"But from where?" she asked, breathing deep, congested, a rattle in her chest. She looked into his unshaven face, a million questions threatening to tumble from her mouth all at once. Most of them about the machines. About what happened to them. But she couldn't ask them here. Not now. "How did you get out of the car?"

"I was pinned," he began to say, picking grit from his face. Isla shoved a bottle into his hand, the tops of his knuckles bruised and bloodied as though he'd been in a terrible fight. He tipped the bottle, guzzling, coughing steadily while forcing the water down. His skin was the color of ash and his cheeks sunken and skin shriveled like dried fruit. White and gray hairs gleamed from above his ears and there was stubble on his chin. And though it had been nearly two days, he'd put on a year of worry, his eyes more tired than she'd ever seen. Was that possible? What happened to him out there? He drained the bottle, licking his thinned lips, and continued, "My leg. I was pinned in the accident. After a day and night out there, I finally loosened what had me. I think the metal was soft from working it or from the—"

"Mom," she managed to say. Did he know? The thought of telling him was like a kick in the gut. Heart sinking, she said, "Dad, the accident... the car you hit. It was us, and Mom." Emily saw Isla and Nolan and Peter passing a look, a sad understanding shared. These were the details she hadn't told anyone.

"I know," he said, voice choked as he gently touched the cut on her head. "I saw it when I got out of the car."

"How did you survive?" Nolan asked, breaking the moment. His brow furrowed. "Nobody survives in whatever this is."

"Staying low," her father answered, leveling a hand above the floor. "The fog is lifting just enough to stay beneath."

"It's lifting?" Peter asked sharply, heels clacking, back straightening. "It's over?"

"N-no, that's not what I meant," her father answered, stammering a little. "It'll never... what I mean is that it's changing. The density."

"Sammi was hurt—" Emily said abruptly, the questions risking them finding out her father worked on the machines. "But we're both good now."

"I'm so proud of you," he said, struggling. She pressed the pads of her thumbs against his cheeks, drying them, a crooked smile appearing. "You saved your little sister. Do you know that? You saved her, and you saved yourself." He kissed her forehead, whispering her mother's name, but she couldn't make out what else he was trying to say.

"This is Peter and Isla and—"

"Name is Nolan, sir," Nolan interrupted. He donned his cap and took to shaking her father's hand vigorously. "It's good to have you, sir."

"You are army?" her father asked, searching over his shoulder.

"I'm on leave, sir," Nolan answered, dimples flashing when he looked at Isla. "My fiancée Isla, we got caught up in it."

"Good to meet you all," her father said, a grin forming. He grimaced, adding, "Circumstances and all."

"Agreed," Isla said, shaking hands briefly before her father returned to the service tunnel's opening.

"What were you guys doing down there?" He looked coldly into the dark hole like it was a grave. "Don't get me wrong. I'm glad you were there. Otherwise... well?"

"We were looking for supplies at the Food-Mart," Peter answered. "We need medicine and food. Shit, we need anything we can find."

"We got a couple bags," Emily began, fingers splayed, empty-handed. "We would have had more, but the roof caved in."

Understanding slowly dawned on his face. "That's what I heard," he said. "I thought one of the service tunnel pipe stems collapsed. It's why I rushed to go the other way."

"You were in one of the branches?" Isla asked, her gaze fell to the floor. "How far away was that?"

"Not far. Could have been farther, though," he answered, looking relieved. "When I heard voices, I had no idea it was you."

"Sir, how long were you in the tunnels?" Peter asked, chin rising to look at the bodies, the cordwood. If Emily didn't know any better, she was certain Peter was looking at the man without any burns, the one she believed was at the machine. Her father saw the dead bodies, the grimace returning. "We're trying to understand where the service tunnels go."

"We're trying to map the branches," Isla added, her skin shiny with a bronze color, the mugginess building. She swept the bangs from her face. "Maybe you could help?"

"I can try. I got in through one of the storm drains—" Emily shrank inside when her dad glanced at her. "—I've been down there since the accident."

"The fog doesn't go below ground level," Peter commented.

Isla's face twisted as she asked, "Was there anyone else down there?"

Emily's father shook his head, answering, "Other than some rats, you're the first I've seen."

"Would you guys mind if we pick this up later?" Emily asked, maternal instincts knocking. "I'd really like to get my dad some help and for him to see Sammi too."

"Sure, yes, of course," Isla said, taking Phil Stark's arm while brushing dirt from his face. He had a tender look in his eyes, appreciative. "We'll clean you up before you see your girl."

"Thank you," he returned. Silence settled across them while he looked at them. His neck was red, a flush rising. "It's, it is so good to see there are survivors."

"Come on, Dad," Emily said, latching onto his arm. And as she forced a step to lead him away, his shoulders slumped forward, his face hidden behind his hands. She didn't know who the tears were for or if it even mattered. He was alive when so many had died. That scared her more than anything else.

SIXTEEN

Sammi's laughter and fast talking bounced throughout the play area. She hung onto their father's arm, hugging and staying as close as she could. It was good to see her sister and father together. But it was sad too, the loss of their mother, their home, the loss of everything. What else was gone? Emily surveyed those circling the reunion, certain they were asking the same questions.

"And Daddy... and you, you slept with them rats?" Sammi asked, awestruck by the idea of it.

"I did. I did sleep with them," their father answered, brushing a hand through Sammi's hair, doting.

Sammi's eyes grew and looked like giant marbles. "Ew! That's gross, Daddy!"

Laughter rose, Sammi spinning on one foot to see the gathering faces.

"They weren't so bad," their father said, curling his fingers into the shape of a claw. Sammi leaned back, giggling helplessly. "And do you know what else they liked to do?"

"What?" Sammi asked, hands drawn, anticipating what was

coming. When her father didn't answer, Sammi's voice chirped with a squeal, "What did they like to—"

"They liked to cuddle!" her father growled playfully, tickling Sammi. "And they crawled on me, running up and down on their funny-looking feet and whipped their funny-looking tails!"

Sammi roared until her face glowed a sweaty bright red, laughter disappearing in a wheeze of throaty clicks.

"Dad," Emily warned when her sister fell over, breathless. The sight warmed Emily. It warmed everyone.

With fresh water and food in him, her father looked better. His color returned some, the dark pouches carrying his eyes softened. She'd never seen him unshaven, white whiskers flecked against a dark beard. To her, he looked less academic, less engineering, and more rugged too. And maybe that wasn't such a bad thing. "Water?"

"I'm good, thanks," he replied, the scratchy rasp less noticeable. Sammi settled down, sitting with her back against the wall while their father took a guarded look around. Emily followed his gaze, as he commented with surprise, "I didn't realize how many made it."

"Uh-huh. It's a good number," she muttered, half listening when catching the stare of a small group with Jeter. They'd taken to standing opposite of the play area, just beyond the food court. It was close enough to see them, but not much else. There were more survivors with Jeter, his small group growing since the assembly. In it, there was a mix of old and young, and an even split of men and women. None of the faces were familiar to Emily. They stared ahead, soundless, the mall's windows casting a shadow across their faces.

"Emily?"

Her father's voice.

"Huh?" She turned to see him waiting.

Discreetly, his gaze drifted toward Jeter, and he took her

hand, a price tag dangling from the sleeve. "Do you know them?"

"Not sure we want to know them," Nolan answered, overhearing the question. Her father regarded the comment but didn't reply. Emily knew he was assessing. That's what he did. It was how his mind worked. He was assessing the situation. All of it.

Peter plopped onto the short wall, sitting next to them with a pair of Air Jordans in hand. "Thought you could use a pair of sneakers. Size elevens?"

"Ten and a half, but close enough," her father answered, grinning. He winced taking off a shoe, the sole on it beaten, the air sucking on a bloodied sock. "All that walking. I'm gonna have blisters on blisters for a month."

"They've been asking about you," Nolan commented in a matter-of-fact way.

"Asking?" There was concern in her voice. Emily searched her father's face, but it remained empty. She knew, though, and added, "What he said at the assembly?"

"Probably," Peter answered and lowered his chin while unraveling the laces. He stopped when reaching the plastic tip, showing it off like a prize. "Any idea what that thing is called?"

"It's an aglet," her father answered. Like Peter, he wasn't looking at the sneaker or them. He was frowning ponderously, a look she'd seen a million times, lips moving while counting the number of people around Jeter. "The assembly, huh. What did he say?"

"He went off about the machines and the one on the beach," Nolan answered. "I don't know a lot about them, other than carbon capture, something-or-other from the atmosphere and all."

"The old guy, Jeter, is saying the machines are the cause of the fog," Peter said, looking at her father this time. Emily saw the questions on Peter's face as he added, "Also saying that he's seen you at the machine too."

"Seen me? Is that right?" A pause, shoelaces lashing the air. "Well, there's a lot of people involved in that project. Hundreds per machine across the world. I'm not sure it was me he saw," her father answered, adding doubt.

At first, she thought he was dismissing what was said. Ignoring it the way he sometimes arrogantly did. But what she heard was concern, him hiding who he was to those machines. Emily felt the concern about their fate, and that was all she needed to watch over her little sister like a mother guarding her young.

A pair of women moved out of the shadows, out of hiding, Jeter following them until they stood closer. Jeter was at the center of the group, his thin frame rocking back and forth while speaking. Nolan asked, "Anyone read lips?"

"Always wanted to," Isla answered. Feet shuffling across the tile, she'd been listening too and sat next to Emily's father. "Not sure it helps, but they've been asking me and Nolan a ton of questions. Like we're in charge or something."

With that, Emily's father broke his stare. He turned to Isla and asked, "You don't think that you are?"

"Seriously?" The corners of Isla's mouth dropped with an upside-down smile. "It was just chance that we happened to be here first."

"It doesn't matter," Emily's father said, twisting around to see the survivors. "Emily told me how you guys organized a meeting and got everyone assembled." He nudged his chin at the survivors. "People are looking to you two for guidance."

"We didn't sign up for that, sir," Nolan commented gruffly. He handed Isla half a candy bar.

"Phil. It's Phil, there's no formalities here," her father said, insisting. "For what it's worth, it doesn't matter what either of you think."

"He's... I mean Phil, he's right," Peter added. "Everyone is looking to you two."

"I'm gonna change out of these," Nolan said, brushing the front of his fatigues like he'd spilled coffee on them. "The first chance I get."

"It won't matter," Emily told him, feeling what her father was saying. "You guys are naturals at this. People are drawn to it."

"I think it could be what our friends over there want," her father said, gaze returning to Jeter. When nobody replied, he added, "They need to see leadership, so they have someone to blame."

"Yeah, he's been complaining about—" Isla began to say, brow rising "—shit, just about everything."

"At the assembly, he said he lives by the machine," Peter commented, his voice lowered as if being cautious. "He's been saying he's seen a lot going on there."

"There's lots of people on the beach," Emily countered, heart sinking. *So they have someone to blame?* The words fired through her mind like a bullet. She clutched Sammi, bringing her closer. Her father noticed, eyes consoling. Jeter continued listening to the two women while picking at his fingernails. They stopped abruptly with a nod, and he lowered his arms, looking in their direction. A dark fear stole Emily's breath, Jeter's face turning bright with a grim smile that revealed a black chasm where a few teeth hung desperately. She didn't want to ask, but leaned close enough to whisper, "Dad, have you ever seen him before?"

"I might have?" he confessed, speaking close to her ear. Her eyelids grew wide. He dipped his head and slipped one of the Air Jordans onto his foot, the new socks already stained. "But it would have been in passing. That's all."

Nolan cocked his head, listening. "Well, Phil, from the

questions and the looks you're getting, it appears that the guy knows you."

"It would appear so," her father agreed, holding out an open hand, Peter handing him the other sneaker.

What if her father was right? They were looking for someone to blame. Emily drew a short breath, heartbeat thumping. She knelt in front of Sammi, working her sister's shirt and pants which were a size too big, the coverall straps needing to be cinched. A man joined Jeter, his face a resemblance, a cousin or brother perhaps. His clothes hung slack from his shoulders and his skin was pasty, a sickly yellow. Two more men came from behind them, with the same blocky head, the same squat faces, their noses, mouths, and chins squished. They were family, Jeter's sons or grandsons.

Her father returned his attention to Nolan and Isla, saying, "Not that it'll matter much to them, but we're in this together."

"I hope they feel the same way," Isla said, words edged by uncertainty. "They're—" she stopped, staring hard, Emily following to see that the group had disappeared.

"They're gone," Emily stuttered, standing against the ache in her legs. She got onto her toes and craned her neck. "Where'd they go?"

"Could be a hundred different places here," Peter said, climbing onto the short wall. He jabbed a finger into the air, saying, "Pick a store. Any store."

"Tell us more about the rats!" Sammi asked, thick hair clinging to her round face. The smiles and laughter were gone, though, her face turning serious, lips pouty.

"Another time," Emily's father said, answering with a kiss.

"You said the fog was lifting," Peter asked, handing over some clothes. He looked to the glass doors, one of the mall entrances. From where they were, the fog stayed low, leaving no room. "Where? I don't see it."

"We're slightly higher than the service tunnels. We'll see it lifting soon." Emily's father took to his feet, lifting each foot, testing the sneakers which made kissy sounds against the floor. He went on to explain about the day of the accident, the pockets in the fog he'd found after his escape. She saw his descriptions in her head, having had no idea there were tunnels beneath the road. If they weren't there, he might have been dead like her mother too. This thought caught her with a quiet sob, and she was grateful Sammi had gone on to play with the other kids. Peter saw it, though, and rubbed her back, comforting her while her father continued to talk about culverts for the creeks and the safety of them. Without thinking about it, Emily leaned into Peter, marrying their curves like she'd seen couples do. The move didn't go unnoticed by her father, his voice stopping subtly but then continuing to tell of the world beyond the mall's concrete, stone, and glass. "We'll continue to see pockets filled with fresh air. Eventually, we'll see it up here too."

"For now, the service tunnels?" Nolan asked, rummaging through one of the Food-Mart trash bags. A moment later, he unearthed a box of bandages and handed them to Isla. "Could be the pockets will be enough to revisit the market. If we have to."

"Dibs on few of those," Emily said, asking. She motioned to the cut on her leg, adding, "Got a few scratches there."

"More than a scratch, I'd say," Isla commented with a cringe. "I'll help you clean and bandage it."

"Could I borrow your charger too?" Emily asked. Glancing at the emergency lighting, the power severely limited, had she ever thought she'd feel guilty for something as trivial as charging a phone? "If we can spare it."

"I think we can," Nolan commented, his attention on his fiancée. Nolan was looking at Isla, worried for her and the supplies. Emily felt the compassion in his face and answered without thinking, "I'd go." When she saw the objection on her father's face, she added, "If it was needed."

"I'll go too!" Peter said without hesitation, sitting up, cool air rushing to replace where his body had been. "Kinda curious what's left. Also, I know the layout."

"What happened to Mom?" Emily asked, the question pressing. It might not have been the right place or time, but there was no taking it back now. "Is she still out there?"

Her father brushed her cheek, eyes welling. "I couldn't leave her there."

"That's good," she said, voice breathy. He went to say more, but she waved it off. It was enough to know her mother wasn't lying dead in the road like an animal, like roadkill.

"Did you go beyond the mall?" Isla asked Emily's father, cardboard ripping when she peeled open a box of children's aspirin. Her father nodded to Isla without offering more. "Did it lead you to the beach?"

"It's where the town's storm runoff goes," he told them. And as her father continued answering questions about the tunnels, Emily tried to think of something other than the images of her mother. She shut her eyelids and felt Peter's chest against her back again. Her body rose and fell to the tide of his breath with images of summers past flashing in her head. She was on the beach with warm sand between her toes, the surf breaking around her feet.

"The sun? When are we going to see it again?" Emily didn't recognize the voice and opened her eyes with a start. It was the older man who was a retired doctor. He'd changed his soiled clothes, replacing them with a greenish jogging suit made of velour, the bottom and top the same color, shaping his body like a pear. His arms were crossed and resting on his round belly. "Word is going around that you know something about what's happening outside."

"He doesn't know that!" Emily blurted. A dark intuition

leaped inside her: what if others heard the same. What then? Voice pitched high, she continued, "Nobody does!"

"It's okay," her father said, the consoling look returning. She hated him in that moment. How could he be so careless when their fate was in the hands of so few. It wouldn't take much for them to turn on him and Sammi and her if they knew he'd worked on the machines. Other than Peter and Isla and Nolan, they didn't know these people or how they'd react.

"Do you?" the retired doctor asked, lower lip trembling. "I want to know what it was exactly that killed my wife."

A cough echoed from one of the wounded, Nolan explaining, "Doc, when we learn more about it, we'll share the information." He held up his hand like a Boy Scout. "I swear it."

"Soonest would be best, understand?" The retired doctor motioned behind him, saying with a nod, "It could be something helpful to treat these people."

"Absolutely," Isla began to say. But the doctor didn't wait and returned to the sick.

"I started drawing up a map of all the service tunnels beyond the mall," Emily heard her father tell Peter and the others. Heart pacing nervously, she watched the retired doctor working with one of the injured. Near him, one of the women who'd been with Jeter sat on a cot. They were waiting for answers too. "I can't promise it'll be all that accurate, though."

"Better than nothing," Peter replied. "We only went the one leg, is all. To and from the market."

"The culverts are the tricky part," Phil explained, doubt on his face while drawing the lines, pencil lead scratchy.

They were alone then, the group dispersing to hand out the food and what few supplies they were able to get before the market was gone. When she went to join Peter, her father called her name, "Emily." It was all he had to say and she knew to sit across from him and listen. She gave him her attention, his voice low, telling her, "Listen, we've got to be careful. Understand?"

"I do," she answered, made uncomfortable by the concern in his voice. "You do too, you know."

"You're right, I do." He took her hands in his. "We both do."

"They'll be gathering soon for a status update. Internet connection, power, that sort of thing—" A pause, Emily cleared her throat. "—Dad, I think they're going to ask about outside." He heard the worry in her voice. "They're going to ask about you. Could you help them understand any of it?"

"Believe me, I would if I thought it would help," he said. And at once, she recognized the tone. It was the same used with her mother when he tried explaining. He shrugged and looked apologetic. "They'll want answers that I won't know until I can get to the machine."

"That's what you plan to do? Go to the machine?" she asked. Her voice was sharp, alarmed. "I heard you and Mom talking about how you'd fix this and—"

"Emily, listen to me, for your safety. For Sammi's too," he interrupted, his expression bleak. He glanced to Sammi and then back. "It's very important that nobody knows what I said or that I was the architect. Not until I know I can do something about it." For a moment, she let the silence fall between them, the tension growing thick like a static charge.

"I understand—" she finally began, eyes damp. Her father was the architect, and they were in danger because of it. "Just thought you'd still be able to help answer any questions, is all."

"I might be able to help in other ways?" he said, half asking. "Like with the engineering, the Wi-Fi or something. But it's the machine I need to get to."

Emily flipped around the map he'd been working on and pointed to the service tunnel entrance that led to the Food-Mart. "The ocean is in the other direction, right?" A nod. "Then to get back to the machine, the service tunnel can take you to the beach."

"Right, beyond the ladder we came up," he said, leaning

over to turn and look at the coast. He couldn't see the ocean, but in his face, there was recognition, a plan forming. "That's the best way to get there."

"Dad, listen," she urged, preying on a possibility. "Do you think the chances are good that you can fix the problem?"

Her father gazed over her shoulder, staring for what seemed a long time. Though he seemed to be looking at nothing in particular, she knew his clockwork gears were in motion. An architect thinking. "I have to get there first. If I reach the beach safely—" he began, lips continuing silently. "—Then yes! With some protection, I'll get to the machine and fix this."

"We?" she asked, wondering if he wanted her to come with him.

He shook his head sternly. "We—as in me and one more. I'd need the extra hands to help." Her father tapped a finger against his chin. "What about your friend Peter? What do you think? He looks plenty strong enough."

At the mention of Peter's name, a new kind of concern leaped inside her. She scowled, a terrible stew of regret and hope churning. "Well? I mean, maybe. He's been kind of an amazing help around here."

"Or... I might need someone older, more mechanical and experienced and all. Maybe someone like Nolan?"

"Yeah. I think he looks mechanical," she commented without any idea of what that meant. "Definitely older."

Her father placed a hand on hers. "Don't worry, I get it." A smile lifted the corner of his mouth, a flush of embarrassment hot on her cheeks. Her father knew but said nothing more about it, the smile turning serious. "Don't mention any of this. Not until I figure it out. People are hurting, and when they're hurt, they're apt to react."

"Maybe someone can help figure out how to protect you from the fog?" she asked.

"Maybe," he answered, regarding the suggestion and gazing past her again. And again, she didn't think he was looking at anything at all—just thinking through the problem. "We just want to be careful about who we ask."

SEVENTEEN

Emily saw them coming, her wishes for a quick meeting dashed. There were more now than before, the shuffle of feet growing, the count rising. Nolan and Isla were already standing on the short wall, their voices steeped in the crowd's low chatter. From the approaching faces, the strain of the disaster was wearing. This wasn't like the other times when a hurricane drove them to the safety of the mall. Those were more like fun sleepovers with board games and hot food and warm cots, even a movie playing on a makeshift screen. This was different. And the looks on the faces showed it.

Peter stayed close and nudged her elbow when seeing the men and women arrive with Jeter. Her father saw them too, a few trading glances and nudging a chin in his direction. There was some news, though. Good news perhaps. She showed them her phone's screen, the icon in the upper right saying the mall's Wi-Fi was back up. The cables had been strung into place, the emergency generator delivering power to enable the network access. But what good was Wi-Fi without the Internet? She was sure there were some things they could do, but it was the Internet they needed.

"At least *we're* online," her father commented, emphasizing the word "we're" with a shrug. "Once the local backbone comes back, we might see other survivors."

"Let's hope," Peter said, facing Emily with a reassuring smile. His gaze lifted to the ceiling, to the beige-painted girders and beams and the dozen or so birds that'd escaped the fog. They sat perched together, fluffed with their heads tucked. The skylight windows were darkened by the fog, the time on the mall's courtyard clock saying they were nearing sunset. *The stars and moon*, she wondered sadly. Like the sun, the fog stole them, too, and like old friends who'd lost touch, it wasn't until now that she'd thought about them. They were still there, though, the distant galaxies whose light had been extinguished long ago. What did they look like now?

"Thank you for joining us," Nolan told her father, his voice breaking her stare. Like the people gathering, she saw the wear of the disaster on him. She saw it on Isla too. Their eyes were half-lidded and bloodshot with dark circles pouched beneath. Had they slept or rested at all?

"Glad to be of help," her father answered, wiping his mouth with a paper napkin. He motioned to the table. "I started to map the service tunnels, the pipe stems and the culverts I was in."

Nolan peered over at the paper, his attention short. "Isla said something about the beach? You guys were talking about it." Her father hesitated, glancing over while Emily tried recalling who was around them when they were talking. "If you think it'll help, we could get a volunteer to verify and see if the access is safe?"

"We know it's safe from here to the Food-Mart," he answered Nolan, looking around them first. "I think we should concentrate on the other passages and get them mapped."

"I suppose," Isla said, leaning in as she carried on a second conversation with a survivor. The mall groaned then, a lull dawning over the crowd. It was subtle at first like the yawn of a sleeping giant. Emily braced herself against the table, hand slapping the map while a rattle shook her. In the distance, breaking glass splashed across the tiled floor as the quake trailed off and died. "That's another one."

"How many is that now?" Nolan asked, speaking to Isla, more annoyed than frightened. The quakes came and went like a restless sleep, turning and kicking and rolling over. "They're getting on my last *effing* nerve."

"A bit hangry, are we?" Isla quipped and lowered her chin, brow furrowed. Nolan didn't answer but leveled his eyes at her. She sighed and added, "Yeah, me too, babe."

"At least it wasn't as strong," Peter said while a shiver of dust clouded the air. Emily looked to the ceiling, the birds flying in circles, escaping what was unescapable. The debris drifted like paper snowflakes; her immediate worries rested when seeing the skylights were intact. But for how long?

"They look okay," her father said cautiously, joining. "Still in place."

"I don't think that one was another explosion," Nolan stated, searching as if seeing the mall for the first time. "I know what an explosion feels like."

"You're right. It wasn't an explosion," her father agreed. "I think it was the last of the Food-Mart collapsing?"

"Let's hope some of it is salvageable—" Emily began, footsteps ascending with a heavy clop. From behind a row of the makeshift beds, Ms. Newl appeared. Her graying hair sat lopsided and she desperately tried straightening it. Her cheeks were flush and pooched with each panted breath. She waved, motioning for them to come over.

"Now what do you suppose that's about?" Nolan asked, annoyance returning. He turned to face the meeting, the gazes following. "Listen up. I'm sorry to delay, but we'll get this thing started shortly."

"I can see the Wi-Fi," someone yelled in the back. "Any luck with those CB radios?"

"Nothing yet," another voice answered. "Just static."

"The Wi-Fi is a start." Isla gave a thumbs-up, adding, "Thanks for your patience."

They didn't run. Didn't jog. But they did hurry away from the meeting place. Emily followed close behind her father, Peter by her side, arm brushing hers. Ms. Newl was still out of breath when they reached her, the waddle beneath her chin quivering. "Outside—" she started and choked back a rattle of spit. "There's something going on outside. I didn't want to scream it out, though. Thought it'd be safer with fewer ears."

"Outside?" her father asked, stepping around the woman, leading them in the direction she'd come from. Emily took his arm, but it slipped from her fingers as he continued forward. "How do you know?"

"It's at the carousel," she answered, hurrying alongside him while pointing. "You know, the old merry-go-round. Behind it, the windows. Go, and you'll see."

Muscles tight as they rushed, their footsteps were a voiceless parade. Others soon followed, Ms. Newl's attempted discretion lost. No less than a dozen were following with more added as they passed through the food court and play area. It was like a snowball rolling down a hill, and what was small at first grew dramatically. The patter of sneakers and flip-flops and Crocs and all different shoes joined them. The low drone of inquiring voices followed too, Emily's father becoming aware as he glanced over his shoulder more than once.

"We've got company," Peter said, his chin near her shoulder.

"I see that," she replied, the carousel coming into view. By the time she was close enough to see the majestic eyes of a brown horse she rode as a child, Emily thought everyone had followed. And at once, she was afraid. She was terrified of what Ms. Newl had discovered.

The carousel looked exactly the same, but in her memories, it was bigger and more colorful and more exciting than anything else she'd ever seen. To see it now, to see it in the deep breath of this disaster, the carousel was alone and unused and forgotten. The shine on the carriages had paled and the gleam on the painted horses dulled. All that had made the carousel bright and happy was tarnished and discolored by the fog's odd light. To see it like that broke her heart a bit, the sentiment making her feel a little childish.

Peter was first to reach the windows, their dark glass swimming from the floor to the ceiling and spanning two levels. These were the largest windows in the mall, the sheer size of the glass making her nervous. Her father must have felt the same way, stepping forward carefully, fingers splayed, palm gently pressed against the surface.

She caught Peter's eye then and he waved excitedly to her, saying, "You gotta see this!"

"What?" Emily asked, peering over to her father who gave an approving nod.

"Hurry! Hurry, before it's over." Peter smiled and spoke loud enough to draw more than a few closer to the glass. She caught the excitement, which stirred a flutter in her belly.

"Over?" she asked, standing next to him. Then she saw it. It was water. But it wasn't like the condensation from steam or clouds or the fog. These were raindrops. Plump and blooming, a wind sweeping them toward the mall. "Is that rain?"

"Rain," her father answered bleakly. "I'm afraid it is."

The flutter in her belly died when the direness emerged on her father's face. Emily got to her knees, the daylight dimming with the end of the day, but it was enough to show the pavement. Just as her father had told them earlier, there was space beneath the fog. It lifted enough to see the pavement and beyond. Her breathing stopped when she came across a pile of clothes, the yellow and turquoise colors clumped in a fleshy red puddle. She moved on and saw the remains of a couple holding hands. A child with a teddy-bear. A family bundled in a hug. Emily cupped a hand over her mouth, the sight driving her back from the glass. Her father stared hard out the window. Did he see it too? A rueful flitter turned inside her, and she hoped that he had.

"The rain? It could be a good thing!" Nolan said, asking. Emily didn't want to see it. Had hoped it wouldn't happen. But Isla and Nolan and Peter were looking to her father for an answer. Even Ms. Newl was waiting for him to say something. "You know, like the way the rain washes things away?"

"Dad?" Emily asked, voice pressing quietly while the crowd gathered closer. He took a step back, feet dragging, and shook his head with another step. He knew something. "What is it?"

"Huh?" She met his eyes and saw trouble in them. He didn't answer but returned to face the window. In the glass, his reflection was exposed, revealing his secrets, telling her that this was bad. His lips moved without a sound, his mind calculating something. But what?

"Mr. Stark," Nolan insisted.

"The rain isn't going to take the fog away," her father finally said. His eyes were glassy, and he half nodded and shook his head at the same time. "The worst of what was in the fog is in the rain. We've got a serious problem."

"What kind of problem?" Peter asked, the earlier smile disappearing behind a frown. He sought out the window corners and where the roofline joined the glass walls. When her father didn't answer right away, Peter asked in a shaky voice, "The worst of what?"

"Acid? Is it some kind of acid or radiation?" Ms. Newl asked.

Isla grabbed her chest. "Oh, Jesus!" she huffed.

"Is it?" Ms. Newl repeated, her face still riddled in thick red and purple blotches.

"Not radiation... sodium hydroxide, chlorine, amongst other things," her father shared with them, turning around to explain. "But with the added moisture on top of any condensation, there's a potential for a higher concentration. Much higher."

"What's he mean?" someone asked, expressions remaining fixed.

"In English, Dad," Emily blurted, even though she knew exactly what it meant.

"The fog *is* poison," he started again, Emily wishing he'd picked another word. Was there any way to sugarcoat this? She didn't think so. He stared blankly and waited for an agreeable nod in the crowd. "But with the rain, it's a lot more potent. A lot stronger. Make sense?"

A puzzled daze.

"He means that you'll get wetter standing in the rain than you would in the fog!" Emily added, desperate to help. She saw understanding pass across the faces, which was quickly swept away with worry. Heart tight, throat closing, she dared to add, "The rain is going to make it worse."

"What's that going to do to the mall?" Peter asked. His eyelids were gone in a flash, eyeballs bulging. "Will it be like the Food-Mart?"

As if to answer Peter, a sharp twang cracked above them, drawing their attention. White and brown and gray blurs fluttered hurriedly as the birds took flight again. Ms. Newl let out a muffled scream while Nolan and Isla backed away from the glass. Emily's father raised his hands, trying to listen.

"That's not the same as the Food-Mart," Emily told Peter, voice grating, intentionally raising her voice for everyone to hear. She pointed up, adding, "Whatever it was, it was small."

"The mall will be fine," her father said. Turning back slowly, he added, "We'll be safe for now. It'd take a lot more rain to be of serious concern."

"Jesus!" Nolan shouted. Heads turned in his direction. He

clutched his army cap, jaw clenched. Isla wore the same expression, Nolan saying, "There's a tropical storm coming!"

"It was forecast for this area. Today! Wasn't it?" Isla asked, searching for reassurance.

"It was. The stronger side of the storm too," Ms. Newl answered, fingers covering her mouth. "That's the more dangerous side."

"It means higher winds and a storm surge," Jeter hollered. The crowd turned in time to see him helped onto a chair. "What'll happen then?"

The crowd's focus returned to her father, his color draining. Emily saw him swallow hard as he glanced back at the window, his fingertips white against the glass. "I... I don't know."

"This isn't just some rain. It's the beginning of the storm? Isn't it?" Peter asked, the question going unanswered. "I was gonna surf it this morning with some friends."

"The rain is coming, folks," Emily heard Jeter say. "It's coming hard too!"

"We're ghosts," a woman cried nearby, hysteria spreading. "Ghosts, waiting for it to end."

The roof boomed to give the threat a fresh voice. "Oh, no!" Ms. Newl shrieked. They waited for more, but nothing came. A hush fell over them, the storm a steady rain patter that filled the silence.

Emily stared ahead, breath hot like fire, pulse racing. Like Nolan had earlier, she was seeing the mall like it was her first time too. The first signs of the storm were here, they just hadn't noticed them until now. Beneath the rainy thrum, a soft wind batted the windows. It was breezy with increasing gusts. With each blow, the poisoned rain pelted the glass, chipping away at the structure, stripping it. The storm was here, and it was getting stronger.

"A tropical storm? The right side?" her father exclaimed, eyes started and bulging, words addressing no one. His voice was a near mumble. "That's too much rain. It won't survive that. Not all of it. The foundation and walls maybe."

His words seized her like a tragedy, the terror in them stirring wildly to anyone else who'd heard him. Images floated in a waking nightmare, tumbling pictures of the devastation they'd face. She saw their mall in ruins. She saw flaming plumes in the sky; giant red and orange fireballs sipping on the generator's fuel like a cocktail. She saw a little girl with lopsided pigtails, her flesh melting from her bones. She saw her father's death; choked by the poison made by his own hand. And then she saw the horrors of Peter's death and her sister's. She saw their end.

EIGHTEEN

Emily peered over at a carousel horse and tried to trick herself into thinking this was all just a nightmare. Her heart ached at seeing the dim shine in its glassy eyes. A tropical storm would consume everything in its path. A monster had been born in the southern bowels of the Atlantic Ocean and was gaining enough momentum to stir itself into a frenzy. When it was ready—only when it was ready—it was going to finish its ride up the east coast by squatting on their little town, spinning over it like a merry-go-round.

"Dad?" But he couldn't answer, his face remained blank. When she dared to move closer, he waved her off. What if he was thinking? That's what he was known for, it was why they sought him out to build the machines. The fleeting hope died when seeing his lips were still, a wet sheen covering his forehead. She saw Nolan and Isla, and Peter closing around him too, wide-eyed and recognizing the panic. Emily could read the intensity on their faces, and it frightened her most of all.

"Mr. Stark? What the retired doctor said earlier about you maybe knowing something. I don't care about anything other than the welfare of Isla and the people here—" Nolan began, a desperate eagerness in his voice which was solemn and small. "Phil? If you can help, then please tell us what to do."

"Dad?" Emily tried again, standing close to Isla, the group pleading her father for an answer. Any answer. She just wondered if he'd say what they needed to hear.

"Emily," he finally said, his voice cracking.

"What is it?" But he stayed silent again, gaze jumping from face to face. Unease like she'd never felt before climbed across her skin. "Please!"

"The service tunnels!" he answered firmly and with commitment. "They may—"

"I know who you are," a voice shouted from behind the carousel. It was Jeter and whatever the old man had been heating up in his mind had finally boiled over. Emily's heart sank seeing Jeter and some others coming directly toward her father. The crowd parted with his approach, four men and two women following. They held a cold stare on her father as Nolan spun around and stood between them. Her muscles turned twitchy, shaky even as Jeter's gang circled around them, blocking them next to the carousel. Peter took to her side while her father pushed to stand in front of them, blocking her view. She had to see and peered out from behind to see the gang's fists were closed, their stances spread. Nolan squared his shoulders to theirs. "And I know what you did too! You and all them other lab coats that'd been out there working on that machine."

Her father turned, his face gray like the fog as he explained, "Emily, Peter—the service tunnels, the beaches and the—" His voice ended with a thwack, his body folding into a shallow pile. There were no words of warning, no questions to be answered. Jeter and his gang had decided the outcome already. They wanted blood. They wanted retribution. Emily didn't realize she was screaming until the raw sting in the back of her throat stole her voice. She jumped to stand between her father and the men, one of them thick like a tree trunk.

It was the son or grandson with the squishy face, his gaze ran up and down her body. Instincts robbed any sense of fear, her arms up, hands fisted. She only knew that she had to stand there and protect her father. Tree-trunk flared his round nostrils like a bull, satisfied. He kicked at the ground, stepping closer, towering over her, reminding her of her insignificance. His hot breath hit her face, and a sudden fluttery brilliance bloomed in her belly. Instantly, her legs wobbled and her lungs collapsed, starving her of the mall's stale air. Her father got to his knees, yelling, "Please, wait!"

"You ain't going anywhere," Jeter hollered, veins jumping out on his neck, his head turning purple. He grinned savagely, saying, "Except outside where ya belong! Son, hit him again!"

"Wait!" her father begged. Without hesitation, Jeter's son swung a beefy fist, throwing it from over his shoulder, swinging hard like a hammer striking a nail. It struck her father's head with a sickening thud, a cut opening in a flash, the blood horribly bright. Her father dropped in a blink, his body lying flat like it had been deflated.

"What are you doing?" Emily spat, anger rising. She crawled to her father's side, vaguely aware of Peter and Nolan fending off the others. Her father's eyes swam dully, trying to focus. "Why did you do that?"

"Jeter!" Nolan screamed, his freckles vanishing in a veil of red. "That's enough!"

"Ain't enough!" Jeter whistled through his gapped teeth. "It ain't never gonna be enough for what they done!"

"All of you, stop this!" Nolan yelled, waving his arms with Peter behind him. "This isn't right. You know it!"

Jeter lifted his chin toward her father, a look of judgment in his eyes. "I seen that one there plenty of times. In and out of that infernal machine. Working it with them others."

"The machines! You're one of the scientists? You were involved and made this happen?" Nolan lowered his arms, brow furrowed while trying to understand. He looked to Isla and rubbed absently at the sting on his arms. "I knew it was something... you should have told us."

"That man done this," Jeter's son barked. He straightened, fists clenched. "My pops says that he's one of them—so that means he can't be one of us. He's an outsider, and that's where he'll go. Outside."

"Hold on," Peter shouted, voice warbling. He was small next to the tree-trunk, but dared to step closer, guarding. The other son pivoted, his build like his brother's, only bigger. Isla went to Nolan's side while a few men lined up alongside of her. Chess pieces in motion, a standoff was building. "You don't know what he was doing there."

"Don't much matter now. We got ways of dealing with outsiders," Jeter continued. "Ain't welcome in here."

"A lot of people worked on the machines!" Emily forced the words, a tearful sob stealing their impact. Her father twitched beneath her hands and then shook his head. *Please don't move.* She gently held him down as he tried pushing to get onto his feet. It was all they needed to see, and Jeter snapped his knobby fingers. The closest tree-trunk balled both fists, swinging and striking her father's back. Air exploded out of him, flattening him to the floor. Eyes stinging and ears ringing, Emily dove on top, covering him, shielding her father. "Please no. Don't hurt my daddy—"

"Outsider," she heard one of them say, two pairs of shoes kicking with deadly accuracy, finding her father, grunts and groans spilling from his lips. Jeter's sons cast shadows in front of her. The bigger—the one attacking—raised his hand again, reeling it back. Emily winced and braced herself. A blast of commotion flew over her head, the sudden rush lifting her hair when it passed. It was Peter, diving to tackle one of the men. "Peter? No!"

But Peter didn't listen, his sandy-brown hair flopping

wildly, his face turning purple while he struggled to hold the man down. The man let out a laugh, his fists blurring, Peter's face bloodied and his head snapping awkwardly to one side. It was enough to send Peter flying onto his back, landing with a hollow thud. His eyes blinked desperately as though suddenly blinded. Emily cried out to him, his stare fading to an absent daze as he stopped moving.

"Please, no more!" Emily begged the men.

"Stop this now!" Ms. Newl screamed. "This is no—"

A thousand pounds suddenly crushed Emily's insides, the rest of Ms. Newl's words replaced by a wheezing breath. Her eyes bulged as she clutched at her chest, choking, suffocating, the carousel spinning and turning sideways. Emily was vaguely aware she'd been hit with a punishing force. Jeter's gang was too much for them. Ms. Newl continued yelling, voice replaced by a loud ringing, her smallish arms and tiny hands swinging at the men. Nolan was in the throes of a battle too, wrestling two of the men. Another strike came, stronger than the first. The ache in Emily's lungs blazed and for a moment she was certain that her heart had stopped. She had no more air to give. No fight either. Jeter's gang wanted her father. They wanted blood. And they were going to go through her to get to him.

Blackness wavered like heat, it crept over her and drenched her mind like the rain outside. A familiar swaying took over, the kind before a sleepy lullaby offered to whisk her away to some dreamy place to leave the horrors behind. Emily fought it, hearing the muted cries of Ms. Newl and Isla. They were yelling and screaming, the voices in an interlude with the uneven tempo of blood rushing in her ears.

The cut on her leg throbbed and planted wet kisses. It had opened again and bled, telling her she was still alive. The men standing over her turned fuzzy and warped, and she understood now that this was the new normal. The days of lawyering and trials and judges had gone. In this world, it was the strong who policed and judged. Emily shoved a hand forward, fingers crawling onto her father's hand, gripping his fingers. But there was no protecting him. The new judges had her father, and the punishment was swift. Another blow brought grainy star lights with flashy tails erupting in front of her. Cold spread through her and her eyelids narrowed while the men pummeled her father like jackhammers. She tried to call out. She tried to beg. And then she tried to cry.

NINETEEN

A gunshot.

"Please no, Dad!" Emily whispered, startled, the boom jarring. Muscles tight, she got to her knees, dazed and stomach threatening. The bleeding in her leg stopped, the bandaging still in place. Sipping the stale air, her father was still, but breathing. Blood spread in a gory puddle around his head. Smeared footprints and scuffed boot-marks circled his body from the men who'd been stomping on him. "God, please!"

"Get away!" Isla's voice threatened, a small handgun poised above her head. A wispy tail of white smoke flowed delicately from the barrel. The fighting had ceased, alarm replacing the grunts and groans and whimpers. Jeter and his sons had stopped too, their eyes fixed hard on the threat. Where did she get a gun? Isla's face was red with fury, and she stomped a foot, warning, "Back away from him!"

"Isla," Nolan said, voice steady but his face a messy twist of fright and concern. He glared at the gun, the barrel wavering. "They'll back away."

"Dad?" Emily said, frozen in place, needing to see more than just his breathing. Jeter's men stayed and rooted themselves next to her father. A chink. The sound of glass splitting, her ears filled with a lightning bolt sizzling through the air. Emily followed the direction of the gun to a small hole in one of the giant windows. Words muffled, she pointed a shaky finger at the faint spider web splintering across the glass. "The windows!"

"Oh shit!" Peter said, dragging himself to his feet, seeing it too. The center of the glass yawned like a hungry mouth, a crater growing, each new split gently racing over the surface like dried leaves skittering across the pavement.

"It's gonna go!" she heard someone yell when a thicker split shot down the middle, popping with a jolting bang. A second and third followed, the crowd backing away.

"Emily," her father said groggily. She went to him, slinking over the floor, staying low, her eyes glued on the window cracks. The fissures formed wildly fast to reveal a giant jigsaw puzzle that towered two stories. The sight of it left her awestruck. Peter joined them, his jaw slack. For one dreadfully long moment, the mall was still, voices muted as the broken window held back the tropical storm's threat.

One blink and it disintegrated like a magic trick, Nolan's reaction as instant as a trigger, swooping beneath the windows and shoving his fiancée clear. Isla's body went flying, whites of her eyes like headlights before she crashed hard on her side. The gun bounced across the floor, metal on tile, and disappeared beneath the carousel like a mouse into a wall.

Emily raised her arms defensively as the glass poured down in a swift landslide, the weight of it crashing onto Nolan in crumply pebbles. Pieces of glass ticked against the floor as everyone watched Nolan straighten, an odd smile on his face. There were minor cuts, but he seemed to have escaped serious injury. Like the broken window, it didn't last. Nolan was wet, the storm's wind entering like an uninvited guest, running its fingers over Emily's fair skin with an instant sting. That's when

Nolan's first screams rose. Her father pawed at her arm as he pushed himself up, saying, "The service tunnels!"

"Uh-huh, the tunnels," she answered, unable to move, unable to turn away from Nolan. "Go there?"

"He's still moving?" Jeter spat. Emily could feel the old man's anger like it was heat. "Hit him again!"

Another gunshot. The men stopped their approach, eyes darting to the ceiling.

But it wasn't the ceiling this time. The smell of spent fireworks wafted beneath her nose. The gunfire real.

"That's enough!" Isla screamed, a terrorized look on her face, the gun back in her shaky hand. Her gaze darted to Nolan as he rubbed at his arms and grabbed at his face where small blisters were rising. White smoke drifted from the end of the barrel which was aimed steadily at the men. Jeter and his tree-trunk sons backed away. "I'll use it if I have to! I swear it. I will!"

"Careful with that thing," Jeter warned, nudging his chin at Isla and then the window. Two of the windowpanes remained, the tropical rains pelting against the glass and running down them in slender wet streaks. Beneath where the third window-pane had been, the one in the middle, Nolan stood in a glis-tening pile of broken glass. "Three strikes and who knows what this place will look like."

"Get to the tunnels," her father gasped, repeating himself.

"Gun or no gun, that man is guilty," Jeter said, the tone remaining accusatory while his gaze returned to the gun. "Guilty as them other ones. He can't be here with us; he's an outsider and needs to go."

"Nolan!" Isla said, footsteps crunching. Her fiancé grunted a painful reply, swiping sharply, body jerking and undulating to put out the burn. "Nolan, honey?"

"Get away from the window," Emily's father shouted. His grip felt like a vise as he jerked her arm to pull himself up. "All of you! Get away from the rain!"

A tropical gust blew a sheet of rainwater inside, the downfall drenching Nolan. Almost instantly, smoke rose from his face, the freckles of his fair skin disappearing behind tall silvery blisters. Nolan spun around, slapping and pawing and batting horridly at his head and face.

"What's happening!" Isla screamed, teeth bared, eyes huge with terror. She stood to run and fell hard onto her knees, her legs stuck. "Help—"

"You can't help him," Emily's father shouted over her screams, gripping Isla by the ankles, holding her back. She kicked, yelling, cursing in Spanish as he pleaded, "I'm sorry, you can't!"

"Dad?" Emily's voice wavered tearfully, coughing from the acrid stench striking the back of her throat. "Dad, what's happening to him?"

"Everyone, move!" he yelled, and by now, Nolan's voice was rising in a scream that drowned all other sound. "Get away from the rain!"

"It's just water," someone said as if trying to convince themselves. Nolan's face vanished in a cloud and his army fatigues wept red, the color unmistakable.

"Oh Jesus!" another person yelled, gagging as they covered their mouth and nose. Next to them, a woman bent over and turned away to retch.

"Help me!" Nolan cried in a low growl, guttural and raw. Isla climbed to her knees, her face a tortured mix of horror and disgust. "It's burning!"

"We have to do something!" Emily shouted, noise from the crowd gaining. Her father stood guard in front of the carousel, a hand on Isla's arm. Emily heard Peter breathing fast, the look on his face like a nightmare. She grabbed his arm, pleading, "Peter, we have to do something."

"What?" he answered, questioning. "What do we do?"

Nolan wore a shroud made of gray smoke, his arms flailing,

hands slapping against what sounded like raw meat. Clumps of hair and scalp dropped to the floor as he circled around like an animal with its tail caught in a trap. Isla got free and ran to her fiancé, slipping on the bloody clumps while swatting to put out an invisible fire. Emily pushed Peter aside, intent to do something, her head down in a run, thinking of a fire extinguisher nearby. She ran to the carousel where she'd seen one, but struck the floor with a wheezing gasp. Pain rifled into her legs, her father's fingers clutching her ankles.

She freed herself enough to reach Isla, jerking her away from Nolan just as another sheet of rain blew through the broken window, dousing Nolan. Her father had hold of her again, his bruised face like stone, and dragged her and Isla to safety. Peter had her hand, helping until they gathered by the carousel and took cover beneath the canopy. Nolan reared up, clutching at the air for mercy as if the rain had been a thousand whips, peeling away his skin.

"Nolan!" Isla screamed through her tears. She fell to her knees, Ms. Newl helping Emily's father, both attempting to save the woman who was willing to die for her fiancé.

"Shoot him!" someone shouted. Heads turned to see it was Jeter making the suggestion. The rest of his gang stared, their faces pale, expressions flat. But Emily saw sympathy register on the old man's face. Maybe remorse too.

Jeter was looking hard at Isla. "If you love your man, you'll shoot him."

"I can't—" Isla began, mouth open wide in a silent cry, cheeks wet, blisters covering the backs of her hands as she held the gun close next to her heart. Nolan's movements became erratic as he got lost in the suffering and the torture of what was happening to him.

"Dad, how do we make it stop?" Emily asked, begging for there to be a remedy, thankful Sammi and the other children couldn't see what was happening. In the back of her mind, she knew there wasn't, though. If it existed, he would've used it by now. Wouldn't he have?

"We don't," her father answered coldly. He didn't turn to look at anyone when he said it. There was a strange sort of awe on his face. "That man back there, he's right."

"Oh God please," Isla begged, moving the gun into position. A sickening quiet descended as if the horrific wonder and tragic heartbreak had stopped time.

Isla steadied the gun, taking aim and saying, "Nolan, I'm sorry."

"Do it!" a shrill voice shouted.

"For his sake, lass!" Jeter yelled, hands raised, waving before turning his back, unable to stand the sight.

Nolan wasn't screaming. Not anymore. Emily didn't know if he was beyond that pain or if he just couldn't. It didn't matter, though. The silence was deafening, save for Nolan's pain-filled groans. Isla burst into tears, slumping forward, the crowd breathing heavy like they were part of a single body. "Nolan! I can't do—"

"Turn away, honey," Ms. Newl demanded. She stooped and took hold of the gun, bracelets clanking. Her face had gone pale —ghostly white—she shook her head, glancing at the gun, daylight glinting off the barrel. Emily felt her old school-teacher's gaze and saw a thousand words in the woman's eyes. Emily understood at once and coaxed Isla to turn away. Isla followed while Emily watched. Ms. Newl braced herself, legs set apart, arms steadied, she wasn't the schoolteacher Emily remembered. She aimed the gun at Nolan, one shot ringing out, its echo joined by Isla's crying screams.

All life was gone. Nolan fell onto his chest, the last of his voice gone in watery rattle. Ms. Newl lowered the gun, sigh-ing. A grim satisfaction stole the concentrated expression on her face. Emily held Isla and saw that the rainwater continued to feed on Nolan, eating at his skin, melting him until she thought nothing would remain except a puddle of gore.

"You have to go!" Peter shouted, ending the quiet. He busily covered his arm, tending to the burns, but puffed out his chest with the intention of being heard. The words were directed at Jeter who flicked a glance in his direction. "You're the outsiders. All of you. Understand me!"

"Now hold on a min—" Jeter's brother began, but then stopped.

"No! You hold on," Ms. Newl interrupted. She held the gun —steady, strong—as if she'd been handling guns for years. And perhaps she had. "You beat this man and hit this child, and it was your actions that caused another man's death!"

"There's no room for you here!" Emily shouted at them, Isla's sobs gaining. Try as she might, Emily couldn't stop looking over at Nolan, looking at his remains. If she didn't stop, she'd burst into tears.

"I can't be here!" Isla said, meeting Emily's eyes. In them, Emily saw heartbreak and agony. She saw rage too, Isla yanking herself free. Without another word, Isla stormed away, her face hidden. Emily followed a step, her father holding her back. The crowd moved for Isla, stepping aside, their heads lowered as though it were a funeral procession. She didn't say another word and navigated around Jeter and his gang, the top of her head disappearing past the food court.

"No more of this!" Ms. Newl continued, mouth twitching. Jeter didn't flinch, but some in his gang looked away shame-faced. "I don't care where you go, as long as you're far from here."

"The service tunnels," her father mumbled, his lips bouncing with his words, pouching out in a painful droop. "Get Sammi from the play area. We all need to go there!"

Jeter gazed around at all of them before his glare swung toward her father, answering, "We'll take the service tunnel you all found. The mall ain't the only place." He raised his arm and pointed at the rainy windows. "But mind me when I say that someone's gotta pay. Ain't free, what he's done. Gotta pay the fine."

A heavy crash raged through the floor and dispersed the group like mice fleeing the light, footsteps sounding in all directions. Emily feared it was the first of many, the place falling apart like the Food-Mart. "Can you walk?" she asked, squeezing her father's arm. He moved slowly at first and gained speed as the crushing noises followed them. "The rain? It's tearing the mall apart. Isn't it?"

"It is!" A bigger thud, heavier and denser. Dust sifted from above and the stink of plaster was like their garage when it was destroyed. The memory was fresh—the sounds, the smell—yet it felt like a lifetime ago. Before he could say another word, the sound of metal twisting, popping and shearing from its welds, spilled down from the roof. His eyes huge, he continued, "But I think I can stop it. I think I can save the mall, maybe."

"Stop the rain?" Ms. Newl shouted, pacing next to them, cheeks ruddy. "The fog too?"

"Maybe. I don't know," her father answered, shaking his head. "I can't stop the tropical storm, but the rain and fog. It has to do with the density. I just need to get to the machine."

Ms. Newl peered over to where Jeter and his gang had stood. Emily saw that they were gone. She looked to the puddled remains of Nolan and then back to her father. "Then what they said was *true*?" she asked. There was rigid disappointment on her old teacher's face. "How much of it is true?"

"Some," her father said, confessing.

"We defended you!" Peter blurted from behind, dismayed and hurt.

"Wait," Emily interrupted, heart sinking. "Just wait and hear what my dad has to say." But shame filled her, and she wondered whose side was the right side, or if there should be one side to take at all. They were picking up speed, breathing fast, Sammi's outstretched arms reaching for hers.

"Listen, it's true I worked on the machines," her father began to explain. "But what I did has nothing to do with the tropical storm."

"It doesn't matter when or where you were, Mr. Stark," Ms. Newl said angrily. "What matters is what to do about it now."

"I agree," Emily's father said, shoes shuffling faster, gaze shooting in the direction of a crash. "We can debate it another time. Let's get everyone into the service tunnel."

"We can move down there, and even move our supplies too," Peter added.

A raindrop struck Emily's arm. It was plump and heavy and it burned, a welt forming instantly, "Peter, the scuba gear!"

"Scuba gear?" her father asked, confused.

"If the other tunnel reaches the beach, you'll need the protection," Emily continued, the welt rising into a blister. It burst, the pain immediate. She let out a sharp cry.

"Here, lemme take Sammi," Ms. Newl offered, fingers grasping. She lifted Sammi in a single motion, breath heaving. "You go and help your father."

"The wetsuits will protect you in the rain," she offered. "That way you can get to the machine."

"The gear I found won't fit him, Emily," Peter exclaimed, a fresh bruise glowing around his eye.

"What about an umbrella?" Ms. Newl suggested.

"The material from tents," Peter added, "From the sporting-goods store."

"Now you're thinking," her father nodded, and she could see him working the numbers in his head. "Duct tape too. It'll buy me enough time."

Ideas flew back and forth between Peter and Emily's father while they made their way to the center of the mall, hurrying people along to relocate. Emily kept an eye on the darker corners, searching the shadows for Jeter and his gang. But they'd gone and she hoped it was the last of them. Sadly, Isla was nowhere in sight.

Beyond the food court, Emily found dozens of people milling about. She realized that they were still preparing for Nolan and Isla's status meeting which had never happened and never would. Peter was looking too, and with him, she waved her arms to get their attention.

A few gasped when seeing her father, and questions and concerns volleyed. He didn't answer any and did his best to explain the circumstance. She did her best to help, especially when another hundred questions sprouted like weeds. Ms. Newl joined her father, voices hurrying the questions along.

Nothing motivated the group more than the sounds of the mall beginning to collapse. Emily shrank when a crash shook the floor and thought the Food-Mart was a simple shack by comparison. There was no outrunning the mall if it came down on top of them.

TWENTY

Shallow daylight crept into the service tunnel, hope stirring that her father was right about what was at the other end. Emily squeezed her fingers nervously, wringing them out like a damp towel. They'd find the beach there, but what else would they find? Each step taken with caution, flashlights beaming on the walkway which was dry and free of the storm's runoff.

End of the rainbow, she thought nervously. But there wasn't going to be a pot of gold. There'd be a machine nearby, and a chance for her father to stop this thing that was happening. Behind them, voices drifted in echoes, the mall survivors helped into the service tunnel, relocated safely below ground where they'd wait until the storm passed. Sammi was with them, Ms. Newl keeping her safe.

Distantly, Emily thought of the rats stuck in the service tunnels. She didn't know what they were going to do if the mall didn't survive. How many? How long could they stay? What about the supplies? She didn't have the answers. Nobody did. Emily braced the wall and found an odd comfort in listening to the soft chatter. The sound kept her connected to them. It kept her connected to Sammi.

"What about the storm's runoff?" she asked, taking a step, her father next to her, his head down. The walkway was dry, but for how long? He beamed his flashlight back and forth, swinging it. "Like, if the tropical storm dumps a ton of rain, is it going to come through here?"

"I think we would have had something by now," he answered, carrying a packed tent. "Could be the storm drains and culverts are blocked enough to divert it."

"Let's hope so," she replied, pinching the fabric tight, holding it as he tore a strip. "Otherwise—"

He shook his head. "One problem at a time." Brow rising, he said, "Okay?"

"Yeah, one at a time." Another strip, bigger this time. She joined it to the others draped around her father's neck.

Footsteps approached, Peter's shaded face appearing. "Everyone is settling."

"They'll be safe down here," her father said, peeling a roll of duct tape. It ripped through the air, and he handed her a long strand while Peter wrapped the material around his arm. "A little tighter."

Emily continued forward, eagerness building to reach the end of the tunnel. She tried to listen for a breaking wave, but nothing came. *Too far?* she wondered. *Maybe the tide is out.*

She jumped with the sudden echo of a crash, the sound like a cannon blow. It bounced between her ears and made her crouch for safety. Screams from the survivors raced behind it, turning distant before fading. Doubt ticked in her heart about the mall's survival. Her father couldn't be right about it. It was like the Food-Mart, the crushing sounds telling her it was being consumed by the rain. She imagined the walls tumbling in on themselves, the place becoming a grave to those she'd helped put in the back: out of sight, and out of mind, so to speak.

That included the man with no burns. His face was unaffected, and it was the reason she thought he'd come from the machine and through the service tunnel. Her father would know exactly where it was, too, and Emily suspected he might have even known the man, perhaps worked with him. Standing, she glanced at the concrete wall in front of her, moisture reflecting the gray daylight, holding onto the secrets of those that had traveled the path before them. And if the man with no burns did come from the machine, was he looking for her father?

"Are we there yet?" Peter asked. Emily stopped, a tug of exhaustion telling her to rest.

"You sound like my little sister," she returned with a soft chuckle. Now wasn't the time for levity, though, her lips thinning to hide the smile.

"The tunnel's getting brighter. Can you see it?" Her father's words echoed from behind.

"I see it," Peter answered. "I thought I was seeing things at first. You know, like my eyes were playing tricks on me."

"No tricks," Emily assured him confidently. Now if she could only convince herself. "That's the beach."

"No rats either," Peter added, sounding grateful. "Glad those little fuggers are gone."

"Where did they go?" her father asked, stopping. "If they're not here, and they're not between the Food-Mart and the mall, then they've got to be somewhere."

"Dad, you're the only person who's been in the other tunnels leading to the roads. It's a mile from the mall, maybe two? What do you think?"

He regarded the question, picking at a cut beneath his eye. Shrugging, he finally answered, "It's got to be the new office buildings? A couple miles is not that far. They're tall and staffed with cafeterias, some of them may have food."

"Well, I guess I really don't care where they went," Peter said in a fearful voice.

"We could go there," Emily suggested, stopping mid-step.

They turned to face one another, huddling in the tunnel. "Like you said, Dad, the office buildings are new."

"And they've got those gigantic parking garages beneath them," Peter added excitedly. "All concrete."

"Sounds like a good plan," her father said, a gritty sound rising from their feet as they turned to face the light.

"The beach," she said with relief, kneeling to swipe her hand over the sand. Ahead of her, the fog hugged the tunnel's entrance, rolling in folds, revolving silently.

"And the fog," Peter continued.

"We're at the opening," her father said. "Just a few more steps but be careful."

"What are they doing?" Emily asked. Footsteps rang out from behind them. Ms. Newl following perhaps. But she had Sammi, and they were supposed to have waited. Emily stood in silence with her father and Peter, the fog rolling in a mindless cycle, around and around, but never coming in. Uncertain if the others would hear it, Emily called out, "Wait back there. We'll come for you."

"Hey guys?" Peter began when there was no reply. "Is it me or does it look too dark?"

"You're right, I see it," Emily returned and then reached into it like a child tempting a candle flame.

"What are you doing!?" Peter jumped, yanking her arm but not before the tips of her fingers broke the barrier. He held her hand in his, his warm breath on her fingertips, asking, "Lemme see! Did you get burned?"

"A little, but it's more like an itch," she answered, frowning with questions. "Dad, it's different than before, isn't it?"

"The fog's getting weaker," her father answered. "But the rain, it's still dangerous."

"Guys?" Peter asked, his eyes growing brighter as if by magic. It wasn't magic, though. It was light from beyond the tunnel.

"What is that?" Emily asked, the walls coming alive with shiny colors, graffiti art with signatures as tall as she was.

"What's going on?" Peter asked, amazement on his face, a colorful glint in his eyes. "Is the fog lifting?"

"Not the fog," her father answered. "It's the tropical storm."

"What do you mean?" she asked, not understanding.

"It's the eye of the storm," Isla exclaimed, her voice suddenly with them.

"Isla?" Emily asked, surprised to see Nolan's fiancée. But when she saw Isla's face, her heart went cold. Sorrow and heartbreak had aged the woman whose name was Spanish. Her chestnut hair was disheveled, her cinnamon skin like ash. Isla was barefoot and wearing jeans and a thin T-shirt with nothing beneath it. It wasn't cold, but it wasn't hot either, Isla wearing less than she should be. Emily dared a touch, Isla's skin damp with goosebumps rising. "We've got tent material, can I cover you?"

"No," she answered, an ugly sarcasm in her voice. Isla forced a smile. "It's time."

"It's time?" Peter asked, confused. Isla walked around them and stopped at the opening, the fog swirling slowly around her ankles. She turned to put her back to the fog, Peter repeating, "It's time for what?"

Isla dipped her chin, gaze pivoting to each of them before she finally answered, "It's time to leave."

"No!" Emily screamed when Isla stepped backward suddenly, the fog circling her arms and legs before swallowing her chest and head. A second later and the woman was gone.

"Jesus! What are you doing!" Peter yelled. Emily rushed past and lunged forward, arms disappearing up to her shoulders. She touched fabric and a tangle of hair, taking hold with a squeeze strong enough to hurt. Emily felt the shirt in her hand, Peter's voice ringing in her ear, "You got her?"

"Isla?" Emily screamed, her father's arm crossing her

middle, holding her. Raindrops struck with a sharp burn and might as well have been a lance slicing through her arms. Emily let go of Isla's shirt, the pain unbearable, retreating. "Oh God, Dad. Save Isla!"

"You can't," he answered, hugging her, pressing her head to his chest. "We can't."

"What the—" Peter began and dropped to a knee. "She just went into it."

"Why? Why would she do that?" Emily cried, begging to know and forced herself to look, forced herself to turn around and see her friend suffer the same fate as Nolan. There was only the fog, though, and the sound of rain tattling its stinging secrets from the other side. It was what Emily couldn't hear that was more heartbreaking, more gruesome than anything else. Isla went into the caustic rain and never made a sound.

TWENTY-ONE

Emily lost track of the time, the mourning for the dead stealing the minutes. The weight of losing her mother, and now Isla and Nolan, was too much. It broke something inside. She couldn't put a finger on what it was. Maybe it was shock. Maybe she'd been in shock since the car accident. But she felt there was going to come a point when all of this was too much.

She didn't move, her shoes were planted in front of the foggy wall. The rain slowing to a steady patter, and then, as if someone had hit a switch, it stopped. The walls began to change too, the graffiti's colors turning livelier, shimmering and moving like some kind of living mural. It wasn't her shaky breathing or the heavy sobs causing it either. The colors were different, and Emily realized it was the eye of the storm on the move.

"If we're going to do anything, we've got to do it now," her father demanded, seeing the same. "I know it's tough, but I need you two to help me. Understand?"

"Yes, sir," Peter answered, unfurling a large swath of tent material. He tore through half, dressing her father's arms and legs, the material crinkling. "Emily?"

"What?" she snapped, still staring. Peter reared back, hurt by the tone. Instant regret left her without words.

"We need duct tape," he said, placing the spool in her hand. He didn't look at her, but continued, "Peel off enough to wrap around his arms and legs."

She moved closer to him, close enough to plant a kiss if she wanted. He stopped when she dipped her head, their eyes meeting. "Peter, I'm sorry."

"You two can make nice later," her father said sharply. His face was like stone, eyes as wide as could be and fixed on the tunnel's opening. She saw his lips moving, calculating how much time they had before the storm passed. "If I'm right, I can travel inside the eye. Go south to north until I reach the machine."

"You won't hit the rain?" Peter asked, lowering his arms, draping the tent across her father's back. He blinked fast, thinking it through. "I mean, you'd have to time it just right or you'd—"

"I know what'll happen," her father returned and motioned to the material. "Could be the eye of the storm is big enough. It's a risk."

"But what if you get it wrong?" Emily asked, scared for him. An image of Nolan's remains flashed in her head. She shook it off as her father ignored the question. Metal clanked as he rummaged through a duffle bag filled with tools. "Dad, you know how far the machine is, but you can't know the size of the storm's eye. Can you?"

"Emily," he said without answering.

She looked in his face and saw the answer. Her stomach knotted, the familiar taste of loss rising in the back of her throat. "It's... Dad, it's too dangerous."

"We don't have a choice—" he began to say, chatter erupting behind them, a parade of shuffling steps. The gray daylight had extended its reach far into the service tunnel and touched the survivors. The empty space filled with footsteps and voices. Emily squinted to see a small spark flickering, the light bouncing. A second sparked. A third next. And finally, there was a row of them, flashlights bobbing, her father exclaiming, "They're coming."

"They see the daylight! That's why they're coming," Emily said in a reproachful tone. "Dad, they think it's over. What if they think they can go outside?"

"You guys have to hold them in here," he answered, imploring, the significance cracking in his voice. "Send them back!"

"But how?" Peter asked, gawking at them in sudden terror. "They'll run right over us."

"I don't know how," he answered, kneeling, the duffle bag's zipper tearing in a rush. He stood up, covered with tent material, and surprised Emily with a peck on her cheek. There was a weary look in his eyes with a hint of a goodbye too. It was happening. The moment she knew might come. He was leaving again. Emily seized her father in a squeeze, her arms barely able to reach around him. He kissed the top of her head, and told her, "I love you, Emily."

"I love you too, Dad—" she said, choked by a cry. The tent material slipped out of her arms as he turned and disappeared into the fog.

"Holy shit!" Peter shouted. "I didn't think he'd go now! Why did he do that? Why didn't he wait?"

"Because he had to," she answered, daring another touch, fingers following where her father's body interrupted the fog. The fog *was* different. She rubbed her fingertips together and brought them to her lips.

"Don't do it," Peter warned, grimacing and slowly easing away.

Emily put her fingers to her tongue anyway and tasted salt. "It's different now," she told him. "Like Dad said earlier. It's weaker. A lot weaker."

Seconds turned into minutes while they faced the fog. Emily expected to see her father appear at any moment, exclaiming it was too much, too dangerous. But he never showed, and the minutes turned into a quarter of an hour, and then a half hour. The chatter and approaching noise grew steadily until the quiet of the tunnel was lost.

"They must think it's safe?" Peter said, the whites of his eyes shining. "We gotta hold them back."

"It's the light," Emily said, uncertainty building. She shook her head, feeling helpless while watching the nightlight sparks turn into individual shapes, and the shapes turn into a group of people. Two dozen or so had followed the storm's eerie light. Hands raised, Emily shouted, "It's the eye of the storm, don't—"

A large man ignored her, cupping his hand and scooping the fog like it was ice cream. A wispy tail followed as he declared, "It's safe. The storm must've cleaned the air."

"The storm! It's coming back!" Peter shouted. But the man didn't listen, his round body disappearing into the fog. He emerged a moment later to wave on the others. "No, stay in here!" Peter said.

The slow shuffling became a stampede as more survivors crowded around the opening, testing it, teasing the fog with their arms and legs. "It *is* safe," Emily heard again and again. Rows of survivors pushed then, the space becoming suffocatingly tight, her back shoved against the wall. Emily saw Ms. Newl near the rear of the pack, holding the side of her face like she had the beginnings of a toothache.

"You okay?" Emily asked, searching for what was wrong.

Ms. Newl, dazed and confused, cried, "They pushed me down back there!" She slumped against the wall. A grizzled old man tripped past them, caught himself mid-fall, and continued forward.

"Sammi? Where's my sister?" Emily returned, voice rising as a new band of survivors passed swiftly, air buffeting while they disappeared one by one into the fog. "Ms. Newl?" But the woman only looked up and down and around, searching absently.

"I got her!" Peter shouted. He hoisted Sammi into the air, the top of her red hair nearly touching the tunnel's ceiling. "You're safe now."

Without warning, a tickle traveled up Emily's legs and into her belly, a vibration careening through the service tunnel floor. It wasn't the mall collapsing or the storm's wrath. It was mechanical. "My father!" she shouted as a terrible sound swept into the tunnel like a roaring freight train. At once, they dropped to their knees and covered their ears. Emily groaned and then tried to scream, but her voice was lost in the sound. For a long, cold moment, she was certain her father must have failed and that the machine exploded. But this wasn't that. Peter stared wide-eyed and astounded, Emily mouthing the words, "It's the machine."

Sammi dropped onto the ground, sprawled out, stretching every limb, shaking. *A seizure?* But Emily was shaking too—they all were. She could feel the tremors rushing through her like sound ripping the air. The wave of vibrations suddenly stopped, releasing its hold. Emily collapsed next to Peter, gasping for air. She shut her eyes and stayed there until the trembling eased from her strained muscles.

"Oh my God!" Ms. Newl said, words eking through her ringing ears. "Do you see that? Do you all see that?"

Emily rolled over, holding back her insides. The vibrations left her dizzy, and she knew from before that she'd have to wait it out. The sound of someone retching confirmed how she felt.

"Emily?" Peter asked, his hand warm on her arm. "You gotta see this!"

The excitement in his voice pulled on her, and she swallowed, trying to stave off the nausea. If she was going to vomit, then she was just going to have to vomit. But before Emily opened her eyes, she felt heat cast over her face. *I'm dreaming this*, she told herself. *I'm dreaming.*

A tear crept into the corner of her eye when the bright sunlight bled through her eyelids, convincing her of what was the truth and what was not. "It's wonderful!"

"Emmy," Sammi shouted gleefully. "Look, Emmy! Look!"

"Is this real?" Emily asked, opening her eyes to see what she'd never expected to see again. She blinked away a glowing afterimage, the sight convincing along with the touch of sunlight on her face. Nobody answered her as they stood shoulder to shoulder, staring at the ocean. The sun busily cut through the fog, parting its gray folds while peeling back the clouds like a rind on some forbidden fruit. "This *is* real."

Fingers clutching hand in hand, Emily held Sammi and Peter, running from the tunnel until they were struck head to toe by the sunshine. She felt like a child again. They all did, their shoes and shirts coming off, discarded into a pile. Sammi and Peter ran and danced and chased each another while others kicked up the ocean's foamy surf. It was the laughing that made her heart swell the most, stealing the gloom of the tragedy and stuffing it somewhere far away.

"It's over!" Peter shouted, celebrating, grabbing her hands and spinning. "Your father! He stopped it!"

"He really did," Emily yelled, throwing her head back, drinking in the sunshine. The sky had regained the deep blues and reds and purples she'd come to know while growing up near the beach. The winds returned, too, but were only a light breeze, the kite-flying steady blow would come later as the temperatures rose. Around and around she spun, digging her feet into the warming sands. Emily pulled on Peter's hands until they were face to face. And though surrounded, they were alone in the moment. "Not all things have to end," she told him, letting the moment take her. Peter leaned in and kissed her. Her arms melted into his, she held him, lips pressing.

"Emily!"

Peter pulled back, recognizing the authority in the tone. Her father raced toward them, the tent material hanging loose, corners of it whipping. He joined them, breathless.

"You did it!" she yelled.

"Thank you, sir," Peter said. "Thank you."

"It's only temporary," her father said, his jaw slack and his eyes empty. He pointed to the south where a wall of black and purple clouds were marching across the sky. "I stopped the machine's reaction, but I can only hold it long enough for the storm to pass."

"What? But what does that mean?"

"The machine, it's still running, but it won't impact the rain," he answered, motioning behind him. "The rain will pass without any more damage."

"So, why can't you just turn it off?" she asked. Was there more to what her father was saying?

He shook his head, peering over his shoulder. "It isn't that simple, Emily."

"But it is that simple, Dad," she yelled, wind gaining, sweeping through her hair. "Just turn the machine off!"

As if to emphasize what her father was saying, the vibrations returned, the sand quivering and burying her toes. "Emily, I need to go back before it's too late."

"Too late?" Peter yelled, asking.

"What I did is only temporary, lasting short periods," he told them, searching the beach, his gaze finding Sammi. "I have to do it in cycles. Start then stop and then start it again. Understand?"

"That means none of the machines can be turned off?" Emily asked, and pinched the emotion creeping in.

"I—they—designed them to run perpetually," he confessed, and then Emily saw the truth in his eyes. She saw that this was forever. That it was always meant to be forever.

"But, Dad?" And before she could say anything more, a detonating sound trumpeted from the coastline, a shockwave racing over land and sea, rushing through them like a bullet and causing them to fall back. Her insides rattled and shook, the clouds trembled and the sunlight flickered. "What's happening?"

"You've got to get back inside!" her father screamed, spinning around wildly. He staggered, racing by everyone until he found Sammi. Emily watched them, heart aching, her family together for the last time in her life. *This is it*, she told herself. *We'll never see him again.*

Emily joined her father and sister, taking hold, throwing her arms around them. And at that moment, the sound died down. She heard none of it, listening only to her father's words to her and to Sammi. His voice cracked amidst broken sobs, telling them to be good to one another, to be good people, and to survive. Sammi kept her ears covered but focused on Emily and then her father, terrified by what was happening.

A shadow touched her arm.

Cold.

The blue and orange and pink in the sky began to fade, the golden sunlight retreating until it turned white. Gray rainbows emerged high up above them, climbing into the sky in massive arches.

"Look at that!" Peter yelled.

The gray rainbows jutted from the ground, scarring the sky like a knife opening a wound. The colors vanished from the world, leaving behind stale shades that moved with the dimming sunlight. The color of the sun was stolen too, becoming a fuzzy white star perched alone. The sight was both beautiful and terrifying at the same time.

Emily glanced over in time to see Peter disappear in the fog. A blur of bright white rode the arch of a rainbow, their sun vanishing as more of the fog closed in. She glanced at the service tunnel, fixing her eyes in its direction. *I can't lose where it is.* Commotion and chaos came with the fog's sudden return. Legs and arms flew in every direction, staggering, and trying to run in the loose sand. Her step was hastened by the screaming and crying, terrorized by the memory of the first time the clouds fell.

"I've got to hold off the storm!" her father screamed. "Remember what I said, Emily!"

She didn't know when she'd taken hold of his shirt, but Emily tightened her grip, refusing to let him go. "No. Please, don't go, Dad," she cried, but knew in her heart that he had to leave.

"You'll understand one day," he told her and tucked something into her shirt pocket. He gazed at whatever it was with guarded and heartbroken eyes. And for a long moment, he said nothing and instead hugged her until the fog completed its return. "Please remember: I've always loved you and Sammi. I'll always love you!"

Her father pulled away, and immediately she lost him in the colorless cloud. Emily pinched what her father had given her, recognizing it immediately. It was her mother's wedding band, the sight and feel of it filled with both pain and gratitude. She'd cherish it forever. She grabbed her sister's arm, gripping Sammi until she heard her cry. Her father's voice was suddenly in her ear then, startling Emily like a bee that had flown too close. The last thing she heard her father say was, "Whatever you do, don't get lost in the fog!"

"I won't, Daddy," she answered, but thought he'd already gone. "I'll get everyone back. I'll take care of them." And that was what she did. That was what she always did. With Sammi at her side, she found Peter and then used her voice to guide the rest of the survivors back into the service tunnel.

Phil Stark ran, Air Jordans slapping the wet sand, the shoes and socks soaked with seawater as he stayed close to the ocean. The clouds were falling, the gray mist chasing him back to the machine. His chest ached, his heart broken with the loss of his wife and children. It was the world he was trying to save now, and to right a wrong that he never saw coming. This was his fault.

"Stay in the surf," he said to himself. It was the only way to know the right direction. He glanced over his shoulder, a gray rainbow narrowing into a spire, its light threatening to stab him, skewer him for having made such a horrible mistake. "I'm sorry. I'm so sorry—"

Phil struck something solid and tumbled head over heels into a watery somersault. Breathing hard, the fog itching his lungs, he got to his elbows and felt around. It wasn't a rock or boulder. When his foot struck, he heard a grunt.

"Who's there?" he begged, thinking one of the survivors must have wandered north. Phil got to his knees, his face aching painfully from the beating. He swiped away the dripping seawater, eyelids peeling to see beneath the fog. There was only a shallow clearance, barely visible, but it was enough to see bare feet and jeans and a wet T-shirt. "Isla?"

"Who?" she managed to say, groggy, disoriented. Phil lowered himself closer, her light brown skin was swollen with blisters. He could see the lumps beneath her wet shirt too, welts making her skin bumpy.

"It's me, Phil Stark," he told her, startling when his focus returned to see her staring up at him. "Sammi and Emily's father."

"Let me die," Isla said, turning away. "I don't wanna live without Nolan."

"I can't do that," Phil answered coldly, realizing then that she was only moments from dying. He pressed his finger where her pulse should be, her temperature low. He found her heart rate, barely. It was slow. Too slow. He sat on his heels, the ocean's surf washing over them, lips moving. He decided then on what to do and drove his hands beneath her. A chill rifled into his arms as he felt Isla's life slipping. "There's been enough death already."

"Where?" Isla asked, her voice breaking in a breathy rasp. "Where are you taking me?"

"The machines," he answered, feeling her body let go, feeling her take a last breath. He looked straight ahead and trudged forward, surf spraying as he told her, "They'll bring you back!"

TWENTY-TWO

Peter stayed with her, waiting through the remaining daylight. And again into the evening. Emily knew her father was gone, but her heart couldn't let go or wouldn't let go. Emily didn't know the difference. *He'll come back*, her heart said, lying with each aching beat. "He's coming back," she'd whisper tearfully to Peter, the hours passing. But her father never returned.

In the distance, the great machine breathed a grating reminder, the noise telling them it was running. They didn't need to hear it chewing on the air to know. The fog was thicker than before, the machine spitting it up faster. She imagined her father working inside, twisting knobs and pushing levers like he was the Wizard from Oz. She imagined him watching a panel of blinking lights, his lips moving as he spoke to himself, trying to lower the machine's poison breath so that their world might survive.

With the children safe, Ms. Newl joined them once, bringing food and offering Emily a blanket and a huge sweater she'd gotten from the department store. She'd even cut out the security tag and added a matching scarf. Emily gratefully accepted, snuggling as close to Peter as she could, sharing the blanket while waiting for the unknown. Hours later, they were told the mall was surveyed and the survivors were moving back inside. The mall's foundation and walls made it through the storm like her father said they would. A tiny thought came to Emily, one she'd find comfort recalling in the years to come—the survivors would remember her father as the one who'd sacrificed his life to save them.

When the night came, and her breath turned white in the chilly air, Peter pleaded that they leave the service tunnel and go inside. He told her that he didn't think her father was going to come back. Tears puddled in her eyes, and she said nothing and laid her head on his chest, holding him.

"I understand. We'll wait," he told her, and dressed his fingers with her hair, staying for as long as she needed him.

In the dark, they couldn't see the fog rolling or folding and unfolding the way it did. Something shined bright enough to catch her eye. To Emily, it had to be from her father. He was still working the machine, tuning it, trying to get the levels right.

"Look, over there," she said, the hour deep into the night. A spark lit up in the far blackness where a wrinkle formed in the fog. Her heart lifted in anticipation. But the spark was too high in the sky, and she understood then what it was. "Peter, it's a star!"

The spark flickered, its brilliance lasting for just a few moments, winking at them as if to say good night. And when it was gone, a pain settled in her heart. Loss. That was the last star she ever saw.

PART TWO

TWENTY-THREE

The sound of the ocean came to Emily, stirring a memory like a visit to a graveyard. *Has it been another year already?* More memories surfaced then, rising until she could taste them. Some sweet. Some bitter. And some, she'd hoped, would never come back. The walk to the machine this year was going to be an emotional one. It always was.

Rubbing away the ache in her hip—broken years before while scavenging for supplies—Emily leaned against the service tunnel wall, taking care not to slip. She glanced at her shoes: tattered and worn, patches sewn on from linens that hadn't covered the surface of a table in more than a decade. She eased the first shoe from her foot, letting it fall with a quiet thud. But when she tried to grip the other, her fingers stopped. Fifteen years felt like fifty. There was a time when your early thirties was still considered young. But that time had passed, changing in so many ways. She squeezed her hands and felt them creak like a hinge and winced at the labor of what survival meant today. That's what they were, survivors.

"My feet look like I feel." She laughed to herself, grimacing at her toes. A thought of keeping the shoes on ran through her mind, but she dismissed it. "The beach is for bare feet... you know that."

She slipped the second shoe from her foot and placed the pair against the wall and side by side, just as she'd taught the children in her classroom to do. Only her shoes were alone today and looked sad and small against the service tunnel's large wall. The graffiti she'd remembered was still there. The last of it hidden beneath years of grime as if it were some secret message that only a few in their commune would recognize.

She touched the names of those she'd added after the clouds fell. These included Isla and Nolan, and Peter, Sammi, Ms. Newl and her own. There were others, those first who'd survived in the mall. A few were gone now, but some remained to build the commune and seek out others.

There was her mother and father too, but both were gone. Emily tried remembering the sound of her mom's voice but could only see her face. The absence of her words was a sad reminder of the years that had passed. Her father? Emily slumped forward, the weight of remorse heavier this year. She couldn't remember the sound of her father's voice either, or anyone from those early days.

Emily had pictures, though, and looked at them almost every day, the images recovered from her old phone during the early days when the mall's stores were still ripe with supplies. A short laugh stirred in a wheezy puff, thinking of how the stores had been plucked clean soon after the clouds returned to stay.

Across much of the wall was the mark of the Outsiders: a red swath painted in a long bowing arch that stretched above a large black oval. The oval was faded, which told her that it had been a while since they'd last been around her commune. She'd been told once that the Outsiders symbol meant they were watching. Always watching.

And maybe they are, she shrugged. But that didn't matter to her: they'd already caused her and Peter a kind of pain and heartbreak that she'd never imagined was possible. *Let them watch. What more can they do to me?*

Sammi told her not to go to the beach today. And especially not to go alone. "Reports of Outsiders—" she'd started to explain, but Emily quieted her younger sister's words with an impatient wave, telling her that she'd be fine.

After all, if given the chance, she'd take on a visit with the Outsiders. Emily reached down and felt the outline of her knife, hoping that if the need came, she'd have the element of surprise. *I certainly wouldn't have much of anything else.*

Facing the outside, the fog rolling silently, Emily stepped closer and dipped the tip of her finger into the gray stew. She breathed a sigh of relief, the fog less caustic. It'd been years since it burned the way it had that first time. Though it was still thick and blinding, she didn't hesitate and entered with one long step forward.

Cool air rushed over her toes, and the sand on the ground felt scratchy. But she'd greet the fresh sensation over the sweaty shoes any day. She even slipped the jacket from her shoulders, the old rags mended from fashions whose styles were long forgotten. She glimpsed the sight of her bare feet—toenails trimmed, some crooked—and tried to remember what they used to look like.

An hour. What she wouldn't give for an hour back in her bedroom with the window open, the smell of nail polish, and fixing to paint her toenails... only to clean them and paint them again. She wiggled her toes, the loose sand drifting between them, and tried recalling the name of the nail color she liked best. *It was glittery, and purple. Was it called Frenzy Sequin?*

Images of Peter came to her, and she thought of the day they'd married, and the first time they'd made love. Young and beautiful, their bodies wrapping as one. But that was a long time ago, and in this world, you wore your age hard. She let her mind see her hands and feet as they were when they'd first met—

youthful and pretty. She waved and pulled a streamer of fog, and then made fists with her toes, enjoying the lie that she was telling herself.

The beach was where she came to remember the tragedy. It was where she came to never forget, and then to respect what was born of it, what came afterward. It was a new way of life. A new world. In the gray daylight, she focused past the fog, adjusting enough to see the sands. That was what life became after the tragedy: adjustments. They adjusted how they lived and how they ate. They adjusted how they worked and grew food. They even adjusted how they produced energy. She didn't know what they would have done without Jerry, the nerd from their original group of mall survivors. While nobody ever browsed the Internet again, Jerry fashioned a dozen exercise bicycles to generate electricity. Within months, Emily had been the fittest she'd ever felt.

She smirked, knowing that she could very well make this walk blind. Playfully, Emily closed her eyes and let the sound of the ocean guide her. After all, she'd walked the same path the last fifteen years. She knew every step, the sand passing beneath her, the ocean surf running over her feet. The image of her toes blurred, and she squinted, but it didn't help. If she had known any better, she would have grabbed more from the pharmacy that day in the Food-Mart. A pair of reading glasses perhaps: the kind that magnified everything. She laughed then, trying to remember the last time she actually read anything on paper.

Her toes disappeared into the black sand, and she longed for the days when the beach was bright and the sands were hot. They'd lost a partner in life: the sun. The fallen clouds had changed a lot of things, including the beach, turning the sand darker with each passing year. Within a decade, they were as black as coal. She wondered if it was the dead: the world's population having turned to ash, their remains washing up onto the shores as a reminder. Or was it the machine? Pumping whatever it was pumping, changing the world with each breath.

Emily rubbed her hip, which never mended quite right. There was enough of a seasonal chill, the pain harsh and biting. But it was better than most days, and she took her mind off it when her fingers landed on her wedding band. She turned her mother's ring, and whispered her father's name, thanking him for having tucked it into her shirt pocket that last day. It was time soon. Time to give Sammi their mother's wedding ring. Sammi was of age and already had her sights on a boy. Emily let out a chuckle. Declan was more a man these days than a boy. He was also one of her first students and would always be a fetus in her eyes.

The expansion west, she thought suddenly, recalling Peter's fight to lead it. He'd invented a way for them to travel between buildings since the service tunnels only went so far. He went on to lead the reclamation projects, traveling blindly into the fog, going farther than anyone else dared. He brought back food and medicines, and technology. It was on one of the trips that Peter returned with families lost in the fog. Declan was just a boy back then, joining the classroom Emily had set up, sitting alongside Sammi to learn their multiplication tables.

The ocean rushed over her feet, washing away the black sand. Her skin glowed like the white morse lines connecting the buildings, pasty and white like alabaster. Declan and Sammi meeting was like serendipity, a dozen events happening to bring them together. It was the same for her and Peter too, wasn't it? Emily stopped and pressed her feet firmly into the beach, grim thoughts of the child they'd lost surfacing. Round and round she twisted her mother's ring, her heart aching.

"James," she whispered and clutched her chest, a familiar pain passing like a cold shadow.

Their only son's name was James, but she used to call him Boo. He was one of the first children to be taken by the

Outsiders. Just two at the time, he was still more clumsy than not and had been by her side. And then he was gone. A hundred or more from the commune searched, but he'd never been found. Rumors, horrific rumors, came then. They told of tales about the Outsiders eating the children they'd stolen or using them as bait when catching feral dogs and other wild animals. Emily shook, knees turning weak from the rush of emotion. She couldn't believe such things, refused to believe them, and told herself that her Boo had tragically wandered into the fog.

After that, commune children were tethered, keeping them close to their parents when traveling between the buildings. It was a simple idea, and one she wished had been thought of sooner. As for her and Peter, they were never the same. They tried. Emily squeezed her eyelids tight, emotions raw. How they tried. Thank God for the classroom and the dozens of children there. Peter moved on to join the leadership, finding a career and climbing the ranks, traveling far and wide while she stayed behind. They never spoke of Boo again.

"Gray rainbows," Emily mumbled. She saw the image of it in her mind, sending the memory of her baby boy to that special place. When her father disappeared into the fog, going back to the machine to stop the storm, the clouds fell again just as he said they would. But this time, the vapors from the machine caught the storm, creating an odd light and casting wondrous gray rainbows into the sky.

Those that had ventured from the service tunnel were suddenly struck by the beauty of the sight, becoming frozen in place, standing on the beach with mouths wide open. But the clouds continued their collapse around them. Peter was the first to pull away, grabbing at Emily's arm and then grabbing others. She remembered yelling at Ms. Newl, and then slapping a woman to break her trance.

"We got most of them back inside, Dad," she told her father, hoping that he was somewhere listening. Some had gotten lost in the fog and were never seen again. "Most of them."

Over the years, teaching the history of what had happened, she'd drawn the gray rainbows a hundred times on the blackboard. Pencils and pens were scarce, but soft writing stones like charcoal were plentiful. She'd draw on a piece of parchment, perfectly fitting the colorless bands, the remains of the sun riding on the curvy end before disappearing forever.

Emily came upon the great machine, swiping errantly at her hair and brushing the lint from the front of her coveralls. She stepped from the fog, leaving the mist behind her just as she'd done every year since the first. The machine straddled the ocean and the beach, looking like a beached whale, as old man Jeter had said. A shudder. That was a name she hadn't thought of in years, and she was glad about that.

Someone's gotta pay, Jeter's voice rang in her head.

"Mr. Jeter, we all paid. Every damn one of us."

The machine was enormous, reaching the height of a skyscraper, lying across the beach and jutting into the ocean. Emily squinted, trying to find the end of the machine, but it was too far. And if she hadn't known any better, she'd think the machine had gotten even bigger since her last trip.

The fog rolled around the silvery giant but never touched it. And the waves seemed to avoid the machine too, the white surf breaking before reaching it. It was a phenomenon that she never could understand. The void showed the entire machine to anyone that dared a visit. And like the waves, an old tickle of anxiety swelled up from deep in her gut.

When she looked toward the top of the machine, the sky cleared just enough for her to see a hint of blue. But the large vents that breathed like a dragon, puffing white smoke, kept the world's old sky hidden from her.

The machine was taller than she remembered it being, but then again, everything was. Emily was certain that she'd become shorter over the last year. The hard years and age have a funny way of doing that to you. Her mind wandered to the farming floor, and her wanting to pick some apples yesterday, just like she'd done a thousand times before. An apple dangled out of reach, touching the tips of her fingers, tempting her with its ripe shine and smooth skin.

Emily!

Emily startled, thoughts of the farming floor lost. She spun around, alone. The woman staring back at her from the belly of the machine said nothing. *Silly girl.*

She was hearing things and hadn't recognized her own reflection. Emily pulled at her skin, finding a couple of new wrinkles around her eyes. She groaned with disappointment, seeing that her hair had lost some of its color too. There were strands that had gone pale white like a seabird's wing. The image of herself made her want to cry, but she laughed it off, recalling the hair dye kit tucked beneath the sink in her room. There were a few things still on the old store shelves.

A gentle breeze, the ocean spray on her cheek turned cold. Emily looked toward the sea, welcoming the rush of air on her face. Wind of any kind had been scarce for as long as the sun stayed stuck behind the clouds. But the unexpected gust only lasted a moment, and Emily faced the shadow of her past, hoping that this year she'd see her father. She eased a hand forward and touched the metal beast. And like before, the touch was surreal and felt unfamiliar. The skin moved outward from her finger, growing wide, rippling like a stone breaking the stillness of a pond.

Emily waited.

Silence.

She pushed a clump of black sand with her toe, giving the knock on the door a moment. That was what she called it: a knock on the door.

She knocked again.

Silence.

The only hope she'd ever had that her father might still be alive, still be inside the machine, was that the machine looked the same. Not just the same, but identical. The world had changed. The beaches changed. The people changed. But the machine never changed, and after so many years, she'd begun to wonder if the same were true on the inside. A tear ran long, staying warm until she plucked it from her chin.

Standing in the half-light of the gray machine, Emily suddenly saw her father standing with her.

"Dad?" she blurted and grabbed her chest. She fixed her eyes on the reflection in the machine, watching his tall frame approach. He was as handsome as he had ever been. "It's you!"

She felt the touch of his hand on her shoulder and saw that she was young again, like she was before the clouds fell. Slender, and beautiful with hair spilling a red sheen over her shoulders. Her mind was lying to her and this time the lie hurt too much. She closed her eyes tight, letting the tears wash away the painful stain.

"Emily?" she heard, and felt a gentle squeeze on her shoulder, nudging her. "Are you okay?"

When she opened her eyes, the machine was still there. Her reflection was still there, her sister standing with her.

"I'm fine, Sammi," she answered, turning enough to pat her sister's cheek. "I ever mention how much you look like me when I was your age?"

"Yeah, like all the time," Sammi answered, gaze traveling up and down the machine. "What are you doing out here?"

"Waiting," Emily answered, a shot of embarrassment turning her cheeks hot. "And didn't I tell you that I'd be okay by myself?" Her words were stern, but hollow, and Sammi knew it.

"I know you did," Sammi said apologetically. "I knew that you'd be fine by yourself, but... well, maybe I wasn't."

"That's sweet," she told her.

Sammi gave the machine another look, asking, "Anything this year?"

Emily shook her head, biting back the emotion. She let out a heavy sigh and turned around to face her sister. "You know what?"

"What's that?"

"I have some work on the farming floor. Maybe you wouldn't mind helping? Maybe pick an apple or two or three?"

"Fine," Sammi answered. "I can help before my date later."

"Declan?" Emily asked, looping Sammi's arm with hers and leading them away from the machine. Emily took with her the memories of her years, the good and the bad. But there was still, and always would be, the mystery of the machine. She'd have to leave it behind her, knowing that she was finally ready to let it go.

Phil Stark watched his daughters. He watched Emily and Sammi from inside the machine, surrounded by a hundred mindless bodies, the machine's workers paying him no attention. The lights on a nearby wall flickered a quick message, telling him that there was work to do. But Phil shrugged away the request, choosing to see his family again, sadness wrestling with the choices he'd made.

It didn't help to tell himself that he'd made the right decisions, that the machines would save the world. It didn't help because he wasn't sure who they would save. The lights flickered again, more demanding this time. Phil shook his head, defiant, intent on watching his daughters.

They're grown. So beautiful, like their mother, he thought sadly, and glanced at himself in the shiny metal. *But I look the same.* He hadn't aged a day in the years since the clouds fell. *It's a punishment for what I've done.*

Phil pressed his hand against the skin of the machine and shuddered. He had traded the warmth of his family for the cold love of an idea. *It's a lie. Isn't it?* He heard the question in his mind, and a feeling of betrayal squeezed his insides.

"Just once," he mumbled, wishing that he could step outside of the machine and tell Emily and Sammi everything. He had wished the same every year, every visit. And as if Emily had heard his wish, his daughter raised her hand, placing it on the machine with his. Phil's heart leaped. "She can see me!"

But the moment was brief, and his heart quickly sank when Emily backed away, taking the arm of her sister, and then turned to leave the machine. Fire coursed behind Phil's eyes, and he reeled around, shielding his face from the light. The sudden burn was a warning for having touched the machine. Another sharp light stabbed in his direction, and a vile taste of regret filled his mouth. He swallowed hard and choked it back, knowing that his penance was forever.

They're watching, he thought and quickly emptied his mind, disconnecting it from the years they'd monitored his existence. He went to that place that was safe. It was the same place his nightmares crawled to in the moments before waking from a long sleep. But sometimes the days were his nightmares, confusing him with what was real and what was not. That happened more and more as time marched toward his annual expirations.

A mindless zombie. That's what you've become, he told himself. *No. That's not fair... that's not true. I am aware,* he argued.

"I am aware," he spoke out loud. His voice was unfamiliar, almost feeble. And the sound of it filled him with shame.

From his white coveralls, he found the sharp metal wedge he'd tucked away earlier. The lights were busy, paying him no mind.

One jab, he considered. *Just one to know that I'm not imagining them, that this is real.*

He hesitated. *I need to know they're real.* The blade's warm edge slipped inside his neck. A small gush of relief spilled from his pursed lips.

One more.

The cutting continued, falling silent like the crashing waves.

"Goodbye, my girls," he said, wondering if he'd see them again next year. He stayed a moment longer than he should have, watching, until the very last glimpse of them had disappeared into the world he'd helped create. "I'll come out one day, girls! I swear it. I will."

But the promise to his daughters had been carried shamelessly on the ripples of a long history, a history he'd created more than fifteen years earlier.

Another jab, he insisted. *Just one more to make sure this is real too!*

Blood ran, and another gush of relief slipped from his mouth. But the sight of his daughters also left him frightened. Remorse came like the waves, filling him with sorrow, and the heavy regret crushed his heart and mind like a vise.

At once, the lights on the walls flickered, blinking rapidly, instructing the others that Phil Stark had stopped his work and needed a correction.

"I'm working," he screamed hurriedly at them, waving his arms. "I'm working! Can't you see that?"

The lights flashed a jumble of sequences that Phil had grown to know and loathe. The nearest machine worker, a zombie body he called them, was set into motion and approaching him.

"You don't care, do you?" he cried out with resignation. Tears stung his eyes, and spittle ran from his mouth.

A jab. Solid. Stoic. Pouring.

"You've never cared! Look at what I built for you! Just let me stay until they leave!" But when he turned back to face the outside, his daughters were gone. He pressed his hand against the cool shell of the machine, wondering if they'd really been there at all.

They couldn't have been here, he thought, realizing the lie was in his mind again—the lie was always in his mind. *It's impossible.*

"One jab!" he cried out with a raucous laugh and stabbed the metal wedge deep into his neck. Blood sprayed instantly, covering the only window to the outside. He heard the rush of blood in his ears, his heart thumping hard while fighting for the life that he did not deserve.

I shouldn't be here, anyway. None of us should.

Another push and his neck opened like a fountain. The welcome smell of blood came to him. Powerful and engrossing: the machine had no smell at all. The other mindless bodies turned their heads and sniffed at the air, wondering about the strange coppery odor.

"That's called life," he gargled. "Dumb fucks!"

And soon, the taste of blood was on his tongue and filled his mouth. The end was coming. His smile stretched across his face, and he lay on the floor to wait. He stared up through the window, straining with the last of his strength until the star he had tried to find earlier winked at him.

"There you are," he said. "I know you." But Phil also knew that the star might not be a star at all.

"What does it matter, anyway," he muttered in drowning laughter. "They're just going to bring me back."

TWENTY-FOUR

Declan Chambers took to the seventh row of the class, ears perked to the whispering he passed along the way. They weren't talking about him, though. There was a buzz of excitement, a flutter blooming in his gut. As much as he tried dismissing what day it was, for fear of disappointment, there was no avoiding what was spreading.

Ms. Stark stood at the board and picked up the chalk, the energy catching. It was like electricity, the charge raising goosebumps on Declan's arm. Ms. Stark glanced over her shoulder, eyes gleaming at the class, her gaze landing on him and then her younger sister, Sammi. Giggles brewed into laughter when she waved a stick of chalk like a magic wand. Today *was* a big day and Declan decided not to deny the joy that came with it.

"Come on, Ms. Stark," Declan said, anxious to see the words. "Write it already."

"Now now," she warned, facing the class briefly. The younger children in the front rows stirred cheerfully while the older kids groaned impatiently. Arm raised, Ms. Stark drew the first line, a chalky shrill making the class yell while she jokingly shook. "Okay, seriously this time."

"Emily! It starts with, *End of,*" Sammi shouted with a touch of sisterly snark. "I mean, Ms. Stark."

"I know what it is, Sammi." Ms. Stark returned and touched the chalk to the board, the powdery tip rising and falling in tall, loopy letters. A lull fell over the class while she finished the words, spelling: *End of Gray Skies.* While the announcement had already been made to the entire commune, this was a celebration for the classroom. For Declan, it was an excuse to get excited and do less classwork. Under the words, she waved her hand again, producing a thin swirl to emphasize what day it was. When she was done, she plopped the chalk onto the sill, the classroom erupting, children whooping and hollering.

Looking from face to face, there were smiles brimming, hands clapping and waving, a few kids covering their ears. Ms. Stark waved them to quiet down, the voices lowering to a gleeful rumble. When the chatter grew again, the fever gaining, she took to her desk and sat, the old chair creaking. She clasped her hands together and rested them, fingers interlaced tight enough to turn her knuckles white. Declan joined in and clapped his hands. *Why not,* he thought. *Anything is better than the classwork.*

A shove, innocent and filled with affection. Sammi was clapping, too, while Ms. Stark shook her head at them, seeking their help. Unlike most days, Ms. Stark's red hair was fixed high in a bun, pinned back, the scars of the past showing on her neck and chest. She didn't try to hide them. Neither did her sister Sammi. Declan brushed his arm where the caustic rains had left their mark, the memories too powerful to forget. There were others in the class who'd never know what it was like the day the clouds fell. And then there were those who would never let it go.

For the children in the first row, it was their first time hearing the announcement. For Declan, it was his third. But, at seventeen, he couldn't remember the first End of Gray Skies announcement. He remembered the second, though, like it was a bad dream. And he recalled what followed. Eyelids clapped shut, he heard the memories of his mother and father crying. He heard his sister too. That moment of failure just about crippled the commune with a harsh disappointment that held no boundaries.

It was a disaster, with stories of other communes and their descents into lowly times, stories of a mass exodus into the fog, depression, and suicide. While the memories dimmed in the years since, the chance to try again never died. By the end of today, there'd be a chance to erase what happened five years earlier.

Maybe... maybe this time, the End of Gray Skies will be the last announcement. Declan blinked and held the wishful thought for a moment. But only for a moment. He was older and knew better now.

"Let's settle down, people," Ms. Stark said, raising her voice and standing, chair dragging. Desks opened, pitted metal screeching while the class settled into the morning routine. Declan did the same, the top sticking, the left-side hinge broken. "We've got a long day. Everyone get some paper out."

Declan fished through his desk, fingers nabbing the remains of a monthly parchment allowance. Ms. Stark still called it paper, but it wasn't. He hadn't seen real paper since the time before now. Brushing his fingers over the wrinkles and the frayed edges of the pulpy fabric, Declan shoved a thumb into the black smudges staining deep in the fibers. He'd have to clean it during the evening's chores. How many cleanings was that?

From the front pocket in his coveralls, Declan found the black nub of his only writing stone. With a sigh, he gazed around the room to see if anyone noticed. He'd been writing again—more than usual—and now there was only enough of it to get through the day.

"Huh?" he asked, a soft touch on his back. It was Sammi, his heart swelling.

Her petite fingers appeared below his elbow. "Here, take some of mine," she whispered, opening her hand, a piece of writing stone in her palm. He caught the sweet scent of apples on her breath, a favorite of hers. *I'll bring her one tomorrow*, he told himself. "Go on now."

"Thanks. I'll be more careful—" he started to say.

"Sure. You won't, but I don't mind," she sassed him. Declan picked up the stone, but before turning back, he held her hand until Sammi closed her fingers around his. His heart swelled a little more.

He still remembered the day she first walked into their classroom. She was lanky and clumsy and awkward like one of the newborn goats from the farming floor. Back then, he supposed they had both been like that. But in the years since, time had turned her into a young woman; and to Declan, she was the most beautiful person in this glum, gray world of theirs. He caught himself staring into her green eyes and heard *Sammi Sunshine* in his head.

It was the name the school kids teased with. Sammi was different to them. She had hair and skin like her sister: white as the chalk on the blackboard. Next to his darker skin, her delicate fingers shined bright. But it wasn't just Sammi's skin that made her stand out. It was her hair too: fire-red, like a flame. It hurt to remember how the kids teased. She was just six that first time, the older children pouncing cruelly, leaving her to stand in front of the class, crying.

Maybe it was the locket of hair. They all wore the same gray coveralls, but Ms. Newl had made Sammi's a little different for her first day: she'd taken some of her sunny red hair and had made a small bow out of it, pinning it to the front. It was color; and color was different. Declan loved that Ms. Newl had done that. Declan's gaze fell to the locket she continued to wear and said, "Thanks for the stone."

"Stop writing so much," she smirked, and shooed him away.

"Okay?" he mumbled humbly, brushing a hand over the parchment. It was the same exercise every day, his charcoal words lifted and lost. They'd mix in a flow of tepid water, carried down the drain into the waste-recycling units. How many words were trapped in the filters? How many stories lost in a mash of recycling pulp, never to be seen or read?

"Attention," Ms. Stark said, demanding silence. There was a time when she'd towered over him and his friends. There was also a time in his life when he'd feared Sammi's sister. That changed during the last year when his mother and sister had gotten sick. It was the flu, and their dwelling was quarantined for fear of a spread. But Ms. Stark visited to help care for them. And when they died, she was the one who held him as he cried, telling him that it was okay and that, in time, the pain would pass. Declan looked down two rows in front of him to the empty desk where his sister, Hadley, had sat. It was still empty and a part of him was relieved about that, even though he knew she'd never be back. The pain never passed. It stayed with him.

"Are we ready?" Ms. Stark asked, desktops closing, arms at attention with stones in hand. She directed her voice toward the youngest in the class, asking them, "What day is today?"

"It's the End of Gray Skies," they answered, voices out of sync, some trailing off.

"And can anyone tell me what that means?" she asked, focus broader.

"Don't pick me," Declan mumbled, shrinking into his seat. To his surprise, Rick Toomey's arm bolted into the air. He was a few years behind them, short kid with lopsided hair and a toothy grin.

When Ms. Stark gave the okay, Rick jumped from his seat

and spun around, speaking directly to the class. "The End of Gray Skies is when the five Oceanic-VAC-Machines will change our Earth back to the way it was." He finished with a stern nod.

"Thank you, Rick. That is correct," Ms. Stark said, motioning for the boy to sit. "Now, who can tell me *why?* Why is this of interest to us?"

Ms. Stark's eyes crawled across the room, searching for someone. Declan shrank back again, but her eyes settled on him with a grin, satisfied with her selection. "How about you, Declan? What can you tell the class about the End of Gray Skies, starting with what happened?"

Silence. Declan hesitated and didn't say a word. He felt a tiny jab in his back, Sammi teasing. When he didn't budge, she nudged him harder. With a groan, he straightened and stood. "End of Gray Skies—"

"Actually, come up here so that everyone can hear you," Ms. Stark said, waving him forward.

"Go on, *Dick-lan,* go on, now," a mocking voice shot from the back row.

"Yeah, *Dick-lan,*" another teased.

"Don't mind them," Sammi comforted. "You'll do fine. You always do."

"Fine," Declan told Ms. Stark and eased into the first step, nerves putting a lump in his throat. When his mouth went dry, he turned back to see Sammi urging him forward. The youngest of the children sat without interest, twiddling their fingers and staring absently ahead. One of them made lip-smacking noises, clapping a hand against her open mouth. The older children were a little more attentive but not by much. The senior students sat in the back rows, including Sammi, a hard stare coming from Harold Belker whose scowl seemed permanent.

Declan cleared his throat which was ripe with an itch, the fog more irritating today. He went on to explain about the VAC-

Machines, the original purpose of them, and then about the disaster. It was the words and his being careful. What happened *was* a nightmare, but to the smaller children in the front rows, they'd only known one world. Today's world.

"Nobody knows exactly what happened that day—"

"Why didn't they just turn the machines off?" a boy in the third row interrupted.

At some point, Ms. Stark had taken Declan's seat in front of Sammi. She was slouched forward with her chin resting on her hands. "That's an excellent question, Stewart. Very good," she complimented. Stewart smiled, his eyes beaming.

Declan glanced to Ms. Stark standing up from his chair, blocking Sammi. A moment later, red hair appeared, Sammi mouthing the words, "They could not..."

Brow lifting, Declan continued, "Because the machines *couldn't* be turned off. Well, they tried, but the machines were designed to keep running, which may be why turning them off didn't work."

"That's right. Thank you," Ms. Stark said, and then added, "Thank you too, Sammi." The class let out a laugh. Declan went on to continue, but a skinny, pale arm sprouted from the fourth row.

Before Ms. Stark could call on her, Tabby Wetton began to speak. "Hi, Declan," Tabby started to say, dimples showing through a bashful grin. Chewing on her lower lip, she asked, "What happened with the poison? Why didn't anyone know there was something wrong with the machines?"

"They *didn't* know until it was too late. Turning the machines off by then wouldn't have made a difference."

"But how bad did it get?" Tabby continued. "I mean, what happened?"

"Well," Declan began, seeking out Ms. Stark, seeing emotion in her glassy eyes. "It changed everything. The fog was toxic. It was heavy with salt that choked life from people and machines and... everything. We used to have cars and buses and trucks, but they died and filled the roads: rusted corpses now. All the traveling stopped. Even travel on foot was impossible for a time.

"Families got separated and buildings fell, the food and medicine got scarce. It was chaos and pandemonium. And it wasn't just the people. The animals suffered. The birds stopped flying, most of them died off. Thousands of species vanished. It was the end of the world. Murder, and torture, the outsiders, and..." Declan was gone. The details of carnage spilling from his mouth.

"Declan!" Ms. Stark yelled.

"Huh?" he jumped, a chuckle rising from the back row.

"Thank you, I think you've shared enough," she spoke in a low tone, nudging her chin where he saw the children wide-eyed, their mouths hanging open. Tabby stared, too, hand cupping her mouth. Declan realized he'd scared them. Unsure of what to say, he went to them and took a knee while forcing a smile.

"Listen, it was an ugly time, but it's also a part of who we are. And you know what? We survived! We found the tall office buildings and made a home in them. And we found animals and birds that had survived too. There's fish in the ocean... we even found seeds, so we can grow our own fruits and vegetables. Sometimes, sad stories do have a happy ending. We're here. Your parents are here. Your families are here. We still have some of the things from the old world. Not a lot, but some."

"Then why do we need an End of Gray Skies?" young Rick Toomey asked. "Why do we have to change anything if everything is fine the way it is now?"

Declan faced Rick Toomey, the question heavy. His gaze lifted to the rest of the class, as he wondered how many felt the same. The world today, as they knew it, was their home. Should they try to change it? "Why don't we let Andie show us?"

At once, the class jumped and began to chant, "Andie! Andie! Andie!"

Ms. Stark smirked at him and went to speak, but the cheering grew louder. She was never a fan of the robot-looking thing which had been a staple in the class for as long as he could remember. Declan knew it to be a glorified movie projector, recovered for parts but adopted for the school. The kids loved the thing.

"Someone is going to have to get on the cycle," she demanded, joining Declan at the front. "Gotta charge its batteries."

"Sorry, couldn't help it," he told her, leaning close.

"You know I can't stand that thing," she answered, eyes leveled with his. "Do we have someone to cycle up? We need a few minutes, at least!" Ms. Stark shouted. The chanting faded, a low rumble continuing, while older students sought out a volunteer to hop on the cycle. When nobody in the class stood up, Ms. Stark addressed them. "No cycle, no Andie!"

"I'll do it," Charlie Tabbot finally answered and reluctantly stood. The classroom applauded and broke out in a cheer. Declan shrank from the deafening noise. Charlie saddled the bike, metal clinking, the old parts scrounged from the ruins. He pumped his knees up and down, angling his skinny legs to clear the handlebars. The motor behind the cycle began to hum, the sound quieting the room, a thin yellow light burning. Charlie saw it and cycled faster, the light growing hotter and brighter, Andie powering up.

"There, you see. That wasn't so bad," Ms. Stark said. "I know *I* wasn't getting on that thing."

Declan readied Andie, sleeving the charging cables behind the chairs, dust clinging to the wires. He rolled it to the front of the classroom amidst oohs and ahs, making a place to project the light. In the back of his mind, he heard Ms. Stark from his earliest days when Andie was still a giant to him. With his finger cradling the switch, he asked, "Who's ready for Andie!?"

The class screamed in unison, "We are!"

TWENTY-FIVE

Memories are a fickle thing. They come and go, and sometimes show things we don't want to see. Sammi glimpsed some of them while Declan spoke to the class. She saw the play area in the mall, and the food court with the merry-go-round and the colorful horses. She saw the other kids with her, the ones playing duck-duck-goose, the rules of the game distant now. Metal clinked sharply and a rubber belt whirred while Charlie Tabbot huffed and puffed. His long legs spun, and the bicycle's charging light glowed brightly. He was one of the kids at the mall with her. There were a few others in the class too. They were family now, like cousins. Hers and Emily's.

There wasn't much she cared to remember from before the mall and the home they lived in once. Except for maybe her mom and dad. But the memory of their faces came more from her sister's phone these days. She couldn't see them in her dreams anymore. Not like she used to. Old feelings rising, she touched the locket pinned to her front, the hair the same color as her mother's. It was one of the better memories. The one with Ms. Newl—Auntie Jane, she called her. Pinching the fraying hairs, it was getting time to change this one.

The carousel. Sammi cringed thinking about how the man died. She could smell that memory, and its bitter taste made her want to spit. It was bad. One of the worst. Especially the screams, the sound of them. *What was his name?* Nolan. He'd melted! That's what the rains did to him. They melted him. There was no forgetting it, or forgetting the woman he was with either, Isla. She disappeared afterward with rumors about how she'd run outside, run into the caustic rain to join her fiancé.

Things were better now, and the mall was just a place where bad things had happened once. It was still there, still a place where some of the kids liked to hang out after school. Sammi looked down a few rows to where Rick Toomey sat, the top of the boy's lopsided hair dancing while he laughed along with the others. Maybe the kid was right. Why end the gray skies? She glanced at Declan, brown hair flopping into his eyes while he wrestled with Andie's cables. *Was it better to leave things the way they were?* To her, what they had now worked. So, why change it?

The saying must be true, she considered, watching Declan joke with the children while horsing Andie to the front of the room. *Sometimes, we do find our soulmate.* Declan swiped his brow, a sheen glinting in the gray light, arms flexing beneath his coveralls. He glanced over at her and caught Sammi staring, her heart shooting into her throat. She didn't turn away, though. There was a gleam in his eyes, his smile validating what she'd been thinking about nearly every waking moment. She'd tell him about it soon. And when she did, it was going to change everything.

Her face warmed at the thought and the word, *soulmate*. The sound of it made her feel giddy too, the idea of it a new one. She'd never heard the word before. Not until reading one of the sappy romance novels Ms. Newl nabbed from the mall's bookstore before all the paperbacks were taken by the other survivors. There were seven in the series, and all of them were deliciously good, like a sugary dessert for her eyes. In her bag, Sammi felt the outline of the sixth book, the others consumed in a single read and returned to Auntie Jane's little library. *Soulmate*, Sammi thought again. That was what Declan was to her.

After reading the first book, she'd asked about the funny shaking in her belly, and the strange way her heart ran fast, thumping a rappa-tat-tat. The old woman laughed silently with a huge smile and told her that the feeling was butterflies in her belly. Sammi had never seen a butterfly; not a real one, anyway. She'd seen them in the photographs and videos, though, and sort of understood what Auntie Jane was saying, but wanted to feel it again. Declan raised his arms to rile up the kids into a grander chant for Andie, Sammi joining in.

"He's so handsome," she mumbled. *Ms. Newl, I'm feeling the butterflies*. She laughed at the silliness, gaze darting around with hope that nobody noticed.

Innocent round faces with childlike eagerness followed Declan while he crossed the room. Their lips were pursed and their brows cocked in anticipation. If Declan didn't hit Andie's switch soon, Sammi thought the first three rows in the classroom would explode. She'd been like that once—they both had. She'd sat in the first row with Declan, squeezing his hand as they waited to see Andie. It had all been terrifically exciting.

Declan tousled a boy's hair, and then another while teasing the button that brought Andie to life. He was good with the children and that meant more to her now than it ever had before. She'd seen him with them plenty of times, but now it was different. Sammi was seeing *him*. She glanced at Emily and tried to see if their mother's ring was in her pocket. The classroom light was dim, but even in the gray light, she thought there was the shadow of an outline. Sammi's time to choose was soon. Everyone knew it too. Who she picked was her choice, but she already knew... she'd always known it was going to be Declan.

Her eighteenth birthday was less than a month away. It was

a big day for a girl—even bigger than the End of Gray Skies announcement. From her perspective, anyway. A girl's eighteenth birthday was the day that she could begin a family. It was the space and the limited rations. There were only so many rooms and food and water, the count of mouths to feed in the commune a constant worry. The executives had rules in place, which included limiting how many children a couple could have. They added the number of years too, thinking it would curtail the volumes. But people will be people and too many had broken those rules, the living space busting at the seams. How many children were there now? Too many. The worry hurt, but Sammi didn't want to waste any time and couldn't risk missing their chance. Maybe one day the rationing would get expanded. Or maybe it'd be abolished entirely.

One could only hope, she thought. An ache tugged on her heart when she looked at Emily and thought of Peter and their son James. If the rules were different, would they have tried for another baby? Sammi frowned when thinking of Peter. She'd seen him recently, his face pale and sweaty and doughy, he'd given her a cursory look when saying hello, but quickly moved on to the executive floor without another word. They'd been family once. What happened to him? To him and Emily? Maybe her sister was mad because Peter could have changed the rules and chose not to?

Sammi's gaze returned to Declan with a question pressing. *Does he know I'm going to choose him?* She chanted Andie's name louder. Loud enough to hear over the class. A cold, hard possibility caught her breath. *What if he wants someone else... someone like Sheila Myers?* Sammi glanced over to Sheila, her voice quieting. Sheila *was* beautiful. She might even be the most beautiful girl in their commune. Teeth clenched, jealousy tapped Sammi's heart with its ugly finger. Sheila played with her hair and pushed a lock of it behind her ear. Had Sammi ever seen Declan notice Sheila? She couldn't think of a single time.

Stupid girl, Sammi thought, feeling silly. She turned back to Declan who was yelling, "Do you *really* want to see Andie?"

The kids roared together, chanting, "Andie! Andie! Andie!"

"Are you *sure?*" Declan taunted. Sammi shouted with them, pumping her fists in the air.

The roar grew louder, her sister covering her ears while the class stomped their feet and banged their desks. Declan swung his arm wide, finger landing on the giant, faded green button. He pressed it and a lull instantly quieted the classroom. Andie sputtered, shook, and whistled a mechanical yawn as it came to life. The children clamored another cheer, seeing life return.

But Sammi heard Andie's age, felt it too, and saw it reflected in Emily's worried face. When was the last time they turned it on? As Andie struggled with powering up, it turned and bumped into the side of a nook. One of the motors was failing, the sensors glitchy. But despite the struggle, the children ate up the dreamy technology from decades past and clapped when Andie sputtered again and inched toward them.

The classroom filled with the clanking plastic and metal thumping, gears spinning with a pitchy whine that joined the children's enthusiastic hollers. Andie circled, and stopped, and then circled once more. Its chassis was mottled with heavy rust; more than Sammi remembered seeing, the salty air aging it fast. But its colorful lights and beeps were just as they'd been that first time. Wonderful.

"Hi, everybod-dy!" Andie sang in a playful tune. The children yipped and yelled, pounding their feet and clapping their hands.

"Almost a full room! I love, love, LOVE a full ROOM!" Andie sang, mechanized words trilling. As it elevated its perfectly round head, a motor ran with a clicking whir. Andie turned left, and then right; two silvery eyes studying the class. "Recalculating. Recalculating. Are there students missing?"

"Very good, Andie," Ms. Stark answered. "It seems we've

lost a few." Sammi couldn't be sure, but thought she heard relief in her sister's voice. It was Harold Belker and his two sidekicks, Norm and Richie. Sammi hadn't seen them leave, but they were gone, and relief came with a heavy breath that made her shudder.

He has the face of a hog, she remembered thinking that first time. Harold had beady eyes and an upturned nose; his face was like those of the hogs on the farming floors. There was a meanness to him too, which seemed to seep from his pores. How many times had he put his hands on her? How many times had Norm and Richie held her down in the corner of the classroom, hidden out of sight from everyone? The thought of his groping fingers made her want to vomit.

"You'll be mine," Harold had told her recently. Sammi shook as if grabbed suddenly by a ghost, his words haunting. "It's your time." He'd lifted his piggy nose and sniffed the air. "You're ready, I can smell it," he'd said, and then snorted a piggy laugh. "When the time comes, you're going to choose me."

Revolted, she'd scoffed at his proposal, if that's what it was supposed to be. He dipped his face, his lips thinning into a sinister smile. And before she could get away, he snatched her arm, jerking her close, the motion jarring and violent. Sammi let out a cry loud enough to stir the class. But the fear Harold held over them had them looking away, his gaze threatening.

"You *will* be mine," he said, the sneer savage and unflinching. Before letting go, he'd laughed evilly and warned, "And if you choose Declan," (only it came out sounding like *Dick-lan*) "I'll hurt him. I'll hurt him bad. And I might just want to hurt you too."

Sammi rubbed her arm where Harold had grabbed her, the bruises turning yellow and a putrid green. The skin was tender, the welts raised. "Ugly boy," she mumbled, afraid of his threat and his bullying ways. And she *was* afraid for Declan too.

Declan stepped forward. "Andie, would you please show us what the world used to look like?"

"Do you mean Earth? Our Earth? Or do you mean another Earth?" Andie hooted and beeped as its head bounced up and down. The younger kids ate it up, one of them falling over in hysterics.

"Yes, our Earth," Declan answered, playfully nudging Andie. A metallic thwack echoed through the room, and all eyes peered forward when the crown of Andie's head opened to reveal a dark, glassy orb.

"It's Andie's brains!" a child screeched. Sammi let out a breathy laugh. She knew what it was but didn't tell.

The glassy orb rose above Andie's head toward the ceiling. Then there was silence, except for the low hum of Andie's inner workings. Almost unnoticeable at first, a tiny flicker of light appeared inside the orb, making a few of the children flinch, its intensity increasing.

The low hum grew and crossed the room while Andie groaned, the brightness gaining. Andie let out a mechanical cough, louder than before, the orb's light flashing yellow and white, a faint image appearing above Andie's head. The photograph was marred with black crevices and covered with scratches and holes. Declan leaned over and blew on the glass, a storm of dust circling before falling away from the projected light.

"Oh my, that feels so g-good. Again, again, again!" Andie sang, begging for more. The younger kids laughed. Declan blew once more, clearing the dust. "Thank you, dear Declan. Now, let me try that again. Here we go!" Andie said, and began to cough and groan, its voice in a near shout. The flickering light intensified, the classroom holding its breath, brighter and brighter, until a glorious colorful eruption flooded the room.

Mouths fell open, eyes opened wide. Even the older teens

hushed, except for the sounds of reverence and wonder. It was the same show that Sammi remembered from years before, the one with the butterfly. She searched for it in the mural of animated light, finding the winged miracle almost within reach of her hand.

Faint specks of dust shimmered in and out of the light's path, the photograph covering the entire room. Sammi focused her eyes past the light, and to Declan. He stood next to Andie with a look of amazement on his face. Even Emily stared, sadness and wonder mixing in her glassy eyes. Sammi held onto her desk as the view showed an enormous valley in front of her; her perspective coming from high in the clouds like she was a bird in flight.

The sides of the classroom were lined with rocky slopes and hills, the space in front filled with deep green fields and lush trees. Birds of every feathered shape, color, and size flew across the valley, landing on bowing limbs and leafy branches. A tapered creek wound through curvy hills and into the valley, and Sammi thought that she could almost hear rushing water, morning light twinkling from the surface of the creek in a feverish dance.

What Sammi saw next brought a heartache so powerful, it reminded her that some things are best left unseen lest we feel the pain of their loss. It was the sun. Just a hint of it at first; but then, as it slowly emerged from behind a cloud, the brightness filled the room, shimmering in the eyes of her classmates' enthralled faces. The sliver of orange and white fire grew to a half moon, and then was whole. She didn't know why, and she couldn't explain it, but immediately she wanted to cry. It was the most amazing thing she'd ever seen.

The next set of photographs were just as powerful. The classroom saw a city. It wasn't like their city, though. While the remains of their buildings were caked in heavy resin, protecting the concrete and the supporting iron from the salty fog, this city had towering glass sculptures that touched the sky. Highways wove in and out of it like the spun sheep-yarn in Auntie Jane's knitting basket.

Another photograph showed groups of people and families gathering in a vast park. Large blankets were laid with care on the groomed lawns and covered with baskets of food. There were mothers and fathers and children running freely. There was no hesitation when they moved; nobody was afraid to walk or run. There were no worries of stumbling over something, no fear of falling, or of crashing into obstacles hidden in the fog.

The green field's expanse was greater than any distance Sammi had ever dreamed of. She thought of how they measured distance today: by the number of hands before your fingers disappeared in the fog. What was a good day? A dozen hands? Two dozen? *That park was at least a million hands*, she thought wildly and was suddenly saddened by their circumstances. Sammi cast her eyes down at her desk, having seen enough. When she heard crying, she knew that she wasn't alone.

"Thank you, Andie. I think that's enough," Ms. Stark said, her tone anxious. In a blink, the world was gone, and they were back in their classroom.

"Tabby? What's wrong?" Declan asked, but the girl held her palms to her face, a quiet sob slipping.

Tabby shook her head and lowered her hands, cheeks tear-stained and eyes swollen. "It's so big," she said in a shaky voice.

"What is?"

"That world!" she cried. "It's too big! If the VAC-Machines work today, then how could we ever live in a world that big?"

"We've lived in it before," Declan said, trying to console and assure her. Tabby, like most, couldn't remember the time before. They only knew what life was like now.

"I don't want to change," Tabby countered, arms crossing. A second voice said the same. And then a third. Tabby spoke above them, adding, "It's too scary."

"I'm scared too," Sammi said, jumping up, relating to the fears. Heads turned. "Tabby, you're right to be afraid. We don't know what the world is going to be like when the fog is lifted. We don't know if it can ever be like the world Andie showed us. We just don't know." She felt the hard stares and sensed most of the class was feeling the uncertainty too.

"But, Tabby, think about what we *could* find, and what we'll be able to do! Think about being able to run, to actually run as fast as you want! Or to look up into the sky! *Our* sky! Who knows, but maybe the birds will come back? Maybe some butterflies? Maybe we can grow our food outside. Just maybe we can do better than we're doing now." More of the class was nodding, their eyes sharing the enthusiasm.

"And we're going to see the sun!" Declan cheered with a clap. The classroom joined in, as did Ms. Stark. More importantly, Tabby started clapping too.

"Okay, class," Ms. Stark yelled over the cheers, voice straining. "We're calling it an early day so that we can all prepare for this afternoon. We're about seven hours from the End of Gray Skies. That leaves plenty of time for you to go to your dwellings and do your check-ins with your floor advisors. They won't mind that it's still early—not today, anyway. But, keep in mind, in seven hours, you'll want to be with your families and friends, and..." Ms. Stark stopped mid-sentence. The interruption pulled Sammi's attention to find her sister's eyes. Sammi gave her a smile to say that she'd be there when the time came. "In seven hours, you'll want to be with your families and your friends to see the sun come out."

"Are you ready?" Declan asked her, returning to his desk and grabbing his bag. The butterflies yawned and stretched inside her belly, pushing out a broad smile that she couldn't hide, no matter how hard she tried. When she didn't say anything, Declan asked, "What's up?"

"I've got a secret," she said, a tickle rising that made it

impossible to hold. She pinched a smile, admitting, "But I can't say."

"A secret?" Declan sounded intrigued.

"I'll tell you what it is... but not until later."

"Promise?"

"I promise!"

TWENTY-SIX

Abandoning the safety of their classroom, a surprise waited for them outside. Declan wiggled his fingers in the midday fog which was much finer than what they were used to. He glanced at Sammi and saw the same pleasant surprise too. *Less itch and no burn*, he thought, dragging a hand through a hovering patch. The fog wasn't just clearer; it was less caustic.

"It's thinner today," he said, shoes grating on the path, the old sidewalk crumbly. "What do you think? At least three dozen hands. Right?" Being able to see that far spurred a playful temptation to run. Not far. But far enough to feel the speed, the air in his face and hair, something they both hadn't been able to do in a long time. Declan grinned until Sammi joined him. He held out his hand and lifted his foot.

"A run!" Sammi said with a shrill.

"Go!" he shouted, knotting their fingers together, arms out wide, coverall shoes clapping the broken pavement. They ran ahead of the other kids before spinning round and round, bouncing from foot to foot. When they slowed, he glanced over at the other children. They'd joined in the fun too, childlike laughter erupting as they twirled and ran in a game of fast-tag. "I gotta catch my breath."

"Old man," Sammi joked, hair pasted to her face. She was breathing hard too. The neighboring laughter ended abruptly with a dense thud and bodies falling, the fast-tag game ending with a cry. Declan covered his mouth, trying to swallow the laugh rising in his throat.

Sammi slapped his arm and hollered to the children, "No cracked heads?"

"We're fine," a warbled voice returned.

"Okay, then. The fog is gaining, it's best to play fast-tag indoors. Understand?" Her voice was stern as she pinched the laughter. Declan did his best to tease, tugging on her shirt. "Don't make fun of me," she snapped and playfully slapped him and then wrapped her hands around his arm.

"I understand?" he mocked. He turned serious then, thick fog rolling around them, the white mist stealing their visibility.

She put on a glum face. "I guess our run is over."

"Yeah," he said, rubbing his fingers together, moisture between them. "I guess it is."

"Watch it!" a woman shouted from somewhere close.

Declan braced, shoes clapping softly, the child appearing out of the fog, running headlong into Declan's knee.

He struck with a thud, the child's head like stone, a painful shot rifling into Declan's leg. "Whoa, kid!" he yelled, trying to catch the boy who reeled back with a dazed look on his pudgy face. "You okay?"

The boy looked at them, gawking with a starry surprise. He rubbed the top of his head, saying, "That hurted."

"I am so sorry," the mother panted, the fog sliding around her. She had the same round face as her boy, hair flat with droplets forming from the thickening fog. She opened her mouth to say more, another child blindly racing ahead of her. She frowned with weary frustration and took hold of a tether strap, jerking it with a hard swing. The weave of braided goat's wool creaked against the strain, the other child stopping dead, his bottom thumping onto the pavement. "It's tough to slow 'em down at this age."

"It is," Declan agreed, rubbing his knee, remembering his little sister who'd done the same whenever she had the chance. Kids run. That's what they do. But in their world, running into the fog was apt to get you lost. He bent over, shoving his hands beneath the boy's arms, a lump forming on the child's head. "Here you go."

"Thank you," the mother said, taking the child under her free arm, holding him like a package. She dragged the other child out of the fog until he was safely next to her. A giggle coming from Sammi. The mother nodded once more and then briskly disappeared into the fog, silence and blindness finding them again.

"How's your leg?" Sammi asked, the humor still in her voice.

"It'll mend," Declan said, forcing a smile, a limp forming in his step. "Better hold off on the racing for a bit, though."

"Yeah, better," Sammi said, patting her arms, the humor gone. Colorless and morbid, the heavier fog was ripe with a pungent odor that scratched his throat.

"You okay?" he asked, his lungs heavier with congestion. The salt stole the purity of everything good, including the fun. "We can go in?"

"It'll pass," Sammi answered, rubbing less. But he could feel the irritation too, and if he was feeling it, she certainly was. "We'll adjust in a minute."

Survival is about adjustment, Declan thought. That's what Sammi's sister told them over and over for as long as he could remember. *Survival is about adjustment.*

They were close to the ocean, their commune edging the coast. It was on days like these they could hear waves crashing onto the black sands and the whooping and hollering of the fishing parties after they'd landed a good catch. The smell and sounds reminded him of his mother, the memory stopping him a moment. *If not for the fish surviving the disaster, we might not have anything to eat at all.* She'd tell him that whenever he complained about dinner. He'd do anything to hear her say it again, to taste some of the dishes she cooked.

A low hum hung in the fog, and it pulled his mind from the memory. It was tinny and small like a salt-gnat buzzing about. He cupped his ear, asking, "Can you hear it?"

"Hear it?" Sammi cocked her head, focus narrowing with a wishful grin. When the sound reached her, a smile appeared. It was brief, concern replacing it, a look of fear in her green eyes. It wasn't fear of the machine, her family was the closest to it in all the commune. Declan considered what the machine was to her. And to her father and sister, Emily, Ms. Stark. He squeezed her fingers, wondering if she'd want to turn around and go back. She pressed forward, tugging. The sound was mechanical, but to them, it might as well have been alien. "You usually can't hear it at this distance."

"The ocean is calm, the sound carrying," Declan commented. Their world was a mostly silent one, machines of every shape, size, and purpose consumed soon after the clouds fell, the disaster leaving behind rusted skeletons, withering reminders of a time forgotten. *Extinct*, he thought. *Like the dinosaurs. But not the VAC-Machines. They were protected; they always had been. Why?*

"Emily still goes to the VAC-Machine," she said. From her tone, the subject was a sore one. She leveled her eyes with his, head dipping as she shared, "Every year. On the anniversary of the gray rainbows."

"Does she think your dad is still there?" he asked cautiously, uncertain how much she'd open up to him. He'd heard the stories of the gray rainbows and the way the machine shut down briefly. But then it turned back on and slammed the clouds against the beach, swallowing everything in sight. "Like, he is still inside the machine?"

"She still does," Sammi said, lips pinched.

"I don't know if your dad is there or not, but the machine is definitely running." Declan knelt and touched the ground, fingers splayed, small vibrations coursing into his hands and arms.

"Whoa, you can feel it. This is crazy," she said, following his motions. With concern in her voice, she added, "Usually can't feel it. Not like this."

"It's like the battery-powered motors," he answered. "They shake too."

"Yeah, but nothing this strong." She shook her head, standing. "I think I feel it in my feet too." Sammi offered her hand, he pulled himself up, closing the space between them. "I wonder if there's something wrong with the machine?"

He regarded the question, recalling how his mother had been one of the executives in the commune. She knew everything there was to know when it came to the machines. But it wasn't information she shared often, if at all. Not even with his father. Declan waved away a foggy streamer floating between them, his mother's voice in his head. One of the last memories of her was an argument, her father yelling while she pleaded for him to be quiet. He wasn't, though, neither of them was.

"It's all such a big secret," his dad argued.

"There are some things I just can't discuss!" she yelled back.

"My mom said something that she wasn't supposed to." Declan glanced over his shoulder as though checking if anyone was near. They were alone. As alone as he could tell in this fog.

"What was it?" Sammi asked, squeezing his fingers. There was fright then. "Is it bad?"

"Not bad, I don't think. It has something to do with the way the machines are mining," he finally told her. "They're digging deep, deeper than any other machine has ever gone."

"I thought that was to help put an end to it?" she said, asking. "That's what Peter said."

"It is, every five years, they've mined enough to try to reverse what happened. That's what Peter and the other executives tell us."

"But?"

He shook his head. "But my mom thought there was something wrong. Like there was more going on than what we were being told."

"More going on?" she asked. Sammi raised her chin, more questions forming. "What if it's nothing and they try again? Only, this time it works?" He heard hope, a wishful one.

"It didn't work the last time." He shrugged. Sammi's brow furrowed, the hope gone. "I remember it."

"I remember too." She gazed up at the sky, the sun hidden. "Who knows, maybe it's the sun. Like there's something wrong with it." Her voice was shaky.

"I dunno, not really—" Another shrug, a gentle squeeze, reassuring her. "—I wish my mom were here. She would've known."

"Sorry," Sammi told him and rested her head against his chest. "If it doesn't work, then this isn't so bad, is it? I mean, it's all we've *ever* known."

"Don't you want to see the sun?" he asked, lifting her chin. "I mean, just feel it?"

"Yeah," she answered, straightening. "Of course I do."

"Sammi, I want to see and feel it. I want to have to squint from the brightness of it. I want to breathe it in like the plants on the farming floors do when the fluoro-phosphor lamps shine on them."

Without warning, she pressed against him, rising onto her toes until he felt the wet touch of her lips. The enthusiasm for sunlight waned, replaced by a carnal excitement of what was to be. The surprise kiss took his breath, lasting a moment. She met his eyes, saying, "I like hearing you talk about the sunshine."

"Sammi Sunshine," Declan blurted, a wide grin brimming. Her smile turned upside down with a frown, the humor fading. When he shook his head to apologize, she slapped his chest and mocked his reaction. "Huh?"

"Sammi Sunshine it is!" she exclaimed, smile returning. "I'll eat the sunlight, if that's what it's going to take." She raised her face defiantly and let out a laugh.

"I didn't mean anything by it," Declan said, relieved. "Caught in the moment."

"It was a good moment," she said, her words touching his cheek with a warm breath. "I do like hearing you talk about it, though. I just hope it happens."

"Me too," he said with wishful caution. Declan thought to change the subject, and asked, "Don't you have a secret to tell me?"

Her eyes blazed with a smile brimming. But before Sammi could answer, there was a fast shuffling in the fog. Instinctively, Declan stepped around her, guarding. This wasn't a mother and her children, shoes dragged across the pavement and kicked pebbles, two or three pairs of footsteps circling them.

"Declan?" Sammi whispered, the hairs on the back of his neck rising.

"Shh," he returned, looking deep and long at her until the danger registered. He pressed a finger to his lips, emphasizing it. This was a hunt. He forgot about the question, forgot about the secret, and even about the kiss they'd shared. Declan gripped Sammi's hand, turning them toward the school. The entire building had already disappeared behind the fog. It was there, they just had to get to it safely.

"Let's go," Sammi mouthed, holding his arm close to her.

Visibility had dropped to three hands, maybe four. A hollow ache filled his gut with a toxic stew of unease and urgency.

"Stay close," he told her, stepping forward, the fog circling their legs and arms. They should have gone inside sooner. They should have done so with the first signs of the increasing fog. And it wasn't just about getting lost. It was the Outsiders and the danger of being taken. *Cannibal gangs*, his mother had told him once. Out of the lack of food there'd grown a practice that was a nightmare. Declan shuddered at the thought.

"I don't hear them?" Sammi said, asking, her voice edging panic. The Outsiders wanted the children more than anything else. Declan's mother had told him about the young that had been taken, leaving hysterical mothers to pull back frayed tether straps. Some of the older kids said that it was the cannibal gangs in need of fresh meat. Others said that the Outsiders needed children because they could no longer have any of their own. The fog settled, separating them.

"Tighter," he told her, Sammi squeezing his arm—footsteps moving closer. She came into view, gray mist lacing in and out of her red curls. Declan looked into her upturned face which was filled with fear. They stayed still, holding one another, hidden in the pocket of fog, using silence as a tool. The footsteps shuffled around them again. Declan flushed, heat on his neck, his legs trembling. Sammi trembled too. She motioned to the ground, their feet in view, the fog stopping at their knees.

His heart lifted when he saw what Sammi was pointing at. They were standing on the morse lines: a collection of painted white markings. There was enough visibility to follow the lines, the codes giving them directions to just about anywhere they wanted to go. *Breadcrumbs*; the thought spurred another memory of his mother. She'd called them that when he was old enough to understand. The name came from a fairytale which she'd eagerly recited for him later that night before his bedtime. Declan pointed, lips moving silently, "That way."

A nod, Sammi repeating, "That way." They slowly followed a solid line, which connected to a dash-dot-dot-shaped line that he knew took them to one of the markets. They came across an intersection, the morse line to their building, an ancient concrete box layered with resin. Sammi tugged his arm, pulling his attention back. His heart thumping wildly as hurried footsteps surrounded them. His breathing stopped. Sammi stopped too.

Declan looked at Sammi and said, "They know we're here."

TWENTY-SEVEN

Declan's hand was clammy in hers, knees weak and her chin and lips trembling. Sammi clutched hard enough to hear him groan and braced for what was out there. Was it two or three? Maybe four pairs of shoes scraping along the path, pebbles skittering. A snicker slipped through the fog. And another. They sounded like a jackal's laugh, a recording from one of Andie's lessons that Sammi never forgot.

The footsteps surrounded them and Sammi blinked past the tears to the morse line on the ground. Her heart skipped seeing they were close to home, their building ten minutes away. She swept the back of her hand across her eyes, a chill chasing the tears, and urged Declan to follow. When his eyes leveled with hers, she pointed at the morse lines. With them, they could run in the fog. As long as they could see the lines, they could run. He nodded, understanding, but shook his head uncertainly. Sammi didn't wait and pulled him into their first steps.

Foggy patches drifted quietly past her head and shoulders, the balls of her feet seeming to hit every stone and clump of asphalt. She pushed them faster, moving swiftly, the morse lines remaining in sight. With every heartbeat, Sammi heard blood running in her ears, the weight of terror striking in her chest.

Distantly, she was aware they were following, their footsteps hurried, their excited hunter chants rising. They never showed themselves, though, staying just far enough out of sight. That changed with the thinning fog and Sammi glimpsed someone running, legs blurred beyond the fog. They weren't hiding anymore. Worse yet, they were stomping the ground as if mocking her and Declan. Her heart sank like a stone. The Outsiders were making themselves known.

Sammi stopped and dropped, wrenching Declan's arm, the force driving him to his knees. He bit his lip, trying to hold his tongue, wanting to shout. She pressed her finger to his lips, thinking to buy them time in the patch of fog. She'd lost the morse lines but thought they were close. The fog hovered knee-high in this space and Sammi pointed to it.

Her long hair draped down the sides of her face as she ducked to see the secrets waiting below. Hands pressing against the stony path, Sammi leaned into the ground which was wet and gritty. She pinched Declan's leg when she saw it, a smile replacing the fright. The other shoes were from their commune —not from Outsiders. They were safe. For now, anyway.

She glanced up to see relief come to Declan, a little color returning. It was slow at first but gaining. Annoyed with running, with hiding, Sammi got to her feet and took a giant step closer to whoever it was chasing them.

"You can come out now," Sammi declared, irritation building like heat.

"How convenient!" a scoffing but familiar voice said. "Look at the two of you together like this."

"Harold," Sammi muttered, unease returning. *Do we run?* The fog was on the move, a light patch drifting. Sickening dread filled her when the outline of Harold's big head showed briefly like a shadow. "What do you want?"

Harold and his two sidekicks, Norm and Richie, stepped clear of the fog, wispy tails gliding over them. Sammi made fists, her heart leaping into her throat. Every ounce of her being said they were in trouble. It wasn't just her they'd hurt. It was Declan, Harold's beady eyes locked on him. There was danger *here*, vileness, and they needed to be somewhere else.

She sensed Declan didn't feel it, though, his expression remaining unfazed. She'd never told him about the threats Harold made. Declan glanced at her, concern appearing. He saw that she was afraid. In that moment, she tried telling him with her eyes what Harold wanted. But Declan only shook his head, confused. Harold curled his nubby finger and bounced it in a mock wave, the sight making her feel sick. It was as if all the places he'd ever touched, ever violated had become a claim and he was here to collect.

"You missed the End of Gray Skies announcement," Declan said, breaking the silence.

Harold gazed around at the light fog, arms spread, saying, "I doubt we missed much of anything." He moved suddenly, stepping within an arm's length of Sammi. There was a sneer on his face as he raised his nose and sniffed. "Nope, nothing, yet," he finished, snorting a piggy laugh. Richie and Norm joined in, trading glances and laughing along. Declan's brow narrowed, his focus jumping back and forth unsure of the joke.

"We're late to get home," Sammi told them, lying, shoving off her back foot. When she turned, Harold's lips thinned to a dark line, the sneer vanishing. The jackal-laughter was gone too. Air rushed past her when Harold jumped to block her exit, his face in hers close enough to feel his warm breath. She could smell it, the stink turning her stomach. Primal fear played a coy joke then, her legs stuck motionless.

"What are you doing?" Declan yelled, shoving between them, bumping Harold's chest.

Harold lifted his hands, palms up, saying, "I didn't want you two to leave yet... not until you saw my catch, is all."

"Your catch?" Declan asked, voice calming. Before Declan continued, Harold motioned to Richie and Norm.

The boys weren't alone, and what Sammi saw next made her knees turn weak and her heart sink. She reached for Declan's hand, clutching at the air before finally closing her fingers on his. As if on cue, Norm and Richie pulled three feral cats from over their shoulders, dropping them on the ground, lifeless. The boys had missed Emily's class in favor of trapping wild cats.

She covered her mouth and gasped when seeing the milky-white fur on the paws of the cat nearest them. He was different like she was, a cat she'd befriended and fed from time to time. A tear stabbed and she was quick to swipe it away before Harold noticed. There were no rules about what the boys had done. In some circles it was encouraged. Still, she could remember when the cats were considered house-pets and not food to hunt and catch. Declan may have felt the same, but didn't invite an argument with the boys, saying, "Nice catch."

"Those aren't the only ones." Harold snickered. His chest was nearly touching Declan's, the air suddenly seeming to suffocate with danger. The hairs on the back of her neck stood, Harold shoving Declan, announcing with a hiss, "Sammi is my catch too!"

Harold snapped his fingers, Richie and Norm moving swiftly, each taking a side next to Declan. Sammi grabbed for Declan's hand, striking air before finally closing around his fingers. Not that it mattered, the boys took Declan by the arms, holding him as Harold crashed down with a fist, striking with a grisly thud. Declan's head rocked backward, Harold gut-punching next. Declan's legs crumpled beneath him, Sammi's throat turning raw with a scream, pleading for Harold to stop. Tears blurred and twisted the view, the struggle filling her ears.

She fell to Declan's side and tried protecting him but missed, the boys dragging him out of reach. Harold's arm was in the air again, the sweat of an anxious hunter dripping from his brow.

"Stop it!" she screamed, her voice blood-curdling.

"Fine," Harold answered suddenly and lowered his arms. The boys did the same, letting go, their hands in the air like a stick-up she'd seen in old pictures. Declan toppled onto his side, clutching his middle, mouth in a gasping pucker like a fish out of water.

Harold's snorting piggy laugh was all she heard. It came with the sniggering exchange of satisfaction between the boys, Sammi's temper jumping with a heat that flashed like fire. She leaped to her feet and clawed at the smallest of the three boys first, digging craters in his face and neck. Norm reeled back, arms pinwheeling, the look of fright and surprise a glorious one.

Richie never saw her coming. Shock replaced the mocking smile on his puny gaunt face. Anger spewed in a torrent, her throws violent, his thin frame stumbling in retreat while he tried to cover against the blows. She had a clump of Richie's hair and squeezed it like a prize. She gripped tightly, leverage gained, and threw punches in a wide swing.

Bone crunched against her knuckles, Richie's nose bloodying in a gush, his shouts and cries childlike. The boy jabbed feebly, arms swinging aimlessly to defend himself. He missed, but a massive blow struck from behind, stealing the air in her lungs. She'd lost sight of Norm and paid for it. Sammi's shoulders and back cramped, sharp lights danced in her eyes with starry surprise.

Sammi dropped to her knees wheezing badly, the wind knocked out of her. Her ears filled with the sounds of heated arguing, the view tipping in a spin. A flurry of arms and legs, the boys were on Declan again, but he was ready this time, fighting them off while guarding Sammi.

"Wait!" she coughed out, and then leaped in front of

Harold, a jealous rage in his eyes. Her eyes darted to his fist hanging above her. *He's going to swing, anyway*, she thought. But Harold paused briefly, his hard gaze seeming to soften. It was a chance they had to take, and she swung her leg in a clumsy motion, connecting her shin with his groin.

"Oof!" Harold cried, dropping to his knees. Exhausted, Sammi planted her legs and readied herself for the other boys. Richie and Norm took a step back. Their faces filled with shock and uncertainty. Declan heaved and staggered toward her, Sammi taking hold of his hand and steering them blindly into the fog.

"He's not done," she managed to say, shock and fear crippling her words. Sammi kept her head down, pain rifling across her neck and back, eyes fixed on the pavement, searching for the morse lines. Declan's hand fell from hers as he stumbled to the ground. Seizing his coveralls, cloth ripping, she yelled, "Get up!"

"Trying," he spat, gray mist filling the space around them. Muscles strained against Declan's weight and almost caused her to stumble too, but she kept hold, fingertips burning, his shoes clopping awkwardly behind her. The fog was thicker now and in it, they could find a place to hide.

They ran deeper into the fog, Sammi's heart racing, sipping on a toxic blend of fear and adrenaline. It was enough to carry her another minute until she had to stop. She bent over, her insides threatening to gush. Declan dropped and rolled onto his back, heaving, spittle and blood on his mouth and chin. Sammi took his face in her hands, lightly touching his swollen eye. She peppered the injuries with soft kisses thinking it'd magically wipe the hurt away but knew better. He smiled, though, so maybe her idea wasn't that far-fetched.

"Oh, Declan," she said. "I'm sorry for what they did."

"I'll be fine," he answered, wiping his nose. He looked at his fingers which were coated in blood. "I don't know what got into them." His eyes leveled with hers, a deep concern filling them. "Are you hurt?"

"Uh-uh." She shook her head, breathing heavy and fast, and even grinned a little, the fright edging excitement. Sammi crawled back over the pavement, finding the morse lines and studying the location to figure out where they were. Fingertips tracing the outline of white paint, the touch smoothed by the thousands of footsteps that had walked it. Elated, she sat back on her feet. "Declan, I know where we are."

"The fog's getting thick," he commented. Sammi didn't reply but went to him, bashfulness gone, her hands gripping and helping him up. He grunted but forced a smile, his teeth bloodied, the sight of it alarming. "Are we near our building?"

"Declan, we're at the old theater," she told him with a rush of surprise and relief, the run taking them in the wrong direction.

She saw him put on a guarded look, asking, "The old theater you mentioned with the animals?"

"They won't hurt you," she assured him.

When he didn't move, she faced him, him asking, "Didn't you mention Harold was here a few times too? Sammi, maybe this is where he got those cats."

She had mentioned seeing Harold around here. She nudged her chin in the direction they came from, certain they were safe. "He's back there and we're here. Come on already." Clutching his hands, she urged him on, excited where they'd ended up. This was one of her places. One of her secrets, having found it a year earlier after following the mews of a cat. There was a feral colony and she'd visited the theater dozens of times to bring them bits of food. With resources scarce, it was against the rules to keep a pet and she'd broken a few to help the cats and dogs living in the ruins. Some were still like they'd been in her memories from before, including Socks who began meeting her with each visit. "It's this way."

"Should we go home?"

"In a bit." She found the wall, guiding her by the touch of its brittle mortar and brick. "We're near the entrance."

"Is it safe?" Declan asked.

"This is where Socks lives. The cat I told you about," she answered, pointing to the building. "He lives here."

"Wait," he said, bending his ear behind his palm. Distant jeers and hollers traveled in echoes, Harold and the other boys searching. But their footsteps were far. Too far to be a danger.

"Oh, Declan, your eye is purple!" Declan winced when she dabbed the swelling above his eye.

"Maybe don't do that?" he asked jokingly.

"Sorry," she said, leaning against him, rising to kiss it instead. "Better?"

"Better." He smiled and turned toward the building. "Let's go inside?"

"My thoughts too." A flutter rose in her chest, the kind when sharing something new, Sammi moved along the wall, carefully stepping until they found the opening. It was just a hole that might have once been a door, but the frame had caved in from years of neglect. They crawled through the narrow space. The broken floor beneath her hands and knees was damp and a little stony, pieces of tile scattered like a child's toys. Sammi got to her feet, gawking at the size of the room and what it had been used for. She was too young to remember movie theaters but had seen pictures. "Look at this place."

"Way cool, look up there," Declan said, grunting as he followed her climb over the theater ruins. "Part of the roof caved in."

"Careful. It gets tricky around here. The salt really did a number on this place." She glanced at the decorated ceiling, its center ripped open by neglect, gray light casting faint shadows around them. The fog passed over the theater like ancient clouds, the caustic mist hovering.

"Here, take my hand," Declan offered, his smile sweet, even with the swollen eye and pulp of blood on his lip. She took hold, returning the smile. What Harold and the others had done was because of her, and she stopped to wipe away the grime with the cuff of her sleeve as if cleaning it would erase what happened. "How's that?"

"Ouch," Declan winced, faking the pain while she pulled back with a quick apology. "I'm kidding."

"Jokester, aren't you," she said, continuing. Declan became quiet, his eyes steady. And for a moment, she did nothing but return the gaze, her knees turning weak with a warm flush rising onto her face. She tried to play off the nerves, asking, "What are you staring at?"

"You," Declan answered softly, leaning closer. Before Sammi could say another word, he kissed her. It was as if every muscle went limp, hands dropping with the touch of his lips moving over hers, his fingers bracing the small of her back. She didn't know why, but she loved it when he touched her there. She loved it even more when letting herself fall against him, embracing until she thought he'd pick her up into his arms. Sammi felt the heat on her face where they'd beaten him, the bruises swelling. Declan lifted his head enough to break the kiss and cover one of his eyes. He shook his head, saying, "Sorry."

"No, I'm sorry," she whispered and gently rested her fingers on his. "Want to go back?"

"I'm fine." He pecked her lips, asking, "How about we take a look around and see what's inside?"

"Good idea," she replied, anxious to return and explore a favorite spot. Sammi hurried a nod and turned toward the long narrow stage with a broad screen that reached as high as the ceiling. It had faded to yellow and loomed over the theater seats, a breeze shaking it slightly.

"I think I saw a movie once," Declan said, following the screen while carefully navigating over the debris.

Sammi shook her head, trying to imagine it. "It must have been something," she said and searched out where the projector would have been. In the back of the theater, a balcony lifted high above them, another survivor like the screen, a narrow set of stairs against the far wall. "That's where they showed it from."

"Let's check it out," Declan said, insistence in his voice. He pinched her hand, urging her to follow, passing row after row of antique theater seats that curved around the screen. She imagined what a Friday night date would have been like. Popcorn and drinks. Hand in hand. The seats plush and cushioned. The movie big and bright and larger than anything they'd ever seen. "What are you waiting for?"

"I'm coming," she answered, brushing against the reality of their world today, the fabric rotten, the cloth scraggly and barely clinging to the chairs' frames. Sammi bumped hard metal that edged an open space, large sections of the chairs missing, the remaining posts little more than rusty spikes sticking out of the floor. They were tapered and sharp like spears, Declan maneuvering around them with ease while she took care not to get injured. How many in the commune had died from the smallest of cuts, the infections unbeatable? "Be careful!"

Voice echoing, Declan jerked his head around and chuckled at the strange sound. When it died down, he waved at the theater's old entrance. "I think it's safer in here than out there."

A thump, footsteps stirring. "You hear that?" she asked, crouching at the sudden noise. Surely by now, Harold and the boys were long gone. But there was no predicting the level of meanness Harold directed. How many times had she seen it before? Nervous, she hung onto Declan's hand to lead him toward the screen and the stage. "Let's stay over here."

"But I think we're fine," he tried assuring her, lightly tugging to see more. Sammi planted her feet, stubbornness feeling safer. When she didn't move, he seemed to resign himself to following. "We'll do what you want."

"Good. Now come up here and sit," she offered, jumping onto the old platform, the wood planks moaning. Muscles tensing, Sammi braced for the floor to collapse, wariness flashing across Declan's face. The stage held, Declan joining, stepping cautiously alongside her to stare up, the screen taller than she could have imagined.

"Do you remember going to the movies?" Declan asked, looking on. He had an odd look on his face, sad and happy, jaw slack while watching the screen as if something were playing. "My dad and mom loved them. She used to tell me how we'd go every weekend if there was something new playing. But I don't remember them."

"We've got Andie now? That's something." In her mind, she saw what Andie had showed them, the pictures of girls her age. She saw the newer clothes with the bright colors and styles, no two the same. She considered their coveralls, pinching the drab fabric which had been mended from whatever they could find. She hated them. It was why Ms. Newl showed her how to make a locket from a lock of hair. And it was why the tidy bow was always pinned to her front. "Maybe Andie could stir up some old movies for the class?"

His brow bounced with a nod. "Maybe." She sensed it wasn't just the movie theater and the treats of popcorn and candy. Declan was missing his mother. He smiled at her, agreeing. "That'd help."

"Every little bit helps," she mumbled, recalling Auntie Jane's words and thinking of another of Andie's videos. The one with the girl in the park with the long blond hair. Hadn't Declan seen her too? A pang of insecurity made her wonder. It made her compare. The girl was around her age but looked so different: so feminine and elegant, dreamy even. Sammi especially liked the girl's pink shirt and how it was cut low in the front. She liked the girl's short pants and the braided leather belt that was wrapped around her waist. It was decorative. It was beautiful.

Eyes cast down at the patchwork clothes hanging limp, she combed her fingers through her hair, grimacing on a stubborn knot. Sammi tried to tidy her coveralls, wiping away the dirt and grime, but that didn't help. When she looked up, she caught Declan staring, and thought, *I'll never look like those girls*, and wished that they were in a different time. Self-consciousness robbing the moment, she pinched the lock of her hair again, asking, "What? What are you staring at?"

"You look pretty in this light," Declan told her, his words surprising her as if he'd been reading her mind somehow. "You always look beautiful."

"Sit," she told him, sighing bashfully, embracing his words. When Declan was seated across from her, she took a small candle from her pocket along with her father's flint lighter. The candle wasn't like the ones they made today. It was from before the clouds fell, a gift from Emily, the original packaging with names that had been long forgotten.

"Where did you get that?" Declan asked, jaw dropping. He picked it up carefully and gently ran his fingers over the glass holder and teased the tip of the wick. "I thought they were all gone."

"Emily saved it for my eighteenth birthday. It *is* a big birthday, don't you think?" Sammi asked, voice trembling slightly. The butterflies fluttered awake, tickling her insides. *I'm going to choose him.* She felt the words pressing against her lips, pushing to come out. When he didn't say anything, Sammi told him, "Declan, I'm going to be eighteen."

"I know," he returned and set the candle down. "I've been watching the days too." She thought his voice sounded more confident than hers, but she didn't mind. "Does this have anything to do with your secret?"

The secret didn't spill. Not past the smile she was trying to hide. Sammi liked that he knew, and asked, "How about a game, first? It's a good game."

"A game." Declan straightened while she worked the flint lighter and brought the flame to the candle. Bright glints of yellow and red bounced in her eyes, the light painting him warmly. She placed the candle behind them, its light forming giant shadows on the screen. Declan laughed and played along, arms raised while he wiggled his fingers. When she joined in, shadow puppets dancing, he exclaimed, "Look! It's like our own private movie."

"Emily showed me how to make shadow animals," she said, knotting her fingers. "That's supposed to be a horse. Like in the pictures."

"Cool," he said, trying to form the same. He frowned, saying, "Shit, mine looks more like a rat than a horse."

"Takes practice." When she cupped her hands and flapped, the shape of a bird flew across the screen. "Like the birds in our building."

"More?" he asked, the shadow bird flying around the screen, avoiding the rips and gashes before perching on his head. He spread his fingers to do the same, but when he couldn't, Sammi took his hands into hers and formed the wings with him. "Like this?"

"That's it," she replied, whispering, belly fluttering. This time she felt something deeper in her swelling heart, heat rising on her neck and face. Biting her lower lip, she leveled her eyes with his and watched the candle's flame sway in them. Without giving it a thought, she moved Declan's hand to her breast, adding, "Like this." Her heart raced when she felt his touch, his lips pressing against hers.

"Wait!" he said, a distant bell ringing, alarm shooting from his eyes. It was their commune bell, ringing for the daily check-in: the one that no commune member was allowed to miss.

"The bell," Sammi said, urgently snuffing the wick to pack the candle. The bell rang twice more, Declan handing her the flint lighter. "We've got ten minutes before check-in and we're nearly ten minutes away."

"I can't have another late check-in," Declan said, worrying.

"We have to hurry!" The worry was catching.

"I know," he answered sharply. The tone hurt and when she stopped, he softly added, "Sammi, I'm sorry... I've been late once this week already."

Sammi held his face, and before she could stop it, she said, "I love you, Declan."

The bell rang, but this time, Declan ignored it. "I love you too." He kissed her then. "The secret... you have to tell me!"

"Later," she answered. *He knows.* She was certain of it, and the tease of not saying more was powerful. The bell struck once more. "Right here, before the End of Gray Skies. And maybe we can light my candle again." With a wry smile, she hoped he picked up on the hint. When he smiled back, she saw that he understood.

"An hour after check-in, meet me here," Declan said.

"That'll give us plenty of time." A light giddiness rose inside, stirring first in her belly and then tickling her heart. In a few hours, her life with Declan was going to change forever. She felt a broad smile and imagined the future. It wasn't just the End of Gray Skies she was thinking about either.

TWENTY-EIGHT

Amidst the bustle and commotion of their building's courtyard, Sammi squeezed Declan's hand and said, "I love you." It was the second time those words reached his ears. The second time they touched his heart. Red hair flowing in the glow of the courtyard's light, her alabaster skin was stunning in this dim gray world. And for the moment, Declan thought he'd twirl her, spinning Sammi into his arms to plant a romantic kiss for all in their commune to see. His heart told him to do it, but there were eyes watching. With the commune bell's ring, Harold and his cronies returned too, thankfully looking as beaten as he felt.

"I love you too," he told her, abruptly letting go of her hand. She flinched at the reaction. Declan pulled in a breath and did his best to warn her of the troubles nearby, the eyes watching them. Sammi glanced once which was enough, her arms instinctively rising in a guarding manner. Remains of her warm touch stayed with him as she started the walk across the courtyard. She turned once, raising a single finger high above her, signaling one hour. Declan nodded as she turned away, her figure melting into the crowd. If not for her brightly colored red hair, he would have lost sight of her in an instant.

A workman's yell grabbed Declan's attention, the men working from the upper floors, dangling from the executive-floor balconies. Tethered for safety, they busily mended the building, protecting it from the outside. For them, there was no End of Gray Skies celebration. Sun or no sun, the work details continued. By this time next year, he'd be wearing a single armband like them, indicating his status. That meant it could be him hanging up there. After all, their building had survived where many had not.

Legs weak, his stomach jumped when trying to imagine himself hanging up there. *Could I even do that?* Declan shook his head, sick with the idea. There was work elsewhere, right? There had to be. Something in the lower floors, the levels beneath the ground like the old service tunnels Sammi's sister told them stories about. *I could manage the comm lines. The communications and power lines.* He wiped his brow, jittery at the overwhelming thought of the future... *their* future. *Sammi's secret.* It wouldn't be long before they'd be starting a family.

"I'll find something, Sammi," he mumbled, stretching onto his toes to glimpse the last of her. She was gone already, too far into the crowd to see her. Dropping down to his heels, he thought of the bureau and the executives, along with the elected positions. He gazed up at the floor where his mother used to work. She'd been an executive there, recording births and deaths. But despite her seniority, there came no privilege. She'd died along with his sister and there was nobody from the executive floor to help. "It'll work out, Sammi."

A group of children ran close by, heads down, chasing in a game of fast-tag. There were fewer babies in the commune. Fewer children. That's what his mother had told him when she'd gotten sick. It was something she wasn't meant to say, but the fever had her saying many things. It wasn't the first time his mother had mentioned it. He'd heard his father arguing one night, his mother trying to explain the problem with the commune's population. With fewer children, the commune wasn't sustainable. What did that mean for him? For him and Sammi?

Declan shook off the worry, tucking its darkness away for another time. While it was a worry, there wasn't anything he could do about it. Still, it was what his mother had said in the moments before her death. It nagged him and kept him up at night. She'd told him that it was all a lie. He'd thought it was the fever speaking for her. But what if it wasn't?

Sammi didn't need to know about any of it. And he decided that what his mother told him would stay with him. As if on cue, the children's footsteps thundered past him. Squealing and playing, they were free of tether straps and of their parents. They ran in circles, some of them barefoot, feet slapping the old, tiled floor. Small hands wrapped around his legs when two of them used him as an obstacle.

The courtyard was filled with traders and market sellers today, the noise bouncing. A man with a round head and thinning hair shoved past him pushing a cart, steam rising from large pots, the smell a little sour. "Your left, boy," the man grunted. Declan stepped to the right to make room, his stomach grumbling for a bite to eat. He had a food voucher in his pocket, but just the one. "Declan?"

"Hi, Mr. Gruber," he replied, the man recognizing him. "Anything fresh today?"

The man smirked, fat beneath his neck jiggling. The question was something his mother would always ask. She'd been the one who loved the market, who loved haggling. Mr. Gruber wagged a finger, answering, "You know it's fresh. Always fresh, not like those yokels around the corner." Declan smiled with him until the eyes came. The ones he hated seeing. He braced for the words, his appetite disappearing. In the man's round face and his deep-set eyes, there was sadness. "And how is young Declan doing? You know since your mom and sister—"

"I'm okay," Declan interrupted, a sick kind of heat stirring in his gut, the sympathy too much. He was lost for words, never knowing what to say even though people meant well. Mr. Gruber cocked his head, disbelief on his face. "Really, I'm fine."

"Ya know, I miss your mom." A smile. "Especially the way she'd battle me on the prices."

"Yeah, she liked to do that." He moved closer as Mr. Gruber stirred the bigger pot. "Any leftover bread from yesterday?"

"Leftover bread? Mine? What do you think?" Mr. Gruber answered arrogantly with an upside-down smile. He reached beneath the cart, a loaf appearing in his hand. It wasn't huge, but it was still too big for the single voucher Declan had to spend. Mr. Gruber turned serious, leaning over the soup to say, "Declan, you don't worry about it. I know where your father's been spending your food vouchers."

His gaze fell to the soup, shame filling him, the ladle going round and round. "You do?"

"Declan, listen to me." Mr. Gruber's tone pulled his gaze. Brow raised, he said, "Your father doesn't mean to. You understand me."

"I do... I guess," Declan lied. Since his mother and sister's death, most of the food vouchers went to the spirits, the ones the market offered from the bulky stills that stank of the fermented liquids they brewed. Mr. Gruber meant well and stuffed the bread into Declan's hand, insisting he take it. "Thank you."

"You pay me back some other time," Mr. Gruber said, winking. "You can clean my pots."

"Oh joy," Declan returned with snark, taking a bite. Sourdough. One of the few they could make. "It's delicious."

"Of course it is," Mr. Gruber said, waving him away. "Now get going, I've got customers."

Declan glimpsed the tables with the stills, their surfaces covered with full bottles, a line forming. His father wasn't there. Not that he could see. And that was a good thing. Another bite, the doughiness making him chew faster. He stopped at a table from the engineering floor, a woman showing off chemical glow sticks which had been recovered from the ruins. A nearby toddler tethered to his father giggled and clutched the air, trying to grab one of the glowing sticks, the engineer juggling a few like a clown.

Another table sold fresh vegetables and fruit from the farming floor. There were red apples, mottled with green, the peel on them fresh. Next to it was goat cheese, small chunks ready to be served, the delicacy something they'd never had before. Declan could smell it and thought how good it would be with the bread. A woman bumped him to get by, waving vouchers for first dibs.

The yard was different today, the buzz from the classroom carrying across the commune. The declaration of the End of Gray Skies was reaching a fevered pitch, and everyone had something to buy or trade before the world changed forever. One of the trading tables had a considerable number of buyers waiting in line. Declan immediately recognized the small bags. They held what his father called rotgut, potato juice that was more toxic than it was potent. It was also a particular favorite of his father's since it was cheap.

"Can I offer you some—" a merchant started to say.

"Not now," Declan said, ignoring the merchant while searching for his father.

"—liz-tails? Good for them young bones," the market seller wheezed. He was an older, stout man, with straggly hair that hung past his ears. He grinned at Declan, baring a few teeth and eagerly jabbing his tongue, anxious for an answer. The merchant pushed a tray, winking at him. "They good for keeping things up after you get chosen. If you catch my meaning," the merchant went on to say, whistling between his words.

"No. But, thank you," he answered, glancing at the tray. The merchant moved on to greet another passerby, just in time for Declan to see Sammi's red hair at the elevators which were gone, replaced with what they called carry-cages.

"More rope!" one of the workers yelled from above as Sammi stepped inside.

Declan recognized the man, muscle corded like sinew as he heaved the pulley system alongside a few others, the gears chewing metal on metal. As a child, the man had introduced him to the hidden world of their building. It was the smallest doorway, a vent cover he'd later come to learn of. And it was just big enough to get behind the walls and move across the building's floors. "I'd barely fit in there today," he chuckled. The light-hearted memory vanished when he considered children with Sammi. What if one of their kids got into the ventilation system? He realized then why his mother was quick to scold whenever she'd found soot and dust on his coveralls.

Most of their life was living in the same building which couldn't hold much in the way of mystery. Every building had secrets, but this one had given them up over the years. When playtime was limited to one place, it was easy to get lost in the floors of their home—except for the executive floors, of course. Those were reserved for the leadership, the ones wearing four bands like his mother had. He suspected there were more than a few secrets behind those doors too. Declan lifted his chin until his gaze neared the top of their building. Protected by barriers, guarded at the entrance. He followed a path from the top balcony to the hard floor of the courtyard below, the height dizzying.

Being a senior executive comes with privileges, his mother told him once. He remembered hearing ambition in her voice. She was a junior executive, but there'd been talks that her status could change. She'd also talked about how it seemed unfair to her. He'd seen the offices once, the floors polished, the walls and metal counters clean of the pitted reminders of the outside. There were private bathrooms with smooth, round sinks, and a seemingly endless supply of water. Executives even had their own farming and food reserves, meals catered when meetings went into the night.

Declan got to the carry-cage on his side of the building, the attendant calling out. The salvaged steel and wood frame was just big enough for a few people, the floor wobbling before the ropes tightened. The attendant turned to ask Declan for a floor number but recognized him and saw the bruises.

"Celebrating already?" he joked. "Hope the other guy got his."

"Matter of speaking," Declan returned, gently touching his eye. He shrugged a quick thank-you while stepping onto his floor, the heavy tone of a man's scream echoing loud enough to lull the market. He glanced over the rail to see upturned faces, including Mr. Gruber's. He followed Mr. Gruber's eyes, heart sinking when seeing that it was his father.

Blood covered his father's nose and mouth and dripped from his chin. Two of the executive guards had his father pinned against the door to their dwelling. *Not again*, Declan thought, heat flushing his face. He recognized one of the guards from the executive floor. That meant his father had been up there again. He'd been warned on multiple occasions not to enter his mother's old office.

"Dad," he yelled, moving swiftly, the carry-cage clamoring behind him. Declan's father clutched something against his chest while two more guards ran the length of the balcony. The guards were dressed in all black. There was no band for their ranks. Declan caught the eyes of a younger guard and waved, "I've got him. Please, you can let him go."

The guards didn't listen and turned back swinging, his father wrestling to hold onto whatever he'd taken. The guards towered over his father; they towered over everyone in the commune. No one ever *chose* to be a guard: they were *chosen* for their size and strength. Dressed in their formal black coveralls, with thick belts hanging from their hips, they carried enforcements that only guards were allowed to have. They were an ominous sight next to his father.

They're going to hit him, he feared, four guards closing around his father. Sandwiched between them, Declan heard his father yelling. Sweat rolled down his back, the run taking his breath. A guard reared back and threw his father against the door, his head bouncing with a dense thud. He dropped like a rock, legs folding while gasping for air.

"Stand back!" a guard warned.

"Why? What are you doing?" Declan yelled, voice rising in a cry. He was vaguely aware of the crowd forming in the market below. If eyes were like darts, then he was feeling every one of them like a pin prick. Declan lowered his voice and put his hands to his sides like his mother had showed him. "Please, sir. I'll take him inside."

"Declan, no!" his father wheezed. Without warning, Declan was suddenly on his toes, his airway cut off, the guard's fingers wrapped around his neck. All motion stopped as the guard squeezed his fingers. "Sir, please. He's my boy."

The guard's eyes darted to his father. "He should know better than to charge an executive guard." Two of the guards chuckled, while the younger guard looked to disagree but said nothing.

"He will!" Declan's father said while staggering back to his feet. He made the sign of a cross, hand moving sloppily, and then held his fingers in a peace sign. "I swear it!"

"Fine," the guard said, tightening the grip once more. Stars jumped into Declan's sight, his dad's face fading. The guard relaxed and let go, the weight on his legs coming without warning. He stumbled backward, the younger guard catching him at the railing. As his breath returned, Declan saw what his father held from the guards: his mother's satchel, the one that had been issued to her when she was promoted to four bands.

She'd carried that satchel to and from work every day. It was a symbol; it was authority like the bands on her sleeve. But Declan thought that for his mother, the satchel had become a burden. Each evening, she placed it carefully in the corner of their dwelling, away from everything, leaving it alone until the next day. At times, he'd caught her standing over it, staring at it, her face empty of emotion, except for maybe disdain, leaving him to wonder if she regretted working as an executive.

When his mother and sister fell ill with the flu, the satchel had remained in the corner, untouched until now. His father clung to the stained sheepskin and leaden buckles, his arms wrapped around it, protecting it. The guards had come looking for it before, more than once. It was the property of the executive floor, and his father shouldn't have chanced taking it out of their dwelling.

"He's just a boy, leave him be!" his father pleaded. "He was running to me, that's all. He wouldn't charge an executive guard! He knows not to do that. We raised him right!"

"You okay?" Declan asked, gasping, staggering forward. He reached his father's side and smelled the potato juice immediately.

"He's just a boy... my boy," his father continued, words shamelessly broken by drunken slurs. "Take the satchel. Take the damn thing!" He tossed the satchel, letting it fall to the floor.

"Pick it up!" the guard who held him demanded, a cruel smile appearing. The younger guard, eager to please, took to a knee.

"Not you," the cruel guard scolded. "One of them. Now, like I said, pick it up!"

"That's not our satchel—" Declan's father began, a hiccup interrupting when he covered his mouth to hide a laugh.

The elder guard's brow furrowed, his lips thinning until they disappeared in a snarl. "That's fine. Be funny. Just know that I can take you both to the detention floor. No need for cause. I can do it because I want to."

"Not our bag. Doesn't exist, far as we're concerned," his father persisted, belching. Declan reeled back from the stink. The guard sucked in a deep breath, air whistling between his bared teeth.

Sensing they'd be detained if he didn't act fast, Declan snatched his mother's satchel, brushing the leather bag clean, and placed it in the hands of the elder guard. The man's square jaw gave up another sneer. "You're smarter than your old man," he said, and then leaned forward to sniff at the air. "More sober too."

"Declan—" his father began.

"He's not always like this," Declan said, ignoring the disappointment.

"You know, I could take him in. But I won't if you get him inside," the guard said, the hard expression breaking. "That means get him inside, now!"

"Uh-huh," Declan grunted, mouth drier than he'd thought was possible. When his father stirred, words perching on his drunken lips, Declan shoved a hand against his father's chest toward the door.

"This is what we came for," the guard said, his attention pivoting to the satchel. He flipped it over to check the dimpled buckles, inspecting it. When they were satisfied, they walked away without saying another word.

"Inside," Declan demanded, the door swinging open and his father staggering inside. The room stank, the floor littered with empty containers. His father picked them up one at a time, draining the last of the juice. "You've been busy again."

"Stow it," his father said, stopping in the middle of the room, looking around as if he was expecting to see someone. Declan saw the memories of what it was like not too long ago. He faced the small hallway and kitchen where he'd see his mother and sister at the center table, or in the nook getting food. It was just him and his father now, the dwelling empty and unrelentingly quiet. Declan's lip quivered when he cleaned up some of the mess and came across a picture of his sister on the table. It was a drawing done in the market by one of the artists, the frame sitting on its side. He righted it and cleared the table, his insides stewing in anger.

A tear stabbed his eye thinking of his sister's birthday coming in the next week. Firsts were the hardest after losing his family: first birthdays without them, first anniversaries without them, and first school days without his sister. How many had come to the farming floor for their cleaning and passing? Half the commune? More? They'd offered sympathies and condolences, but nobody had warned him about how hard that first year would be.

Standing and waiting for a family that wouldn't be there, Declan touched his father's shoulder, seeing he was trembling. His father was feeling the pain of firsts, too, and his sister's birthday wouldn't be celebrated, or even spoken of—but it would be remembered. His father reached to take a drink, then hesitated. Instead, he picked up the framed drawing, clutching it. Declan rubbed his father's back and did the only thing he could think to do. He held him.

"Thank you," his father said weeping while smiling awkwardly. His smile was brief when he saw Declan's eye and the bruises from earlier. "Did they hit you, son?"

"No, I got these on my own." Declan lifted his chin as if to show off and winced when he smiled pridefully. Declan's focus shifted to the scattered bags, the mess. His father shrank a little, pulling away, shamed and embarrassed. It wasn't the first time their place looked like this. Sadly, it wouldn't likely be the last either.

"I know what you're thinking," his father blurted, kicking

some of the containers out of sight. He stopped then, a look of forfeit on his face. "I need it, son. I just do."

Declan bit his tongue, keeping what he wanted to say to himself. He changed the subject, asking, "Why did you go to the executive floor with Mom's satchel? You knew they'd arrest you."

A shrug. "I just wanted to be closer to her," he finally said. Confusion eclipsed the blank look while he searched their dwelling for nothing in particular. "But they knew I'd opened it... I... I don't know how they could've known."

"What?" Declan held his breath, heart skipping. An executive's satchel was never to be touched, let alone opened. "Why would you—" the words wouldn't come. He cleared his throat. "—Dad, they'll kick you out of the commune for that!"

Another shrug, the idea of excommunication registering. Only, the look on his father's face told him it was a fate he'd be willing to take. "Might be that I don't care about the rules anymore."

"But Dad—" Declan began. His father wouldn't be the first, though. While their building was big, the walls had a way of pressing. A way of squeezing until going outside was the only answer. Declan decided his father's lapse was the potato juice. His father wasn't arrested, and the guards got the satchel back. "What was inside? Were you looking for vouchers?"

"Maybe." His father lowered his head, ashamed. "I just needed them—"

"Food, Dad?" Declan cut in, his tone sharp and unforgiving. He picked up one of the empty containers, straining his arm when throwing it. The empty pouch slapped against the wall. "Dad, how are we supposed to eat?"

"Don't you talk to me in that tone!" his father yelled. He slumped forward, his reproach lost. "I'm trying, son. I am." From the front of his coveralls, his father pulled out two vouchers. Stamped with the commune's seal, the resin-laminate parchment was still warm from his father's pocket. "I didn't use all of them. I wouldn't do that. Get yourself something to eat before the End of Gray Skies celebration."

"I think Sammi's going to choose me today," Declan said, sharing the news.

His father's sad expression broke into a smile, lips stretching across his rosy cheeks. Without a word, he pulled his son into his arms, his chest heaving as he whispered, "How I wish your mother and sister were here to see this."

They were quiet for a moment, Declan finding the solemn words to say, "I wish they were here too." When his father broke the embrace, he handed Declan a thin card. It was from the time before the clouds fell, the material perfectly flat and smooth, its corners pointed and sharp. The smell of it was crisp and fine—unlike the pulpy parchment they used and reused. Declan pressed his finger against the crisp edge, skin creasing, the card keeping its form. "It's an old index card. What about it?"

"It's what's on the index card," his father answered. "Your mom said it came from the executive floors, and I think it's what the guards were here for."

"But why?" Declan asked, flipping it over. On the other side, he found rows of printed numbers. These were typed with ink, printed by a machine and not scratched in place by anyone's hand. Declan gently ran his finger over the printed numbers, feeling the small indentations and pleats, five sets, each separated by a thin blue line. Why would his mother have this card?

His father's gaze had drifted as he mumbled, "I think your mother and sister getting the flu was intentional."

"What?" Declan asked, the idea striking in his gut. "What do you mean?"

Focus returning with a leveling stare, his father told him, "I think they were killed because of this."

TWENTY-NINE

The smell inside the old theater was musty and dank. Sammi crinkled her nose, thinking it was the fog which had gotten thicker since earlier in the day. Heart whirring, it was beating wildly with the surprise she had planned. Sammi left the commune early while Declan was still in his dwelling. She wanted the afternoon to be perfect.

With her favorite blankets rolled beneath her arm, she'd stopped at Emily's to borrow some of her perfume. The pretty bottle was from before, from when they were at the mall. She only took a drop, maybe two, the smell rich like flowers. When Emily asked what was going on, Sammi could only smile, the giddiness making her blush. It was going to be perfect, she decided, and hopped up onto her toes, eager to set things up.

Aged wood beneath her fingers, the stage and screen were where to put the blankets and candle. The passing fog above the theater's balcony caught her eye then. Declan had wanted to explore the balcony. Wouldn't it be better there? With the seclusion and being closer to the roof, it'd be magical. And what if the promise of the End of Gray Skies came true? It was going to happen soon, and she imagined being on the balcony, sunlight gleaming on their naked bodies.

Sammi let go of the stage, changing her mind. "It'd be the balcony," she said while stepping over the old seat posts.

A tip of a rusted post crumbled, its sharp point tearing into her coveralls. There was danger in the old metal, and she carefully stepped around it, finding the old theater aisle that moviegoers had used long before. The carpet was worn, threadbare, the path littered with the trash of what she thought might have been the last movie shown before the clouds fell. She avoided what else was there, the bones. Surely not everyone made it to safety. She made it past the rotting lumber and to the back where she gently placed a foot on the old staircase.

"You can do this," she muttered, the narrow pass dark, making her hesitate. Glancing to the seats, the rusted carcasses of what they once were, she wondered how the steps fared. Sucking in a breath, she eased a foot onto the first, shifting her weight with a slight wobble, and almost fell backward. She grabbed the railing that hung from rusty cleats and jumped when a handful of spider legs scurried over her fingers. She let out an edgy laugh and moved on to the next step.

Wood creaking, the middle of the steps had gone soft but held. Nerves rested, half the steps behind her, Sammi searched the dark and waited for her eyes to adjust. They didn't. Dust rose from the rotting carpet, stirring around her head and putting an itch in her nose and eyes. A sneeze shot like gun, the sound louder than she'd wanted. A sound stirred from the balcony, stopping her dead. Something was up there and moving around. For a moment, she thought it might be Declan. She thought that he'd shared in the idea of leaving the commune early. Maybe he'd brought food and was trying to get everything just right. But it didn't matter to her; she'd love anything that he did.

The mew of a cat eked from darkness. There'd been the cats she'd fed here before, the colony welcoming. There was stress in the cat's mewling. The cry coming again, adding urgency to her climb. Sammi hurried the next steps, the wood dropping beneath her. She yelped once, jumping over the final step until she was safely on the landing.

A deep sigh, the balcony everything she'd hoped. It was sheltered and private and sat just beneath the opening in the roof. The balcony was closer to the decorative ceiling, their gray world hovering close with its misty vapor passing mindlessly by.

"Psst," she called, searching the darker shadows. They were feral cats but came out to her calls, food a good incentive. "Psst. Come out now."

Another mewl. There was stress in the cat's voice, concern growing and heating the search. Sammi went to the corners where it was darkest, arms stretched to feel in the shadows. She went to the rear next, following the stir, a weak struggle. Her heart sank when she found it. When she found them. There were tether straps strung to the short wall separating the balcony from the rotted seats below. Noosed on one end and tied off above, four of the straps hung empty of any captures while the last one had caught the tiny paw of a young cat.

"So this is how Harold is getting them," she mumbled, thinking of the cat with the white paws. It wasn't just cats either. She'd seen him return with dogs, even a few of the wildlife that had been thought gone from this world.

Her stomach clenched when the cat's green eyes found her. It hissed, warning with its fur standing on end to make itself look more threatening. "Easy there," she told the cat, steadying herself against the balcony's railing. Her fingers clutched the decorative etchings which were worn and smooth. The railing shifted suddenly with a woody groan, warning that it was going to break.

With gentle steps, she finally reached the frightened cat. It reared back, spitting from a mouth full of teeth, swiping at her with its free claw. Sammi reared onto her heels, a cut opening on the back of her hand. The scratch puffed and turned itchy, the irritation a warning of what the cat could do to her.

"Easy," she began, agitated while assessing the noose and how to free the cat. Frustration grew, beads of sweat trickling on her face and neck. When the cat eased a little, ears rising, Sammi slowly reached for the noosed end of the tether strap. The cat lashed out, but it was weaker this time, the threat empty. "That's better. Let's get this thing off your foot. Okay?"

When the floorboards creaked behind her, relief came. Declan must have heard the commotion and come up to the balcony. Two sets of hands would do the job far more easily than one. Maybe they could use her roll of blankets, wrap the cat while they untied the snare.

"Declan, I found where Harold's been trapping the cats," Sammi said, sitting up. "Help me free the poor thing! I just need a—"

"Look what we've got here."

Sammi stopped breathing, the words ending in a snorting laugh. More snickering came then, and her insides melted with the sudden urge to cry. She stared ahead and looked for a place to hide. But there was nowhere except down, which meant over the balcony railing.

Trembling, Sammi was twelve years old again. She was twelve and had been backed into the furthest corner of their classroom, huddled in the shadows and hidden from Emily. Norm and Richie had their hands gripped so tight she thought they might break her arms off. They were giants back then. So much bigger than she was.

Harold threatened to have the boys do more than break her arms if she made a sound. She believed him. She believed they would do anything Harold told them to do. Harold stood over her like a monster preparing to devour its prey and pressed his hands, pinching and fondling. She tried not to cry, tried not to give him the satisfaction by pushing her mind to someplace else. It was all she could do, and it made what was happening to her disappear.

When it was over, she'd returned to her seat, Emily noticing her untidy coveralls and disheveled hair. The locket of hair was missing too. Later, Declan found it. When Emily asked if anything happened, the ghost of the boys' hands had sealed Sammi's mouth tight. She shook her head and left the classroom.

That was the first time. It wasn't the last time. And in this moment, she could see the look on his face. He wasn't about to let her go. Not this afternoon. She was trapped on the balcony with the cat and Harold, both of them exactly where he wanted.

Sammi rubbed her arms where the boys held her that day. It'd been years, but the ache came to her like a bad dream. Carefully, she looked around to find something to protect herself. The balcony floor was littered with ruins but nothing with size and weight. Gaze darting, desperation turning feverish, she poked in the dim light and realized that she was beginning to sob, just as she had when she was twelve, the fear making her weak.

"That's our catch," Harold snorted.

"Harold, you guys should leave them alone," she said, her voice hollow. Sammi could almost feel the heat of their grins. Hands shaking, fright gripped her heart and made it race with huge, walloping beats. "Maybe you should leave."

"I think this is gonna be fun," she heard Harold tell Richie and Norm. The trapped cat bowed high on its haunches and hissed. A murmur of jibes and heckling rose from them, the laughter triggering a rage from somewhere deep inside. Like the cat, Sammi was cornered in a snare of fear and anger, but, this time, she wasn't going to let him touch her. She had teeth and claws, too, and she was ready to use them.

The gray daylight gleamed from a metal rod and, without thinking twice, Sammi jerked it from the floor. She wrapped her hands around it hard enough to make her fingers hurt. She had to do something before Declan arrived. Alone, in the ruins of the old world, Harold would kill him. Spots of rust flaked from the old post, but the metal held its form and kept the weight.

Sammi jumped to her feet with a scream and swung in a viciously wide arc, the ragged end striking whoever was closest. The sharp end raked over Norm's arm, instantly sliced through the coveralls and turned the fabric red. Norm threw himself backward, clutching his arm, crying out with shock. Her eyelids peeled open wide with victory. The triumph made her fingers tingle. She narrowed her focus then, shedding the last fright-filled tears. She never saw the club swinging from her right, but she felt it connect with the side of her head. The formidable blow struck her with a dizzying thud; pain echoing throughout. She reeled back staggering and saw double images of the boys. Grabbing her head, she pushed forward onto the balls of her feet, trying to regain her balance.

"That's for breaking my nose!" Richie yelled, satisfied. Sammi stumbled again, backing away until she was against the frail banister. The railing leaned away from her, the wood moaning against her weight. She glimpsed the seats below for a moment and considered jumping. *Too high*, she wondered, weighing the alternatives. *It is too high.*

Sammi squeezed her eyelids tight, wincing when the back of Harold's hand swung wide. To her surprise, it flattened Richie's bandaged nose, breaking it for a second time that day. Richie fell to his knees, screaming, blood gushing through the bandages.

"Nobody touches her!" Harold yelled at him. "Ever!"

"Please let me go," she pleaded. Harold offered no reply while she held her breath and gripped the railing with one hand, the metal seat post with the other. Two of the boys were down. They were done. It was her and Harold. She braced, tensing every muscle while waiting for him to take a step. Instead, he raised his hands like he'd done before, and motioned toward the stairs.

"The exit is right there. But answer something for me?" he asked with sincerity. Cautious relief tempted her to lower the rod. Maybe even drop it and run.

"What?" She nodded, hoping he'd accept whatever answer she gave him in trade for her freedom.

But then Harold's expression changed to a bitter jealousy she knew. His eyes shifted to the rolled blankets, and he picked them and brought them to his face. He inhaled deeply before tossing them aside. "You were going to choose Declan today, weren't you?"

"Harold, I would never choose you," she said, words scornful, hurt filling his eyes. But she didn't stop; she didn't care. "I've chosen Declan. I've *always* chosen him!"

"Hold her down!" Harold huffed without hesitation. But the boys didn't move; Richie tended to his broken nose, while Norm held onto his bleeding arm.

"Not today!" she yelled. There was fury in Harold's eyes as he advanced alone. Sammi reared up and swung the metal post with everything she had, lungs emptying in a biting heave. The end of it whizzed past his face, missing. The momentum took her balance and spun her into the railing. She felt the frail wood break against her body, the wood splintering. She dropped the post, reaching out aimlessly, her hands clutching the air. As she fell forward, Sammi was certain that a hand was on her, fingers splayed across her back. But she couldn't tell if it was Harold pushing her or if he was trying to pull her to safety.

When the seats appeared below, she pushed her mind to that distant place she'd found when she was just twelve. It was there that she listened to the sweet sound of her mother's singing. And then later, Emily continuing the song in a night-time lullaby. She found the warm touches of Declan's hands on her skin, and heard his voice breathe loving words into her ear.

The theater came to her a final time and she saw the balcony with Harold watching helplessly. Then, when her legs rolled above her head, she glimpsed the stage where she'd shared a passionate kiss with Declan. Finally, she saw the immense opening in the roof as the floor stopped her with a sickening thud. Pain didn't register at first, but she heard bones breaking inside her while the air rushed out of her lungs in a wheezing gasp. Her eyes filled with a white explosion, sharp starry light that stayed brilliant for a moment before fading.

The faint sound of shoes trudging down the stairs stirred her awake. The taste of blood filled the back of her throat and was bitter like the fog. Sammi thought she could get up, but she couldn't move. She blinked away something warm running into her eye, the sting of it escaping down the side of her face.

Harold came into view, staring, mouth pinched tight, a look of worry she'd never seen on him before. When she tried speaking, blood filled her mouth instead. She coughed it, the suddenness of it splattering on him. He swiped frantically as though on fire, guilt replacing the look on his face. Richie and Norm pawed at his shoulders, speaking, but her ears were filled with an incessant ringing. The theater went dark again.

How long, she wondered, chest heaving, her mouth open. Soft fur rubbed under the fingers of her right hand, a soft purr and mewl coming from one of her cats. It was searching for a treat, and she nudged her head wanting to smile but was drifting somewhere between life and death. She wiggled her fingers to invite the cat's affections while sliding closer to death. Blood filled the back of her throat again, choking and forcing her to turn and vomit. She was vaguely aware of the bleeding around her waist, too, but was afraid to look down.

"Gotta look," she grunted, her mouth wet. A shallow scream, Sammi inched up high enough to see the metal remains of a seat post sticking out of her belly. Clenching her teeth, frightened, and fighting the pain that had found her, she realized she was fastened to the theater floor. She was stuck. Another gush. Sickening and warm. She turned her head to cough it out. Her legs were growing cold, and she shivered as bumps crawled up and down her arms. "Declan, where are you?"

The feral cat moved up to her face and laid its body alongside hers. Did the cat know? Did it know she was cold? Sammi welcomed the heat while she shook uncontrollably. A paw gently grazed her chin, and Sammi stared into a pair of comforting green eyes. She was dying and the cat knew. Regrets flooded her mind as the blood poured from the wound in her side.

The cat flinched and hissed, baring its teeth and laying its ears flat. The rapid patter of shoes ran along the floor, the sound approaching. *Harold?* She wheezed a gravelly breath. But it was Declan's muffled voice. It was his eyes she saw next. And her heart filled with the pain and remorse of knowing that he was going to see her die. He dropped to his knees as she shook her head and told him, "I... I want you to leave."

"Sammi!" he cried with a sadness she'd never wanted to hear in her life.

"Go!" she told him, wanting to scream the demand but couldn't. *This can't be how he remembers me.*

"Never, I can't," he cried while the feral cat stayed with her. It approved of Declan's presence and pressed against her body. The pain in her side began to ease and the blood in her mouth thinned. It was time soon, and she looked longingly into Declan's eyes wishing she could tell him all the things she'd ever wanted.

"It's okay now. It doesn't hurt anymore," she told him and felt the fluttery yawn of butterfly wings as she considered what awaited her in death. She reached for the lock of hair, pulling the pin from the front of her coveralls, and thrust it into Declan's hand. "Declan, I choose you."

Tears streamed down his face as he held her hand, his eyes never leaving hers. He nodded and his voice shook as he said, "I accept you as chosen, Sammi... I always have."

THIRTY

Declan couldn't breathe. He couldn't speak. What was in front of him couldn't be real. Could it? Next to the splintered remains of the balcony railing, Sammi was lying on the ruins of the theater seats, a rusty post jutting out her middle. He shook his head, staving off a cry, the sight a nightmare. He decided that it had to be a bad dream. That he had to wake up.

"Declan." Her voice came to him, urging him to her.

"Sammi?" he returned, dropping to his knees, words slipping by the rawness of what had happened. Her broken figure stretched and pulled in his watery eyes while he fought to understand how this could possibly be. "Wha—"

"It's okay now. It doesn't hurt anymore," Sammi said. With her words, he felt the strike of heartbreak. The tears came, the sobs stealing his strength. "Declan, I'll be okay."

Her fingers were cold, and he desperately tried to warm them, bringing them to his lips. He leveled his eyes with hers, never leaving her alone. Not for a single moment while nodding and telling her, "I'll get help, Sammi... you just have to hold on!"

It was a pain nobody should ever endure, Declan's heart aching, his mind breaking when she offered her lock of hair to him. He knew what it meant and pleaded, "Don't go, Sammi. Not yet."

Emotions choked his words, and he wove his fingers around hers, locking them together. He brushed the blood away from her face, only to see more of it spill like tears from the corner of her eye. Declan's gaze darted from her toes to her chest, to her neck, assessing all that was wrong.

Gulping at the air, he had to stop when the count of it all overwhelmed him. One of her legs was turned outward in a way that wasn't natural. Her left arm was pinned beneath her body, and she seemed unaware that she couldn't move it. But what destroyed his hope that she might survive the fall was the metal shaft that protruded from her belly. Blood, terribly dark, pooling beneath her and spreading. With the noticeable smell biting the salty air, he saw what she'd lost already. It was too much.

He carefully crept around the metal rod, trying to find a way to lift Sammi and free her. The cat's ears went flat, and its eyes bulged like marbles. A furry paw swatted, clawing at his hands with a warning. Sammi moaned faintly and groaned whenever he touched the injury. Each harrowing sound killing him a little inside.

"No—" she demanded and tried waving her hand. After a moment, her arm dropped, her fingers returning to the cat.

"I don't know what to do," he cried, caressing her face. Her breathing grew shallow, and then seemed to stop for a moment before blood spewed in a thin spray from between her lips. She'd gone pale too, her skin turning gray like the fog, her mouth a little blue.

"I don't want you to see this," Sammi managed to say. Squeezing his hand, there was resignation. "Just... just be with me." She took another breath, staring into his eyes. "Declan, I'll be okay."

"Sammi," he wept. Her breathing weakened and her focus drifted past him. Her face began to change too, light shining from the opening in the roof. It was her hair and her skin, both turning bright with colors he'd only seen in the murals painted by Andie.

"Declan," she said, eyes huge and glowing, reflecting sunlight, bright and intense. Sammi smiled giddily; her expression was one of awe, and she gave his hand a weak squeeze. Her voice hoarse and strained, she said, "Look at how amazing!"

An odd heat grew across Declan's shoulders and back, its touch confusing. From outside of the theater, he heard the commune bells ringing. He heard people yelling and cheering too. There were loud explosions of laughter, and singing, and celebration. And all around him, the theater was becoming more alive with brightly saturated colors that revealed a time lost years before.

A world of fog held no winds to move weather against the turn of their planet, but with the sudden sunlight, a soft breeze swept over his face. It was breathtaking and he watched Sammi slowly close and open her eyes, seeming to marvel at it. The sunlight in her eyes grew more intense, and he could see the magnificence of her color and beauty.

With the sun on her face, he was seeing Sammi as she was always intended to be seen. Her eyes, her hair, her skin looked purer than at any other time and she seemed to gleam from the sunshine raining down on them.

Declan turned to face the End of Gray Skies. His eyes burned instantly from the direct sunlight, and he had to shut them. Even closed, there was the afterimage of the sun dancing. His skin soaked in the sun's rays like a sponge drinking water. It warmed instantly with an intensity that put a sweat on his upper lip.

"It's amazing! *Absolutely* amazing, Sammi! Isn't it?" he yelled, holding her hand, squeezing it. When she didn't reply, Declan knew that Sammi was gone. He threw his face to the sky and opened his eyes as wide as possible, gazing directly at the sun while screams of anguish and anger gushed from his mouth. He hurt. He hurt with rage.

Declan held her hand against his heart and feathered her face with his lips. Her eyes remained alive, reflecting glimmers of sunlight. Instinct told him to close them, but he left them as they were. Even as the torture of her loss pained him, he wanted her to have every precious moment of sunlight. It was the End of Gray Skies.

A LETTER FROM B.R. SPANGLER

Dear Reader,

I want to say a huge thank you for reading *When the Sky Falls*. If you enjoyed it, and want to keep up to date with all my latest releases, just sign up at the following link. Your email address will never be shared and you can unsubscribe at any time.

www.bookouture.com/br-spangler

What happens after *When the Sky Falls*? What's in store for Emily and Sammi and Declan and all the others? You can find out in the second book, *When the Dawn Breaks*.

The Dark Skies Apocalypse series began as a short story written more than a dozen years ago. The original story focused on the plight of Emily and her mother and sister, and the race to survive an unthinkable tragedy. I was never satisfied with the short story, the characters often thought about. From those few pages, two novels were completed, satisfying the full story. I hope you find as much enjoyment in them as I did.

I would be very grateful if you could write a review, and it also makes such a difference helping new readers to discover my books. You can reach me on my website or social media.

Happy reading,

B.R. Spangler

KEEP IN TOUCH WITH B.R. SPANGLER

www.brspangler.com

facebook.com/authorbrianspangler
x.com/BR_Spangler
instagram.com/brspangler

PUBLISHING TEAM

Turning a manuscript into a book requires the efforts of many people. The publishing team at Bookouture would like to acknowledge everyone who contributed to this publication.

Audio
Alba Proko
Sinead O'Connor
Melissa Tran

Commercial
Lauren Morrissette
Hannah Richmond
Imogen Allport

Cover design
Damonza.com

Data and analysis
Mark Alder
Mohamed Bussuri

Editorial
Jack Renninson
Melissa Tran

Copyeditor
Rhian McKay

Proofreader
Catherine Lenderi

Marketing
Alex Crow
Melanie Price
Occy Carr
Cíara Rosney
Martyna Młynarska

Operations and distribution
Marina Valles
Stephanie Straub

Production
Hannah Snetsinger
Mandy Kullar
Jen Shannon
Ria Clare

Publicity
Kim Nash
Noelle Holten
Jess Readett
Sarah Hardy

Rights and contracts
Peta Nightingale
Richard King
Saidah Graham

www.ingramcontent.com/pod-product-compliance
Lightning Source LLC
Chambersburg PA
CBHW061526210726
48287CB00006B/1841